SAVING MARIA

Also by Lynn Sheft

The Deadly Game

SAVING MARIA

Lynn Sheft

This book is a work of fiction. Names, characters, places, and incidents are the product of the author's imagination or are used fictitiously. Any resemblance to actual events, locales, or persons, living or dead, is coincidental.

ISBN 978-1-7378030-2-7

Printed in the United States of America
Cove Press

For my family — Barry, Valerie, Elijah, and Judy — who support me with love, good humor and enthusiasm.

It always seems impossible until it's done.

--Nelson Mandela

Chapter 1

It was twelve-thirty when Maria parked her Honda Civic in the townhouse community in Pembroke Pines, one of South Florida's many housing developments that bordered the Everglades. As she approached her front door, she heard the telephone ringing. She hurried, worrying it might be her mother calling from Bogotá. It had been two weeks since they had spoken and she missed her mother terribly. She flung the door open and rushed to the phone. She picked up the receiver, but the caller had already hung up.

"*Mierda!*" Maria cursed at missing the call and not having caller ID. As a cost-cutting measure, she had basic telephone service with no extras.

The telephone rang again as she walked to the refrigerator. Her daughters would soon be home from elementary school and she wanted to have a hot meal ready for them.

She answered it after the first ring. "Hello."

"*Mi querida Maria.*" My dear Maria.

"*Ah, madre. ¿Como está usted?*" Oh, Mama. How are you? Her voice trembling with emotion, Maria's mother said, "*Es su papa.*" It's your father.

Maria hesitated. "What's the matter, Mama?"

"Your father is getting worse."

"What do you mean, Mama? I didn't know he's been sick."

"I didn't want to worry you. You have enough to cope with — making a new life in Florida, taking care of Julia and Paula, studying English, cooking, cleaning, all that goes with tending to the house. Oh dear God, I miss my little ones and you, Maria."

Maria interrupted, "I miss you, too, Mama. Tell me about Papa. What's wrong?"

"Your Papa has kidney disease. You know he's a diabetic, so his kidneys have been bad for some time. He's getting dialysis several times a week. His doctor wants him to have a kidney transplant. Who knows when that could happen?"

"You're just telling me now? When did all this start?"

"Right after you left for Florida."

"Mama, that was two years ago. I just don't understand. Why didn't you tell me sooner?"

"Maria, I didn't want to worry you. Besides, your father is upset. Things are not good with you and Jorge."

"What do you expect? When FARC called for the ransom money, he said that I was married so I was no longer his responsibility. He refused to pay. That's what I was told."

"Maria, I don't excuse what your father said. I divorced him over it, didn't I? But now I know things I didn't know then. So please listen to me. He's asking for you. He loves you and he wants to see you. He's afraid he may die before he can get a kidney transplant. Please come home, Maria. He wants to make up to you. There are many things he has to say to you. He'll pay your expenses. Please. Say you'll come home."

"Why can't he just talk to me on the phone?

"Maria, you know as well as I do that some things are better said in person. Please. Say you'll agree."

Maria's deep blue eyes filled with tears. "Do you know what you're asking? I'm here in Florida because I was granted political asylum. Do you remember what it took for that to happen? A long year with bodyguards and driving around in an armored car. I was constantly afraid. Remember we even had to move out of our apartment and find a place where no one knew us. I had to quit the university because of the risk of FARC kidnapping me again. I can't go back. If those rebels found out, they would kill me. And even if I wanted to take a chance and return to Colombia, asylum would be revoked. I wouldn't be allowed to come back and live in the United States. We made a new life here. This is now my home and I feel safe. I can live in peace and not worry about someone taking me or my children for ransom. I just don't see a way, Mama. I have Jorge and my daughters to think about."

"Maria, please. There must be a way. Please think about it. It is very important to Don Pedro that he sees you — his only daughter before ...," Maria's mother's sobs stopped her from finishing.

"Mama, please don't cry. I love you. Oh, dear Lord. Dear Mary and Joseph. Is Papa in the hospital?"

"No, Maria. He's home and we have a home healthcare nurse. I moved back into the apartment so I can look after him. Please, Maria. Talk this over with Jorge. He's smart. He might be able to figure out a way so you can come home."

"But Mama, Jorge would not want me to leave. When those stinking rebels had me, Jorge thought I might be dead. He was so distraught. Now he has a normal life and he doesn't have to worry about living through hell again. Do you realize what you're asking? It's just too dangerous."

"You do want to see your father, don't you? I wouldn't ask you if he were well, but he's not. The fact is, he will die if he doesn't get a new kidney. Dialysis can only give him some time. I'm asking you to come. You may never get another chance. It will mean so much to him."

"Oh, Mama," Maria said as the tears began to flow. "I just — I'll have to call you back. It's just too much to think about. Maybe tomorrow. I need to hang up now. Julie and Paula will be home from school soon. I don't want to discuss this in front of them."

"Not so fast, Maria. Your girls won't be home until two-thirty. It's not even one o'clock now. Let's talk about you now. How are you doing in the ESOL classes at the college?"

Maria sighed, relieved that her mother changed the subject. "I'm making progress. I understand English fairly well when I'm reading and writing. The hard part is having a conversation in English. I tend to think about what I want to say in Spanish and then translate it into English. I want to be able to think in English and speak fluently. Then I can take the TOEFL."

"What's a toe full?"

"It's an exam that measures proficiency in English. When I pass that I can apply for admission to a university."

"You still want to be an accountant?"

"That's right Mama. It'll take years, but it'll be worth it. Then I can get a job and at some point, we'll be able to afford to buy our own home. That's the way it is here. You need two incomes. No one I know of here has a staff of cooks, maids and butlers like we did. You do it all yourself."

"I don't know how mothers do it there in the states. Work all day and come home and work some more. It's crazy!"

"Even so, I'm glad to be here. I just have to practice speaking English. That's what the girls tell me at the dinner table."

"What about friends? Have you made any from your class so you can practice English with them, too?"

"Yes, I have," Maria said. "Several women are also from Colombia, Venezuela, and Brazil. They had the same issues: Kidnappings. Corrupt government and police so there's no one to put an end to it. They're political refugees like me. Lucy, who's from Venezuela, told me that she and her family fled Caracas the same day they heard her husband was going to be kidnapped. He's a doctor and wealthy. They left with only what would fit in their suitcases. Now he's studying for the medical licensing exam so he can eventually practice medicine here. The standards to become a licensed doctor are very strict; it's almost like starting over again. He has to be certified, do a residency program, and take another exam. Lucy said he's always studying."

"Are you still seeing the psychologist?"

"Yes. Once a week. She said the post-traumatic stress crippled me emotionally. She's working on building my self-confidence. That's why I'm taking Tae Kwon Do classes."

"Really?"

"You sound surprised."

"I guess I shouldn't be. You were a strong swimmer in school."

"I like it because it emphasizes kicking."

There was a long pause. "I'm so sorry what happened to you. It was horrible, Maria. The conditions you endured for months. Whenever I think about it, I..., Maria's mother hesitated.

"Let's not talk about it now, Mama. I've got to think about Papa. I need to say goodbye now."

"All right. Give my love to the girls, Maria. I love you. Remember I'm asking you to come home because your father needs you now. I'll wait to hear from you."

"Goodbye, Mama. I love you, too."

Maria ran her fingers through her short brown hair, then wiped the tears from her cheeks.

She was desperate to reconcile with her dying father, yet she feared the consequences. If only there was a way.

She turned and saw the statue of the Madonna in the living room, and instinctively prayed silently, "Hail Mary, full of grace. The Lord is with thee."

She stopped reciting the "Hail Mary" when the image of the Madonna in the abandoned farmhouse flashed before her eyes. She remembered the four brutal months she was held captive in the hills of Colombia. It brought pain and fresh tears to her eyes.

Chapter 2

Two years ago, Bogotá, Colombia
October 28, 1998

At nine-thirty, Maria, her sister-in-law Silvana and Roberto, a classmate of Silvana's, met outside of the university's library and walked to Roberto's car. Silvana had arranged the ride home from the evening class with Roberto since Maria's husband Jorge was at home sick with the flu. As they walked to the car, Maria carried her backpack on one shoulder while she buttoned up her navy cashmere overcoat. She was dressed warmly in a plum-colored wool skirt, matching cardigan sweater, a white silk blouse, and navy pumps. The October evening was cold and when she spoke to Roberto she could see the vapor from her breath. Roberto was a tall, slim man with short dark hair, brown eyes and an infectious smile. Maria guessed his age to be about 21 years old. He was smartly dressed in a caramel leather jacket over a blue turtle neck sweater and faded jeans.

"Roberto, thank you for the ride home," Maria said. "My husband would pick us up, but he's sick.

I probably should have stayed home tonight to care for him, but I hate to miss class."

As Roberto looked Maria over, he said, "Me, too. The professor takes attendance because he wants us there for the class discussions."

They walked to the car in silence and Maria thought Silvana was unusually quiet. As sisters-in law, Maria recognized that they had nothing in common except the fact that Maria's brother Roman was married to Silvana. At one time she consciously compared herself to Silvana. Whereas Maria dressed in classic fashions that were well-tailored, Silvana wore trendy clothes that were usually tight-fitting. The same was true for hair and makeup. Maria kept her long, silky brown hair off her face with a simple barrette. The effect emphasized her dark blue eyes and long eyelashes. Silvana, on the other hand, had curly red hair that fell to her shoulders in ringlets and wore bright lipstick and dramatic eye makeup more suitable for a night club than a lecture hall. While Maria was quiet and almost shy, Silvana talked incessantly about everything and nothing, whatever it took to be the center of attention. Tonight Maria thought Silvana was absorbed in her own thoughts.

"Here we are, ladies." Roberto used his car key's remote to unlock the car doors.

Silvana opened the front passenger door and got in leaving Maria to sit in the back seat of the compact car. After they buckled their seat belts,

Roberto checked for traffic and pulled out onto the street.

"I'm so hungry, Silvana. I only ate an apple and a soda at four o'clock. Do you want to stop and get something to eat?"

"Not really, Maria. I'm tired and I just want to go home. It's been a long day," Silvana said looking in the side-view mirror.

"Are you feeling all right?" Maria asked. "You're very quiet tonight. I hope you're not coming down with the flu, too."

Resting her head on the neck support, Silvana said with a sigh, "No, I'm just tired."

Roberto said, "We can drop Silvana off and stop at a restaurant if you want."

"No, I'm hungry, but on second thought I want to go right home. Jorge is sick and he's caring for our little girls, I hope by now they're in bed sound asleep. I'll find something to eat at home. There's always the microwave."

Rummaging through her backpack, Maria pulled out a pack of chewing gum. "I have gum. Would anyone like a piece?"

Both Roberto and Silvana waved their hands in refusal. Maria popped the gum into her mouth. Then she folded the gum wrapper into a ring that looked as if it had a gemstone on the top.

"I didn't know you're a mother. How old are they?" Roberto asked watching her through his rearview mirror.

"Paula is four and Julie is nine," Maria said. She tried the paper ring on, slipped it off, and then handed it to her sister-in-law. Silvana looked at it and said, "Aren't you clever. Or should I say crafty?"

"Maybe a little of both," Maria laughed.

Interrupting the women's banter, Roberto asked in an insinuating tone, "A child bride, eh?"

"Not really. I was 21 when I married Jorge and within a year, Julie was born."

"What are you studying here at the university?" Roberto asked.

"I'm in a master's program now," Maria said.

"In what subject?" Roberto asked.

"Accounting," Maria said, now getting weary of Roberto with all his questions. His charm had worn off minutes ago.

"*Si*," said Roberto, his attention distracted by the bright headlights reflecting into his eyes from the rearview mirror. Suddenly Roberto slammed on the brakes as he was cut off by another car.

Maria looked outside the window and saw several men with machine guns running around the car. Three of them each opened a car door, dragging Roberto, Silvana and Maria out of the car while the others pointed their weapons at them. Silvana and Maria screamed in terror and Roberto shouted, "What the hell is going on here?"

A man opened the trunk of Roberto's car and instructed the other men holding Roberto and Silvana to put them in the trunk. Silvana was told to get in first, then Roberto. Another man slammed the trunk. Maria saw a man retrieve her backpack from the back seat and hand it over to another man in the second group. Four men got into their car and the driver sped away on the deserted two-lane road, squealing tires signaling their departure. Maria screamed. A man came up behind her, slapped his hand over her mouth and dragged her backward. "Shut up, Maria. Your daddy's going to give us a lot of money."

Maria struggled to free herself, but the man tightened his grip and continued to drag her backwards. She heard a trunk latch release and realized he had dragged her to another car. He then lifted her off the ground and forcefully threw her into the trunk. When he slammed the lid shut plunging her into darkness, Maria screamed again and started to cry. A stream of questions filled her head: What do they want with me? Will they kill me? Will I ever see Jorge or my little girls ever again? Where are they taking me? As the minutes passed, she realized that she was another one of many kidnappings that occurred every day in Colombia. She wondered how much ransom her kidnappers would demand.

As she was trying to calculate how long they have been driving, the car slowed down and stopped. The combination of being confined in the trunk and the exhaust fumes nauseated her. She was desperate to get out. The motor was turned off and she heard the noise of a garage door being closed. Then she heard a tool clanking against the license plate, it falling to the floor and then the squeak of another one being screwed into place. Maria realized they switched license plates. She heard the garage door being opened again. The driver started the car, backed out and they were driving once more. The sound of the road and the bumps and jolts told her they had left the city. Maria was trying to keep track of time so she could figure out where they were taking her, but in total darkness, it was impossible.

After what seemed like ten minutes, the car slowed and stopped. Maria heard men cursing. Then a man yelled that the car broke down and to send another car. She wondered how long they would remain here. Minutes, hours? She was lying on her side in a fetal position and struggled to lie on her back. She was beginning to panic from being confined and she hoped she wouldn't vomit in the trunk. She took in a deep breath and exhaled slowly. She wondered how long it would be before Jorge realized she was missing. What happened to Silvana and Roberto? Were they alive? Where did they take them? Why were they separated? The words "your daddy's going to pay us a lot of money" replayed in her mind. If they get the money, will they let me go or kill me anyway? The daily TV newscasts had numerable stories of kidnappings and murders by leftist rebels who called themselves Fuerzas Armadas Revolucionarias de Colombia or FARC, the acronym. They financed their civil war by dealing in cocaine and kidnappings. It was rumored that they bribed employees of the internal revenue service and banks to learn who were Colombia's wealthiest.

She laid there and thought about Paula, only four years old. She was such an adorable little girl, with soft brown eyes and fine, curly brown hair that she always wore in a ponytail. Her favorite pastime was to have Maria play "horsy" and give her rides upon her back. Maria's eyes filled with tears with the thought that she may never see her again. Then the image of Julie came to her. She had a close physical resemblance to Paula, but her personality set her apart. At nine years old, she was very independent, very bright, and insisted on doing everything herself, including fixing her own hair. Some of the hairdos she came up with made Maria laugh. Julie mothered Paula and sometimes Maria had to scold her for being too bossy to her sister. What will happen to them? What will become of me? How long will it take for Jorge to report me missing?

She then thought about Jorge, her childhood sweetheart. She met him when she was only 16 and was immediately attracted to him. He was four years older than she, tall, with a muscular build, jet black hair, a dark complexion, eyes the color of coal and a broad nose that reflected his mestizo heritage.

She remembered the night she met him. Maria saw him across the room at a birthday party and wondered who he was. Sensing a pair of eyes on him, Jorge turned in her direction and looked at her with a wide smile. Out of embarrassment, she turned away to talk to her cousin, Iliana, and felt her face go warm. Iliana sensed Maria's discomfort and asked, "Maria, are you all right?"

"Is he still looking at me?" Maria asked.

"Who's he?"

"The man standing next to Demetrio," Maria said, gesturing with her thumb to the area behind her.

"I don't see Demetrio. Oh, wait a minute. He's walking over here with a handsome man. Get ready, Maria."

Demetrio excused his interruption to Iliana and Maria and introduced Jorge.

Maria remembered from that moment on, she knew some day she would marry Jorge. Now she wondered if she would ever see him again. Her throat constricted as she tried not to cry. Jorge will know what to do, she thought. He's smart.

Abruptly her reverie ended when she heard the men yelling again, this time in triumph. The trunk was opened and finally Maria was pulled out. One man dragged her over to a Jeep.

"Get in the back seat and lie down, you bitch. Don't speak or we'll kill you!" a repulsive man with a bushy mustache yelled at her. His automatic weapon was aimed for her chest.

Another man sneered at her, "Daddy has to give us a lot of money."

As Maria stretched out across the backseat on her side, she looked at her watch. More than two hours had passed since she left the university. A man reached across and covered her with a dirty blanket that reeked of sweat and wet dog. She wondered where she would end up tonight and if Jorge had reported her missing.

After what seemed like an hour of driving who knew where, she was ordered out of the Jeep. Gone were the street lights and traffic of Bogotá. Now she found herself in a dense forest. The same men who had abducted Silvana and Roberto were waiting for them in a small clearing. The driver of the Jeep drove off leaving the eight of them to walk. Maria had no idea where she was so it would be futile to run off. Now she walked, three men in front of her and four men behind her. The spongy forest floor made walking difficult for Maria, since she was still wearing high heels. She was thirsty, but she didn't dare ask for something to drink. The sugarless gum was drying out her mouth, so she threw it in a bush. The forest was quiet except for the rustling of leaves.

When they came to a small clearing, the leader announced, "We'll camp here for the night. I'll take first watch." He pointed to the man with the bushy mustache, "You take second watch. I'll wake you."

Maria glanced at her watch. They had been walking for an hour. She was exhausted as much from fear as the late hour.

The men settled down, some with blankets, some with sleeping bags that they had been carrying on their backs along with other supplies. There was nothing for Maria except the damp ground. She was so afraid she didn't know if she could sleep. She found a place near a tree so she could put some distance between herself and the men. Fallen leaves and twigs blanketed the ground and she heard a swish as if something was slithering through. She hoped it wasn't a snake. She sat down and felt all the men looking at her. She glanced away and prayed that they would leave her alone.

"OK, get to sleep," the leader commanded. The men obeyed and settled down. Maria lay down and looked up at the October sky. There were a thousand stars twinkling in the heavens. She said her prayers asking for a guardian angel to protect her from these filthy rebels. She wondered if she could escape, but then she remembered they were taking turns watching her. She asked God to bless Jorge, Julie and Paula. Then she prayed that she would be rescued alive. She hoped God was listening tonight. And then she closed her eyes.

Chapter 3

"Do you think they left?" Silvana whispered.

"I think so. I haven't heard anyone since the engine was turned off and the doors slammed shut," Roberto replied.

"What if they're just waiting to see if we try to get out of the trunk?"

"I don't see how we can get out. This is an old car. There isn't a safety release latch here," said Roberto. "We're locked in here."

"What if they're waiting out there, ready to shoot us?" Silvana asked.

"Let's just wait and listen for a few minutes."

"What then?"

"What do you mean? What then?" Roberto asked.

"If we're locked in, how will we get out?"

Roberto sighed, "I'm hoping the back seat will fold down, if it's not locked in place."

"Let's try it now," Silvana demanded.

"You're closest to the back seat. Feel for a latch. See if you can move it," Roberto instructed.

Silvana reached behind her back and felt around for the latch. She found it and slid it down. She arched her back, leaned back, and pushed against the seat. It yielded under her pressure. "I got it, but I have to roll over and face the seat to get it down."

"Go ahead, then. Just don't kick me trying," Roberto said.

After much squirming and wiggling in the cramped space, Silvana was able to push the seat flat. She crawled out of the trunk into the back seat and looked around for their captors. Seeing no one, she called Roberto to come out.

Roberto crawled out and looked at the steering wheel. "We're in luck, Silvana! The keys are in the ignition!"

"Oh, my lord!" Silvana said, exhaling deeply. "Please take me home. I have to tell Jorge and Don Pedro what happened to Maria."

"It's amazing," Roberto said. "They left the keys. Don't you find that surprising?"

"Not really," said Silvana. "They got what they wanted. Come on, let's go."

Roberto and Silvana climbed out of the back seat. Now in the driver's seat, Roberto started the ignition and said, "I can't believe they let us go. They could have shot us. Talk about being in the wrong place at the wrong time."

"Roberto," Silvana interrupted. "Drive, please. Take me home so I can tell Jorge and Don Pedro what happened."

"Do you want to call the police?" Roberto asked as he drove on the deserted roadway.

"They took my cell phone. Let's just go home and let Jorge take care of it. Maria is his wife."

"The rebels said her father is going to pay them a lot of money," Roberto said. "So he's a rich man. I wonder how much money they'll want."

"As much as they know he's worth," Silvana answered.

"And how much would that be?" Roberto asked.

"I wouldn't know. But he owns Fino Foods."

"That's got to be a fortune. Fino is everywhere. How did they know Maria is the daughter?" asked Roberto.

"That's a good question," said Silvana.

"And how did they know where she would be so they could abduct her?"

"I wouldn't know," said Silvana.

"These rebels have made a business out of kidnapping. I've heard they bribe people in the internal revenue service to find out who's rich. That way they only target someone whose family has the means to pay the ransom. I wonder how much they'll ask for Maria," Roberto said, glancing over at Silvana. "What do you think?"

"I don't know," Silvana snapped. "I can't even think right now."

Roberto glanced at Silvana and kept quiet. He continued driving through the streets of Bogotá, where historic Colonial buildings lined the street. The traffic was light, making the trip to Silvana's home in a mere 20 minutes.

"Look, make the next left at the light. Then pull over and park on the street at the second apartment building on the right," Silvana instructed. "That's where we live."

Once Roberto parked the car, Silvana got out and rushed to the wooden double doors of the apartment building Don Pedro owned. Once inside, she yelled, "Don Pedro, come quick! Maria has been kidnapped! Don Pedro. Don Pedro. Hurry! They took Maria!"

Roberto followed her into the tiled lobby and doors were flung open. Those living on the upper floors ran down the stairs. As the news spread, the women became hysterical, crying and wailing. Maria's husband, Jorge, was the first to reach Silvana with Maria's father, Don Pedro, on his heels.

"What happened?" Jorge demanded as he grabbed Silvana by the upper arms. "Where's Maria? I've been trying to call her cell phone but it goes straight to voice mail. Tell me. Where is she?"

"Jorge, let go of me. A bunch of men with machine guns cut us off the road. They made us get out of the car. They grabbed Maria. Then they threw Roberto and me into the trunk of Roberto's car. I don't know where they took her," Silvana said. She tried to loosen herself from Jorge, but it was impossible.

"How did you get out?" Jorge asked, his voice rising. He stared at Silvana, his eyes seeking the answer from her. Getting no response from her, he released her from his iron grip so abruptly she almost fell to the floor. He hung his head and massaged his temples as if to push the pain away.

"We put the back seat down and crawled into the car. The keys were still in the ignition. I couldn't believe our luck!" Silvana said.

"They left the keys?" Jorge asked. "Incredible! I've got to call my friend Sergio at the police station. He might be able to help. Don Pedro, come, please. We can't waste any time."

Silvana rushed over to Mama, Maria's mother, and embraced her. Mama wailed, "Silvana, they took Maria, my baby. My baby girl. Maria, Maria, Maria."

Jorge grabbed Don Pedro by the wrist. "Don Pedro, come!"

Once they were in the quiet of Jorge and Maria's apartment, Jorge dialed his friend Sergio from his cell phone. After two rings, the night duty officer answered at the local police station. "May I speak to Sergio?" asked Jorge.

"I'm sorry. He's got the night off. Can I help you?"

"Yes, my wife--she's been kidnapped. Who can help me?"

"Call GAULA, that's the Special Forces unit that handles kidnap and extortion. Shall I transfer your call?"

"Yes, please," Jorge said. He looked at his father-in-law, a short, stocky man with soft brown eyes, a straight nose and thin lips. Don Pedro removed his eye glasses to clean the lenses. Jorge noticed tears welling in his eyes as he replaced his glasses.

After a few seconds, he heard, "This is Officer Ramirez. Your name, please."

"This is Jorge Alvarez. My wife has been kidnapped. Please, can you help me?"

"You're going to have to come to our station and file a report," Officer Ramirez said. "Do you know the address?"

"No, I don't."

"We're at Carrera 7, number 32-16."

"But that's in Sante Fe," Jorge said. "Should I come now?"

"Yes."

"All right then. I'll leave now," Jorge said as he looked at his watch. It was already midnight. He wouldn't get there until 12:30 am.

"You have to go to Sante Fe?" Don Pedro asked. "That's the worst part of town. Nothing but whores and drug dealers. You're going now?"

"Yes, Don Pedro. I must. You stay here with the family. I'll come back as soon as I can."

"You should take Silvana and Roman with you. Silvana can describe what happened when you file a report. Mama and I will stay in your apartment to watch Julie and Paula. I hope they'll stay asleep."

Jorge and Don Pedro returned to the lobby and the family fell silent.

Don Pedro said, "Roman, Fernando and Salvador, your sister has been kidnapped. Jorge needs to go to the GAULA office now to file a report. Roman, you and your wife need to go with

Jorge since she's a witness. Mama and I will wait in Jorge's apartment."

Hearing her name, Mama wiped her eyes and said, "Roman, get your coat. You don't want to get sick like Jorge."

Roman and Jorge exchanged glances and went to get their coats. In a matter of a few minutes, the men escorted Silvana to Jorge's car and left for Sante Fe with all doors locked. Sante Fe was a run-down, seedy district where all the walls of the buildings were covered with colorful graffiti. Street corners were places of business where young thugs traded cash for drugs. Prostitutes stood in doorways smoking cigarettes and watching the traffic to catch the eye of a customer. Silvana instinctively inched down in the back seat of the car not wanting to be seen. She looked at Jorge as he spoke to Roman, his voice hoarse and cracked. He was blaming himself for not picking up Maria from class.

They arrived at the GAULA office without any problems and went to the reception desk which was behind a glass window. Jorge tapped on the glass to get the officer's attention and explained his reason for coming.

"Have a seat. I'll have to see who can take your report," the young officer ordered. Jorge sat down, but then popped out of his chair and paced the small room. He cursed under his breath, frustrated that he had to wait. Thirty minutes later, the same officer returned to the window and told Jorge he would have to come back at six o'clock in the morning when the officer in charge would be in. He explained that he was away on another assignment. It couldn't be helped.

Jorge made a fist and slammed it into his open hand. "Dear Maria! God help you!"

As they walked back to the car, Jorge said, fighting back tears of frustration. "Damn it! I can't believe we all came down here for nothing."

"There's nothing we can do but go home and get some sleep. I'm exhausted," said Silvana. She started to yawn and then covered her mouth.

"That's all you have to say, Silvana? What about Maria?" Jorge asked.

They drove home in silence. Jorge's nerves were on edge; his stomach cramping with worry about Maria. He tried to make sense of the whole thing. Kidnappings were common in Bogotá, many of them never reported. But now it was his wife!

By the time they arrived at the apartment building, Silvana had fallen asleep. Roman roused her and helped her out of the car.

"Jorge, do you want us to go with you in the morning?" asked Roman with concern in his voice.

"Yes, let's leave at six. See you in the lobby." Jorge said, glad that his brother-in-law offered.

Jorge opened the door to his apartment on the fourth floor and found his in-laws sitting on the couch. Mama's face and eyes were swollen from crying. Upon seeing Jorge, new tears began to flow. Don Pedro put his arm around her shoulders to comfort her and said to Jorge, "So what happened? Are they going to find her?"

"The officer I'm supposed to see won't be in until six this morning. I'll have to go back. Mama, Don Pedro, thank you for staying here with the girls. Go back to your apartment and go to sleep. Can you come back in the morning to stay with the girls, get them off to school? I'm going to leave at six."

Don Pedro nodded in agreement and helped Mama get up from the couch. Jorge held the door open. As they came to the door, Jorge hugged Mama. She sagged next to him, her gray head resting against his chest.

"Go on, now. See you in the morning," Jorge said.

He closed the door after them and walked down the hall to the girls' bedroom. He opened the door quietly and looked in on his sleeping daughters. Jorge went back to the living room, turned out the lights, and went to his bedroom. He undressed and lay down on the king-size bed. He tried to sleep and dozed off only to wake up again. Every time he woke, his stomach lurched remembering Maria was gone. He finally got up at 5 a.m. shaved, showered, and got dressed. His breakfast was a cup of coffee, orange juice and a decongestant. He felt even sicker than yesterday, but he had to file a report if he hoped to ever see Maria again.

At five minutes before six, he heard a soft tap on the door. It was Mama. She was wearing black slacks and a matching sweater which was striking against her light skin and silver gray hair. Although she applied some eye makeup, her eyelids were still puffy. She sighed deeply and said, "Don Pedro is still asleep. I didn't want to wake him. I'll get the girls up and ready for school while you're gone."

Jorge thanked her and left, closing the door behind him. He found Roman and Silvana sitting on the sofa in the lobby with their coffee cups in hand. The light wall sconces cast a somber glow in the room. They were both casually dressed in jeans and sweaters and wore leather jackets. "Did you get any sleep?" Jorge asked.

"Yes," Roman replied. "From the looks of you, you didn't."

"No, I didn't sleep well. I'm afraid for Maria. I need to act fast," Jorge said, the desperation clear in his voice.

Fatigue and the shock of the abduction kept them quiet on the drive to GAULA. When they arrived, they were escorted to Colonel Gustavo Diaz's office and introductions were made. The office was cramped and smelled like stale cigarettes. Diaz was in his mid-forties, slim, of medium height, and he wore his dark brown hair combed straight back.

"Have a seat, please," Diaz said. "I will ask you a series of questions. Then feel free to ask me questions. First off, do you have a recent photograph of your wife?"

Jorge got his wallet out, pulled out a picture of Maria and handed it to Diaz. "This is my wife, Maria. You should know that Silvana, my sister-in-law, was with Maria when she was abducted on the way home from the university last night. She can answer some of your questions as well."

Diaz nodded and put the photo off to the side of his papers. He started going down the printed questions and wrote the responses. Both Jorge and Silvana answered his questions trying to be as helpful as possible.

After 30 minutes of questioning, Jorge was drained. Diaz wanted to pick up Roberto's car for fingerprinting so Silvana gave him Roberto's phone number.

"Any questions?" asked Diaz.

"What happens now?" Jorge asked. He fought hard to suppress his frustration.

"I will assign this case; then you need to be patient, wait, and pray. You know there are 2,000 kidnappings a year in Colombia. And that's just a fraction of what's reported. Many people don't report it and just pay the ransom. That's good for the rebels, but bad for us. I don't mean to be insensitive when I say take a number. We'll work this case with great effort, and hopefully find Maria and bring her home to you. We'll be intercepting all of your phone calls since we know the rebels will be contacting you very soon for a ransom."

"I'm not rich. But Maria's father is. He owns Fino Foods," said Jorge.

Diaz nodded knowingly, recognizing the name. "I suppose the rebels know this. I'm going to bet she's the only daughter in the family."

Jorge nodded.

"Daughters are always special. In this case, the rebels will also be contacting your father-in-law. We will tap his phone as well. The first call to him will be a demand for the ransom. We'll be in touch with him later today. Also, we'll be freezing your liquid assets as well as your father-in-law's. You'll only be allowed to withdraw enough money each month to pay your bills. This prevents your family from caving in to the rebel's demand to pay the ransom. Like I said, be patient. Your father-in-law could be in negotiations with the rebels for months. That's all right. It'll give us time to find out where they're hiding her."

"But how do you find her?" Jorge asked.

"We ask questions, see if we can find informants and track phone calls. Cell phones are harder to track but land lines are easy."

"I understand. What are Maria's chances?"

"I can't say, but know that our squad completed a new program funded by the State Department's Bureau of Diplomatic Security. It's a U.S. Anti-Terrorism Assistance course, which focuses on close combat skills and operational planning for rescue missions. We're well prepared," Diaz said. "We just need to find where they're keeping her."

Jorge sighed and rubbed his forehead. Silvana stared at her fingernails while Roman draped his arm around his wife's shoulders.

"All right, then," said Diaz, standing up and extending his hand to Jorge and then Roman. "Call if you have any questions. I'll let you know if we get any prints off the car."

"Thank you," said Jorge. "I hope you find something that will help."

Jorge, Silvana and Roman left GAULA silently. Jorge worried about Maria and hoped the family would help him take care of their daughters. Then he felt a catch in his throat as he wondered what he would tell Paula and Julie. How would he explain that their mother was gone and he didn't know when or if she was ever coming back?

Chapter 4

Maria struggled to keep the pace walking through the verdant forest in her high heels that were now caked with mud. The sodden ground was covered in seedlings, vines, and fern while the canopy above created by majestic oak and pine shielded her from the sun. The motley group has been traipsing through the woods for several hours. The leader offered her water and bread before they began their morning hike. Maria accepted the water but refused the bread. She had no appetite.

The men spoke among themselves, ignoring her except for occasional glances. Maria studied them. She tried to distinguish one from the other but they looked pretty much the same in their uniforms. They wore camouflage fatigues, army caps, combat boots, backpacks and holstered guns. Their hair was dark and stringy and their eyes held no emotion. Overall, they all looked and smelled like they hadn't shaved or showered in weeks. She guessed their ages ranged from late teens to mid-twenties, except for the leader. His dark face was lined with wrinkles and there was gray at his temples.

When they approached a clearing, Maria saw a primitive farmhouse that appeared to be abandoned. There were no farm animals or chickens in sight. She noticed a cistern at one corner of the house while a brick chimney flanked the other. Three steps led to the porch where a pile of firewood was stacked by the front door. The unpainted wooden structure had been left to weather so it was mottled gray. Off to the left was a vegetable garden long gone to seed and weeds. Four wooden benches and fencing posts in the ground were tangled in dead vines. Whatever was used for the fencing was long gone.

"Welcome to your new home," the leader said, leaning down into her face.

Maria jerked her head back, revolted by his foul breath and blinked her tears away. She wondered how anyone would ever find this place and then realized that was exactly their plan. The leader pushed the wooden door open with his foot and motioned for Maria to enter the one-room farmhouse. There was a wood-burning fireplace with wood shelving on either side where cooking pots, skillets, dishes, cups and utensils were stored. Plywood covered the windows so the only natural light in the room came from the open doorway and cracks in the roof. The leader took Maria by her arm and led her to a closet door. He opened it revealing a bucket on the floor.

"The bathroom," the leader said raising his eyebrows. He had a smirk on his face and his eyes studied Maria for a reaction.

Maria backed away and looked around the one room house. There was no sink with running water or electricity. A large wooden table in the middle of the room with a few chairs around it served as the dining area. The walls were bare. She looked around the rest of the room hoping for beds but found none.

As if reading her mind, the leader said pointing to a wall, "You'll be sleeping over there on the floor. See those rings hanging from the wall? You'll be handcuffed there at night. There is no escape!"

Maria nodded and looked away, holding back new tears.

The leader went outside and called to his men who quickly assembled. Maria watched from the doorway, anxious to know what would happen to her. She looked around the room and focused on the place where she would sleep, manacled to the wall. Evidently, she wasn't the first prisoner to be held here.

Looking around the room, she forced herself to think about her abduction. Obviously, they knew my daily schedule. How long had I been stalked? Was there a traitor among my family or friends — someone who received a bribe? Could it be Roberto or even Silvana, my sister-in-law? How much money would they demand for my release? Would the ransom be paid? How long would they wait to get paid before killing me?

With this last thought, Maria broke down and sobbed. She collapsed to her knees on the dirty wood floor. She covered her eyes with her hands, the tears flowing down her cheeks. More than anything she wanted to be home with Jorge and her little girls. She thought of her mother and father who must be distraught knowing their only daughter was snatched in the night. She was being held against her will and she knew there was no escape. They would take shifts guarding her during the night. Even if she could get away, where would she run? She had no idea where she was. How could anyone find her? She had no way of reaching anyone since her cell phone was in her backpack and it was gone. She continued to cry until there were no more tears left and she was exhausted. She wiped her eyes and looked to the doorway. She saw the leader standing at the threshold, his face hidden in the shadows. Fear gripped her once more and she began to tremble. Now what, she thought?

Chapter 5

October 30, 1998

It was two-thirty when Don Pedro and his wife returned to his office from having lunch. The executive office was richly appointed with a mahogany desk, dark brown leather and wood guest chairs and a matching leather couch along one wall that offered guests a panoramic view of Bogotá. In front of the couch was a coffee table inlaid with exotic woods where a floral arrangement of ginger and bird of paradise lightened the masculine tone of the room. His appreciation of art was evident in the pastoral oil paintings on the walls. His favorite acquisition was a bronze sculpture of an eagle perched on a carved pedestal

He settled into his high-back leather chair and looked for phone messages. There was only one from a job candidate seeking a sales representative position. Since he had already hired someone, he threw the sheet of paper in the trash can under his desk. He had a pile of paperwork to go through, but he was too distracted to concentrate. Maria's abduction had taken its toll on him, her mother, and the rest of the family. Three days had passed while he anxiously waited for the phone call demanding the ransom. Looking at the many framed family photos on his desk, his eyes focused on his favorite, the one of Maria taken in her senior year when she was on the high school swim team. Finishing first in the freestyle competition, her smile stretched from ear to ear.

He pulled open the middle drawer of his mahogany desk, looking for a pack of cigarettes. Not seeing it, he put his hand in the drawer, sweeping the back to bring it forward. The only thing he produced was a pack of chewing gum and pens.

"Are you looking for cigarettes?" asked Anna Marie. His wife arched her eyebrows in disapproval.

Don Pedro nodded.

"You quit, remember? Doctor's orders."

Don Pedro slammed the drawer shut. The color rose on his cheeks.

Anna Marie rummaged through her purse. She walked to his desk and offered Don Pedro a peppermint candy. "Here, have a sugar-free peppermint. Forget about the cancer stick."

Don Pedro took the peppermint. As he started to remove the cellophane, a phone rang. There were two phones on his desk installed by police technicians: a red one with a red light that flashed when there an incoming call. This one was tapped by GAULA. The other phone was black and was reserved for GAULA communications. It was the red one that rang and alerted Don Pedro with its flashing beacon. He picked the receiver up on the second ring. "Hello."

"Don Pedro?" said the electronically disguised voice.

"Yes."

"Listen carefully. We have your daughter. If you want her returned to you alive, the price is six million US dollars."

"I don't have that kind of money. And why are you calling me? Maria is married. She's no longer my responsibility. She has a husband who's responsible for her."

"Look, Don Pedro. I know you're a rich man. Her husband is not. Maria is your only daughter. That makes her special. Surely as her father, you want to see that no harm comes to her."

"How do I know she is alive and well?" Don Pedro asked with a tone of skepticism in his voice.

"You have to take my word for it. You want to see her alive, you have to pay."

"I can't pay six million dollars," Don Pedro stated flatly.

"Don Pedro, don't play games. You want her alive, don't you?"

Anna Marie reached for her husband's hand. He pulled it away and shook his head to stop.

"The best I can do is $50,000 U.S. Where do you want me to deliver it?"

"Not so fast. I'll get back to you." The caller disconnected and the dial tone buzzed in his ear.

Don Pedro exhaled loudly, his shoulders drooping with fatigue. He looked up to see his wife staring at him, tears welling up in her eyes.

The black phone rang. Don Pedro put his hand up signaling she should remain silent. Picking up the phone, he listened to the caller.

"Don Pedro, this is Colonel Diaz. We recorded the call but we couldn't trace the phone."

"Now what do I do?"

"Just sit tight. These negotiations can go on for a while. You'll be hearing back from them. We'll be listening in when they do."

"Do you think they'll go for the $50,000?"

"Not at all. They'll counter offer."

Don Pedro said, "I'd like to shoot the bastards."

"I know you would. But you have us working for you to find Maria and bring her back to you. Be patient. They're prepared to keep her for a long time. I'll talk to you again soon. You know where to reach us if you have any questions."

"All right," Don Pedro said as he hung up the phone. He looked at Anna Marie. Tears were rolling down her cheeks.

She cried, "How can you be so cold about our only daughter?"

Don Pedro threw up his hands. "What? You have to act like you don't care when it comes to business negotiations."

"And now our daughter is a business negotiation? I can't believe you! You're her father," she wailed. Anna Marie looked up and clasped her hands together in prayer. "Oh dear Lord, please help us."

Don Pedro got up from his seat and went to his wife. He put his arms around her to calm her. "Anna Marie, have faith. We'll get Maria back. I promise, if it's the last thing I do."

Chapter 6

December 11th

Maria was reading *El Tiempo*, Bogotá's daily newspaper. She'd been reading the same edition every day since November 17 when the rebels photographed her holding the paper. After taking the Polaroid photo, her kidnappers forced her to write to her father begging him to pay the ransom. The letter, photograph, and Maria's long-forgotten cell phone were put in an envelope and sent to her father as proof that she was still alive.

Now almost a month had gone by and Maria was desolate. She cried every day, mostly at night when she laid down to sleep and was alone with her thoughts. Her two little girls and her beloved husband were always at the top of her mind, and she prayed she would be reunited with them.

During the day, she had nothing to do but dwell on her futile situation. She was left alone in the room and she paced it nervously. The rebels did not speak to her at all, except to say her daddy was going to pay them a lot of money. It was their mantra. The isolation and the boredom were having serious effects on her mentally. The only thing to look forward to was a meal and no one could make a decent one. In fact, the meals were barely edible so she eventually volunteered to cook. That chore gave her some purpose, relieved her boredom, and lifted her spirits.

Over the past month and a half, many of the original group of rebels left and now there were only three people who occupied the house with Maria. Since there was no electricity to power a refrigerator, fresh food was dropped off at the farmhouse every few days by a rebel. At home, Maria had the luxury of a cook to prepare the family's meals and now she was learning to cook by trial and error. Maria typically made soups or stews such as *ajiaco* made with chicken, potatoes, cream, corn, and capers. In place of bread, she made *arepas*, corn pancakes. Sometimes she cooked pork or beef when it was available and served it with rice and red beans. Whatever wasn't finished at lunch was consumed at dinner. Dishes were cleaned by using basins of water, one for washing; the other for rinsing.

Still wearing the same clothes and shoes, Maria was grateful that she could take a sponge bath in the so-called bathroom every four days or so, but her long hair was a stringy, oily mess. She tied it back with twine to get it away from her face. She looked at her watch. It was almost 7:30 p.m. and the date was December 11. She had safeguarded her other jewelry the day of her arrival. With the privacy the bathroom afforded her, she opened up a few threads of the waistband of her skirt and slipped the rings, bracelet and necklace in there. No one was the wiser. But after all, their attention was on the millions of dollars they thought they could get for her.

Just as she folded the newspaper and put it by her blanket, she heard the leader named Carlos yelling that it was time to move on. Maria was surprised because it was already dark outside. All the men had cell phones and two-way radios from which they got their daily orders and updates.

"Gather up all the supplies," Carlos instructed Alfonso and Alex. "We're moving into the forest."

He then sauntered over to Maria holding an Army camouflage jacket, thick socks, and rubber boots. "Here, put these on. Take those shoes off. We'll be doing a lot of walking. Here's a jacket. You'll need it."

Without looking him in the eye, Maria took the oversized coat, said thank you, and put it on over the coat she was already wearing. She took off her high heels and put on the socks and boots. She was told not to leave anything behind so she shoved her shoes into the pockets of the large overcoat.

"Alex, do you have the tarp for the rain?" Carlos asked.

Alex nodded. The rainy season had passed, but there were still some occasional showers. All essentials such as food and water were stowed away in large backpacks. Blankets were rolled, put in a plastic bag and tied to the backpacks. Within 30 minutes everyone was ready to move. Maria was struck by anxiety. She wanted to know the reason they were moving at night and wondered what was in store for her. Is this her chance to escape? Perhaps she could find a way when the rebels were all asleep at night.

They left the farmhouse. Maria turned around to take a last look and felt her throat tighten. She tried to hold back the tears, but it was futile. The rebels ignored her as they always did.

They began walking. Carlos took the lead followed by Maria, Alfonso and Alex.

She noticed Carlos held what she thought was a GPS so he could track where they were going.

As she walked she could see the vapor from her breath. It was cold so she shoved her hands into the pockets of the jacket. They no longer walked in a single line, but instead, Alfonso and Alex flanked her. She felt Alex's eyes on her. Despite his boyish face, she thought he was probably in his late twenties. When he wasn't wearing a cap, he habitually brushed his wispy brown hair out of his face. He stood a few inches taller than Maria and had a slim build.

Using her peripheral vision, Maria noticed Alfonso on her other side. Dark skinned and muscular, he appeared a little younger than Alex, wore his dark brown hair very short and was clean-shaven. Maria had seen him showing off several times to the other rebels doing one-arm push-ups. Now he walked very straight and thrust his jaw forward. Maria didn't dare look at him as she found his coal-colored eyes menacing and calculating.

Maria wondered about these young men. Did they have families? Maria knew that the FARC recruited orphans whose parents were killed during Colombia's decades-long civil war. Were these young rebels here because they had no choice? Maria stopped herself from feeling any pity. They were always armed and they could kill her at any time.

The group continued to walk in the forest, stopping only for rest periods, meals, and sleep. Since the food supply dwindled as the days wore on, meals were not as hearty as when they were in the farmhouse. Alex offered her some of his share of the food after she had finished her ration and she accepted it gratefully. He also gave her an extra blanket when it was time to settle down to sleep on the forest floor. She was exhausted every night and fell asleep quickly only after saying silent prayers for her family.

There was in time and place. She realized that even if she had an opportunity to escape, she wouldn't know where to run. They were an isolated group, never once encountering other hikers in the woods. Finally, after 15 days of trudging over rough terrain in the bitter cold, they arrived at another abandoned farmhouse surrounded by fields that once produced a variety of vegetables. At the corner of the structure Maria noticed a cistern that captured rainwater.

Upon entering the dwelling, Maria felt some relief, as this was an improvement over the first place she had been held captive. Although it was vacant of furniture, there were four rooms, a kitchen with a large fireplace for cooking and heating, and a bathroom. She was surprised when Carlos turned on the overhead light. That was when she heard the hum of a gasoline-powered generator. She also noticed a musty smell in the air and the windows were dirty from neglect. She saw several buckets in the kitchen that would be used to bring water from the cistern into the house for bathing, cooking, and cleaning.

"Follow me," Carlos said to Maria as he walked to one of the bedrooms and turned on the light. "Here is the room where you'll sleep. You can continue to do the cooking. And there's a bathroom at the end of the hall. Better than the other place, but no running water."

Maria looked around the room and she saw no manacles attached to the wall.

As if reading her thought, Carlos said, "Someone will be on watch during the night so that you don't go anywhere." With that comment, he left Maria alone.

She looked at her watch. It was now 5:35 p.m. and the 26th of December, the day after Christmas. She thought it odd that the men didn't celebrate the holiday. She then realized that this was the first time in her life that she was away from her family at Christmas. Maria worried about her daughters and wondered if Jorge had tried to make the day festive. She also wondered how he was managing working full time and caring for the girls. She knew her mother and father would be happy to do whatever they could for their grandchildren, but they both worked in the family business. She wondered how long it would be before she would be reunited with her family. Or if she ever would. With that dreadful thought, she collapsed to the floor and wept. She looked around the empty room and noticed a small figure in the corner of the bedroom. There, miraculously, was a statue of the Virgin Mary. Maria got up off the wood floor, walked over to the corner, and knelt before the Madonna. She closed her eyes, held her hands in prayer and began to pray, "Hail Mary, full of grace. The Lord is with thee."

Chapter 7

At the bathroom sink, Maria stood naked and shivering, with tears streaming down her cheeks. It was just before dawn and she was taking a sponge bath in an effort to wash away the odor of Alfonso.

It was near the end of his watch so he had crept silently into Maria's bedroom, closed the door and took her by surprise. She was sound asleep and awakened by Alfonso pulling off her underwear and forcing himself in her. She tried to scream, but Alfonso clamped his hand over her mouth. She pummeled his back with her fists, but it was futile. When he was finished, he rolled off her and told her to be quiet. She was terrified and shocked that he had overpowered her so easily.

Then he whispered in her ear, "Why don't you join our group? I could have your children brought to you."

Maria couldn't believe he actually said those words. She thought he was crazy. "Not in a million years would I do such a thing!" she said, sitting upright and glaring at him.

Alfonso rose up, his eyes flaring with anger and his hands clenched into fists. Fearful of him, Maria said she had to go to the bathroom and fled the room.

Now she felt filthy and no amount of soap and water was going to change that. She wiped her tears away and looked at her watch. It was January 1, the start of a new year. How long will it be until she would go home? She felt sick to her stomach and decided to pass on breakfast. She returned to her bedroom and sat on the floor. She thought of Alfonso raping her. The only man she ever had been with was Jorge, her husband. Now she was disgraced. If she ever got out of here, should she tell Jorge what happened? What if she got pregnant? What about disease? Would this rape be the end of it or would take her every night? The men hadn't bothered her in the one-room farmhouse, but now things were different. There were separate bedrooms affording a small amount of privacy. Maria prayed that she wouldn't be violated again. She felt sore and bruised.

While the men were having their breakfast in the kitchen, Maria overheard them discussing that someone named Sondra would be joining them to make the household appear more like a regular family. She guessed they were worried about outsiders passing through the area and observing them. They were taking no chances.

Just before lunchtime, Maria heard the men greeting a woman. From their banter, she assumed this was Sondra who they knew for a long time, because they were asking about friends they had in common. Maria emerged from the bedroom to meet her. All heads turned to her. Alfonso said, "There she is. The rich daughter!"

Sondra looked Maria over from head to toe and said, "How much money does your father have?"

"I don't know," Maria answered and looked away.

"I'm sure it must be a fortune or you wouldn't be here!" Sondra said as she placed a five-foot-long canvas duffle bag down on the floor. "From the looks of you, you'll be glad that I brought you some fresh clothes and toiletries. Here, take a look." Sondra unzipped the olive green bag and Maria knelt down on the floor to inspect the contents. There were sweaters, jeans, socks, nightgowns, shoes, and underwear. In a plastic bag, she found deodorant, shampoo, conditioner, toothbrushes, toothpaste, combs, brushes and disposable feminine products. Maria also saw many rolls of toilet paper and bars of soap. Sondra then pulled out a heavy clear plastic bag with a long flexible tube and what looked like a shower head.

"Here's a portable shower for camping out," Sondra announced. "I was told there is a bathroom but no running water. As long as there is enough water in the cistern, we can have a quick shower every few days."

Sondra picked up the bag of toiletries and said, "I'll put these in the bathroom. The rest will go in the bedroom you and I will share."

Maria noticed a clip on Sondra's belt that held a cell phone. She realized this group was well organized and they were prepared to hold her for as long as it would take to get the ransom. When supplies ran out, more would be sent. Everything they needed was a phone call away. She looked at Sondra as she walked to the bathroom. The woman was older than Maria, probably in her forties. She wore her dark brown hair pulled back in a ponytail which emphasized her widow's peak. Her skin was tanned, apparently from spending a lot of time outside and she wore no makeup. She was dressed in jeans, a black sweater, black riding boots and a pea green wool jacket. Maria wondered under what circumstances Sondra joined this band of rebels.

After everyone had eaten lunch and the dishes were cleaned, Maria excused herself to take a long overdue shower. Sondra followed her in the bathroom to set up the portable shower. The plastic bag was filled with water that had been heated when they cooked lunch. Sondra attached it to a hook on the bathroom wall. She showed Maria the shower tubing, pointing out the clamp that would stop the flow of water. Maria was to stand in a large aluminum basin which would catch the shower water. When she was through with her shower, she would dispose of it down the toilet.

"Have you ever used one of these before?" asked Sondra, referring to the shower.

"Never," said Maria shaking her head. "I've never been camping."

Sondra instructed, "First, wet yourself down. Then shampoo your hair and wash your body. Rinse. Use the conditioner for your hair. Then rinse. You're finished. There's not a lot of water so be quick about it."

Sondra left the room and Maria was left to have her first shower in well over two months. She followed Sondra's instructions, but she had barely enough water to finish rinsing her long hair. She didn't have the luxury of a hair dryer, so Maria combed her wet hair and secured it in a ponytail.

When she emerged from the bathroom feeling refreshed and wearing clean clothes, she noticed no one was inside the house. The front door swung open and Carlos walked in. He grabbed her by the elbow leading her outside. "There's something I want to show you."

He led her to the weed-choked garden. Standing there were Alex, Alfonso and Sondra. There were mounds of dirt piled up and shovels on the ground. As Carlos pulled her closer to the mound, she saw the men had dug a grave. "This is where you'll be going if your father doesn't pay us soon. He is a shrewd businessman, and he still hasn't agreed on a price."

Maria looked down at the bottom of the grave and gasped. She looked at each one of the rebels and wondered who would be the one to kill her.

Suddenly she saw Carlos put both his hands up in surrender and shouted, "No, Alfonso. Put it away. Don't be stupid."

Maria froze when she looked at Alfonso and saw him holding a grenade with his finger on the ring ready to pull it free. Alfonso yelled, "She's a bitch who has a father that doesn't care about her. I should just kill us all and get it over with!"

"No, no, Alfonso. Stop. Don't do it. I'll have her write another letter to her father. We'll get the money soon. These things take time. You know that! She'll tell him about the grave. You'll see," Carlos said with authority. "Put the grenade down, gently."

Alfonso shook his head and stared at the grenade. He released if from his hand and it fell on the ground. All eyes were on it to see if Alfonso had pulled the pin. He had not. They were all safe for the moment. Carlos ran over and picked up the grenade, inspected it, and put it in his jacket pocket. He nodded to Alfonso, "Good! Cool down. Take a walk."

Alfonso turned and walked away. Carlos now led Maria back to the house. "Now write the letter. Tell him about the grave we dug for you. That we'll put you in it unless we get the money."

Maria hung her head, crying from the relief that she was still alive. Carlos put paper and pen on the table. "Here, Maria. Write to your daddy. Tell him he must pay if he wants to see you alive."

Maria picked up the pen and through blurry eyes, began to write:

Dear Don Pedro,

Please pay the ransom. Today they dug a grave for me and this is where they will put me if they don't get the money. I am very scared and I want to come home. My love to you, Momma, my daughters, Jorge, and my brothers.

Maria.

She put the pen down and stepped away from the table. Carlos picked up the letter and read it. "Good."

He pocketed the paper and pulled out his cell phone. He speed dialed and when the person answered his call, he said, "I've got another delivery. Come and get it."

He closed the phone and stared into her eyes. Then he looked her body over and came back to her eyes. He reached out to pull her to him, his tongue licking his lips. Maria knocked his arm away and marched swiftly to her bedroom, closing the door. She rushed to the Madonna, stood there, and then genuflected. She took in a deep breath, held it, exhaled slowly and listened for footsteps. She then knelt down and prayed that Carlos wouldn't come after her.

Chapter 8

Jorge pulled up in front of the high-rise condominium in the north Bogotá neighborhood of Santa Barbara, the same upscale residential area where he lived with Maria's family. He was here to pick up his children, Julie and Paula, from Vivian. She was married to Jorge's boss, Sal Perez. Once Sal learned about Maria's abduction, he asked Jorge if he needed child care for his daughters. He suggested that Vivian, a watercolorist, might be able to care for the girls after school since she stayed home to work on her paintings. Vivian was happy to pick up the girls from elementary school and keep them entertained until Jorge picked them up each evening. The routine for Julie, a fourth grader, was to sit down and complete her homework. Once she was finished, she joined Paula and Vivian for painting lessons in Vivian's studio.

Jorge took the elevator to Vivian's floor and walked to her luxury apartment. The first day he came for his daughters, he remarked what a beautiful home she had. Vivian graciously accredited it to an interior decorator whose work was frequently pictured in interior design magazines. Although the colors were all beige tones, the various textures in the furnishings made it interesting. But the eye was drawn to the art. In addition to framed watercolors by Vivian, there also were bronze sculptures, polished wood carvings and art glass prominently displayed in a wall unit along one wall. Even the coffee table in front of the couch was a piece of art: A bronze sculpture of a dolphin supported the glass table top. Adding to the overall elegance of the room were wood floors of polished cherry.

He knocked on the door and within seconds, he heard the muffled voices of his daughters yelling, "It's Daddy. Come, Aunt Vivian. Daddy's here." The children had grown close to Vivian, calling her "Aunt Vivian" as a term of endearment.

He heard the deadbolt release and the door opened. His heart skipped a beat as his daughters reached up to hug him. Jorge scooped up little Paula in his arms and bent down to kiss Julie. The girls said in unison, "Hi, Daddy, we missed you."

"I missed you, too," said Jorge with a touch of weariness in his voice.

Vivian waved her hand for Jorge to come in. "Jorge, you look tired. Come and sit down for a few minutes." Vivian was forty years old but she could pass for thirty. She was wearing her painter's smock over a blue sweater and faded jeans. She walked gracefully in tan moccasins. She had short brown hair, wore no makeup and her soft brown eyes reflected concern. "Girls, why don't you go back in the studio and clean up for me? Please wash the paint brushes and be sure to rinse out the sink."

Anxious to go home with their father, the children frowned and walked to the studio.

"I'll sit for only for a few minutes," Jorge said as he took his seat in the soft leather chair across from the couch. "I don't want to take up much of your time. The girls must tire you out."

Vivian sat down on the couch tossing one of the many decorative silk pillows aside, "I enjoy every minute I have with them. Children grow up so fast. My own daughters are already 18 and 20. They're both attending the university," she said with a wistful sigh.

"Vivian, I don't know what I'd do without you. It's been almost three months since −." Jorge stopped with the painful memory.

"I understand what you're going through, Jorge. Sal said this has been a strain on you and your family."

"Maria's parents are just about ready to get divorced. My mother-in-law wants her daughter home, but Don Pedro hasn't agreed on the ransom. She doesn't seem to understand that GAULA has frozen all his money except for enough funds to pay the bills. We know that the agency is using whatever means available to find Maria. It's frustrating but what can we do? Wait. And pray. Everyone in the family thinks that there is a traitor who set Maria up. So now everyone is looking at each other, wondering. The police even suspected me for a time. But I've been cleared. Vivian, it's really hard to go to work every day not knowing if Maria is alive. And it's even harder trying to maintain a somewhat normal home for Julie and Paula," Jorge said, covering his eyes with his hands. "It's just so hard."

Jorge stood up and took a deep breath to stop himself from breaking down in tears. "I'm so glad to have the support of you and Sal. You're more than friends. You're like family."

"I know," said Vivian who looked at Jorge with compassion. "Sal thinks of you as the son he never had. We're here for you. You must know that."

Jorge nodded in agreement.

Vivian reached for Jorge's hand, squeezed it and said, "I pray for Maria every night for her safe return. Hopefully, you'll have her home soon."

Jorge put his free hand on top of Vivian's and looked at her soft brown eyes. "From your lips to God's ears."

"Daddy, can we go home now? I'm getting hungry," said Paula who suddenly appeared in the hallway.

"Yes, Paula. Get your sister and we'll leave now." Jorge said releasing his hand from Vivian's. "Vivian, thanks for your prayers and for caring for our daughters."

Vivian nodded, pressing her lips together so as not to cry. "Go on now. I'll see you tomorrow. Get some rest. Sal said you have a big client meeting tomorrow."

"That's right. It's a new business meeting. This potential client needs a customized software program. I hope to get him to sign a contract." Jorge said, noticing Julie and Paula had their backpacks and were ready to leave. "All set, girls?"

Paula and Julie said in unison, "Yes, Daddy. Good-bye, Aunt Vivian. See you tomorrow."

Vivian stood up, helped them into their coats, and gave them each a hug. "See you tomorrow. Be good for Daddy."

Jorge and his daughters returned to his car. Jorge opened the car door for them and the girls got in the back seat. Once everyone's seatbelts were secure, he turned the key in the ignition and checked the side-view mirror before pulling out into traffic. The girls were quiet during the ride home. He looked in the rearview mirror at Julie. He noticed that she had gotten very quiet in the last few days after having a heartfelt conversation with her. Julie had asked when her mommy was coming home. Jorge had answered, "I don't know, Julie. And I don't know if she will."

Jorge now wondered if he was wrong to be truthful. He knew she was smart and mature for her age, but now he felt his words had traumatized her.

He prayed that Maria would come home very soon. He didn't know if he could go on without her. He worried that her kidnappers would kill her. With that horrible thought, tears welled up in his eyes, blurring his vision. He blinked and took a deep breath, willing himself to maintain his composure in front of his daughters. They needed their mother, he thought, and so do I.

Chapter 9

Maria woke up to gunshots and shouting. There was a thunderous explosive charge and the heavy farm door collapsed, crashing onto the floor. Swarms of men dressed in black came charging into the dark farmhouse wearing night vision goggles and holding revolvers, ready to fire.

Maria's bedroom door burst open and she screamed, "Oh, my God. Please don't kill me. Please, no. Please."

The farmhouse filled with smoke, and Maria heard shouting, screams and curses during the mayhem. A man picked her up and carried her out of the farmhouse into a waiting van. Maria screamed, fearing for her life. The man placed her on the seat and said, "Maria, we are rescuing you. You are safe. We are the police. Don't be afraid. Your father is Don Pedro and he owns Fino Foods. Your daughters are Paula and Julie and your husband is Jorge. I am going to call your father now so you can speak to him. Then we are going to take you home. You'll see your husband and daughters at headquarters."

Maria looked at her savior, nodded and began to cry. She had thought a new group of rebels had come to execute her. Instead she was saved; her prayers were answered.

The officer pulled out his cell phone, punched in a number and waited for the connection. When he heard Don Pedro's voice, he said, "Hold on a minute, sir. I have your daughter, Maria. She is safe."

With trembling hands she took the phone and held it to her ear. Sobbing, she said, "Daddy. Oh Daddy, I love you. I can't believe it. I can't believe it. I can come home."

The officer left her to her phone call, got in the driver's seat and turned the ignition. Another officer got in the back seat with Maria and another one took his seat up front in the passenger's seat. Maria didn't notice an officer outside the van had his video camera and light focused on her. He had videotaped the entire rescue mission which would be used for training purposes. A copy of it would also be given to Maria.

"Ok, Daddy. I can't wait to see you. Goodbye," said Maria, closing the cell phone. She handed the phone to the officer next to her. She sobbed loudly as she put her hands over her eyes. The officer in the front passenger seat tapped her knee and handed her a box of tissues. Maria took it, and wiped her eyes with a tissue. Then she turned around in her seat to see Sondra, Alex, Alfonso and Carlos being taken out of the farmhouse in handcuffs. They were led to another waiting van by the surveillance and rescue team. All guns were aimed at her captors. She wondered where they would take them.

The driver turned the headlights on, put the van in gear and slowly drove over the farmland. It was 5 a.m. and the sun had not yet begun to rise. As the driver turned the van, the headlights revealed the hole in the ground that could have been her grave. Maria gasped, closed her eyes and when she opened them, they were heading away from the farmhouse and all of its horror.

"How did you find me?" Maria said after a while, finally realizing she was on her way home. She took the bottle of water that was offered to her and drank deeply.

The driver said, "It wasn't easy. They all use cell phones. They're hard to trace. But we had a stroke of luck last night. One of the rebels made a call on a landline. He was ordering food supplies for the farmhouse. We were able to trace the call to his location. We moved in fast and we apprehended him. Eventually, we got him to talk and he disclosed the location where you were being held. We found out how many people were here with you and the time of the shift change."

Maria remembered the shift change vividly. "Yes, 5 a.m.," she said.

The officer nodded in agreement.

"How long will it take for us to get back to the city?" Maria asked. "I have no idea where I am."

"It's about a three-and-a-half-hour drive. All two-lane roads. It's slow going," said the driver.

Maria let out a deep sigh and closed her eyes. In the past few days, she had begun to lose hope that she'd ever see her family again and now, in a matter of hours, she would be reunited with them. She thought about her captors. She had feared Alfonso and Carlos the most. They were short-tempered so she avoided all eye contact with them. She remembered the day they showed her the grave and shivered. She thought of Sondra and dismissed her. When the woman first arrived at the farmhouse, Maria thought she might talk with her for companionship. Instead, Sondra ignored her. The only words she spoke to Maria were, "How much money is your Daddy going to give us?"

Then she thought of Alex. She believed he was fond of her, but he never crossed the line that would get him into trouble with his comrades. He had shown kindness to her, by giving her an extra blanket and some of his ration of food in the forest. He even had washed some of her clothes this last month. She looked at her watch. Yes, it had been a month and a day since they arrived at the farmhouse; three months since she was kidnapped. Now she was going home. The hours couldn't go fast enough.

Now the van was on a paved two-lane road and Maria settled back for the long ride home. She asked, "Did my father get my letters? I wrote three of them."

The driver said, "Three? No, he only got two."

"I wonder why," Maria said, frowning.

"It doesn't matter now. You're safe and going home," said the driver.

"Do you know what happened to my sister-in-law and friend that were with me that night?" Maria asked. "Are they all right?"

"They're fine. They were locked in the trunk of the young man's car. They managed to get out through the backseat into the car and found the car keys in the ignition. They returned to your home and told your family you were kidnapped."

"How convenient," Maria said. She fell silent and thought about that fateful night as she had the many days and night she was in captivity.

Maria wondered why she was kidnapped. Of course, for money, but why her? She then asked, "How much was the ransom?

The officer sitting next to her said, "Six million American dollars. They have been negotiating with your father and the amount was down to one and half million."

Maria grew quiet thinking about the past four months and all that she had missed. The celebrations – Christmas and New Year's Day – Paula's fifth birthday and all the other family birthdays. She thought about her daughters and began to cry softly. She wondered how Jorge managed to care for them and provide for them. She then thought how lucky she was to be alive. She silently said a prayer, thanking the Lord that she was saved by these brave men. She knew from TV news reports that not everyone was so fortunate.

By nine o'clock, Maria arrived at police headquarters. She was told that Jorge and her daughters had arrived at 8:30 a.m. and were anxiously waiting to be reunited. She was also told that a press conference would be held and her reunion would be broadcast on all the major TV stations. They explained what she could expect in the coming days and months. Most people that were rescued lived in fear that it would happen to them again or to some other family member. For security, many survivors acquired bullet-proof cars and trucks and employed bodyguards. Many sought out counseling services. And ultimately, many sought political asylum from foreign countries.

Finally, at 10 a.m., Maria was brought into the room where they were holding the press conference — the blaze of light from the television crew was blinding. She had washed her face, combed her hair and changed into clean clothes that her husband had delivered. The clothes just hung on her since she had lost considerable weight. When she looked into the mirror, she was amazed at how much older she looked. An officer introduced her and then her beloved family was escorted into the room. The cameras focused on Maria as she ran to them, crying. She knelt down on her knees to hug her daughters who simply stood there, paralyzed by the commotion. She didn't want to let them go, but then she reached up to her husband. Jorge wrapped his strong arms around her and let out a sigh. She inhaled the scent of him and found comfort in him. He then held her at arm's length and looked into her glistening blue eyes. Tears rolled down his cheeks as well. He did not brush them away. They were tears of joy. He said, "Maria, I love you. I prayed for this day. Thank God you're home." He hugged her again and then they parted when an officer intervened, telling them they could leave. The camera then cut back to the public information officer to broadcast his closing remarks. Now reunited, the Alvarez family was free to go home and make up for lost time.

It all felt surreal to Maria who was now a free woman. The family held each other's hands as they walked out of headquarters to Jorge's waiting car. The sun was shining; the sky was cerulean blue, and the air crisp. She looked at her daughters and then her husband. Her throat tightened and she swallowed hard. There was so much she wanted to say to them, but for the moment, all she could do was cry.

Chapter 10

Maria wiped her tears with a tissue. Her mother's request to come home to see her dying father left her feeling helpless. She glanced down at her watch. She still had an hour or so before her daughters would be home from school. She turned on the TV and inserted the videotape GAULA had made of her rescue from the FARC rebels into the old VCR. Her tears continued to flow as she watched the events unfold on that memorable day. She was glad to have this recorded history. Although it was painful to watch, it was a confirmation that she was no longer a victim but a survivor.

The tape was short. It opened in darkness with the sounds of shouting and the police breaking the door down. The police ordered everyone down. She heard her own voice crying "Don't kill me!" Finally, a spotlight was on her as an officer carried her and placed her on the seat of the police van. She heard the man telling her she was safe. The tape ended just after she took the cell phone to talk to her father. Then the tape dissolved to the television broadcast announcing a successful rescue of a FARC kidnap victim by GAULA. She was introduced by the police captain and then the tape ended with Maria embraced by her husband and daughters.

That was two years ago. Now her father was on his deathbed and her mother had pleaded with her to come home. Yet everyone in her family knew the terms of political asylum. Once you were granted a green card providing lawful permanent residence status to live in the US, you could not return to your homeland. If you did, political asylum status would be revoked because you demonstrated you no longer had a fear of being persecuted or killed.

Besides that major issue, Maria remembered the phone call from Alex just a couple of months after her rescue. She was shocked that he tracked her down. She told him she didn't want to talk to him. He said he was still in prison, and he wanted to warn her she would be killed if the rebels captured her again. Now she realized that Alex cared about her. His final words were, "Be careful."

After that phone call, Jorge and their daughters moved from the family apartment building to a secret location. She remembered the months of anxiety. Jorge had bought a bullet-proof car and truck for protection while the political asylum application was being processed through the US Embassy.

Now she feared that if she returned to Bogotá, someone would recognize her and inform the FARC rebels. After all, everyone in the family thought there was a traitor among them, but no one had dared to make an accusation.

As much as she knew she shouldn't consider returning to Colombia, she wanted to see her father and make up for all the ill feelings that had passed among Jorge, her mother and him. She wanted to hear what he had to say. After all, he was the one who had to deal with the phone calls from the rebels and the government agency that was working on her behalf. Others in the family had drawn a portrait of her father as an uncaring, shrewd businessman. She had argued with Jorge about it many times without any resolution. She reminded Jorge that her father couldn't pay the ransom since the agency had frozen his bank accounts. Jorge's retort was to ask her why her father withheld financial aid when they were leaving Bogotá for the safety of the US. Don Pedro was wealthy but chose not to help his only daughter start a new life.

Jorge had sold the car and truck for $20,000 and that is what they used to settle in the US. The money wouldn't go far since neither of them had a job waiting for them. They needed to buy a car, rent a place to live, and pay the household expenses. He also reminded her that she would never inherit any money from her father's estate, since that was the Latin custom. Only the sons received an inheritance.

Now she was torn between the duty of being a good wife and mother and that of being a dutiful daughter. She always had a close relationship with Papa. She remembered her father helping her with her homework as a child. She had such difficulty doing math word problems and he took the time to tutor her. She eventually came to love math, the only *real truth* her father liked to say. All through the years he always encouraged her to work hard and follow her dreams. He instilled confidence in her that she could accomplish anything she set her mind to. But now this dilemma. She knew she wanted — no — she needed to see her father before he died. She loved him dearly and she had to set his mind at ease that he was the best father a daughter could ever hope for. She needed to tell him how much she appreciated him and how he helped her to become the woman she was today. But how could she return to Bogotá without getting killed? How could she return to the US and keep her green card? There had to be a way.

Impulsively, she went to the kitchen and called Jorge on his cell phone. He was working in Miami as a computer systems analyst for an international company. It was Sal, Jorge's former boss, who had found him the job. He insisted Jorge was perfect for the job since he was multi-lingual, speaking fluent Spanish, French, Italian and English.

The call went to voice mail. Maria didn't leave a message. She thought it was just as well. She really shouldn't discuss this matter with him while he was at work. It would only upset him.

She took the phone with her and sat down on the couch. The living room was small and from where she sat, she had a view into the kitchen and dining area. There was an expanse of windows that brought in the sunlight and afforded a view of a grassy area leading to a canal. The townhouse provided two floors. The girls' bedrooms were on the second floor along with a bathroom. The master bedroom and bath were on the main floor. There was also a half-bath for the convenience of guests, should they entertain on rare occasions. Her home was a far cry from the lifestyle she enjoyed in Bogotá, but at least she was safe and could live in peace.

Maria rubbed her temples, deep in thought. Once again, her eyes were drawn to the Madonna, looking for answers. How can I go see my father without anyone knowing I am there? How can I return to the US safely to live with my family? Maria wished she could be invisible so that she could do as her heart commanded.

The telephone rang, interrupting her thoughts. She picked up the phone and answered, "Hello."

"Maria, I saw that you called," said Jorge. "What's the matter?"

She started to cry and through her tears, she said, "It's my father. He's dying and I have to go home. My mother called and I have to go, Jorge."

"Maria, are you *loco*?" Jorge said, his voice rising. "You can't go back. Remember why we left? The bullet proof car and truck? You could be killed. Remember the warning from Alex? The American Embassy told you if you leave the US and return to

Colombia, you lose your green card. What are you thinking, Maria?"

Maria let out a deep sigh and struggled to speak. "I just know it in my heart that I have to see my father before he dies. I just have to."

"Maria, pull yourself together. Think about our daughters, Paula and Julie. Think about me. We can't let you go. Please don't even think about it," Jorge said his voice now suddenly weak.

"But Jorge, after all I've been through, I have to see to my father before he dies. I just have to. I was so close to him before — but now there's a wall between us. I know you were upset with him. And so was my mother. But he asked for me. I need to find a way to go. Please help me, Jorge, please."

Jorge was silent. Finally, he said, "Maria, you're not being rational. I've got a status meeting scheduled in five minutes. This will have to wait until I get home."

Maria wiped her eyes and inhaled deeply. Exhaling slowly, she said, "All right, Jorge. Goodbye." She touched the off button on her handset. She looked up to the ceiling and sighed. "Dear Lord, now what? What am I going to do? How can I live with myself if I refuse his dying wish?

Chapter 11

Jorge always looked forward to coming home from work. But not tonight. He had to deal with Maria and her crazy idea of returning to Bogotá to see her father.

As he turned the key in the front door of his home, he heard the muffled voices of his daughters announcing his arrival.

When he opened the door, they were standing there waiting for a hug and a kiss from him. Maria usually greeted him at the door, too, but he heard her moving about in the kitchen preparing dinner. He could smell the aroma of *Cocido Bogotano* cooking, a Colombian beef and vegetable stew.

"Hi, Daddy," Julie and Paula said in unison. They both had changed out of their school uniforms and were wearing play clothes.

"Hi Julie, Paula," Jorge said reaching down to give each a hug and kiss. "Is your homework done?"

"Yes, it's all done," said Julie. Her smile stretched from ear to ear revealing her braces with purple bands.

"Do you want to go out and play?"

"Yes, Daddy.

"I'll call you in when dinner is ready," Jorge asked. "Just stay in the playground area across the street. Don't go wandering anywhere else."

"OK," Julie said as she grabbed Paula's hand. They went out the door and Jorge closed it behind them.

Jorge walked into the kitchen and said, "Maria."

He normally got a kiss hello when he came home from work. Not tonight.She was peeling and cubing potatoes and carrots that she would add to the stew pot. She turned to face him and barely whispered, "Hello."

"Do you want to talk about this craziness now or after the girls go to bed?" Jorge asked, already knowing the answer.

"Later," she said, "I still have more vegetables to cut up and I have to make the salad."

"All right. I'll go change and then watch the news." Jorge went to the master bedroom and changed from his white business shirt, navy tie and gray slacks to khaki shorts, a blue tee shirt and boat shoes. He hung up the slacks and tie in the closet and threw the shirt into the hamper. He then went to the kitchen and grabbed a beer from the refrigerator before returning to the living room. He sat down on the couch and turned on the TV to *Telemundo* which broadcasted in Spanish and gave more news about South America. He watched the reports but his mind was elsewhere. He looked across the room and saw Maria busy at work. She looked tense, moving about mechanically. He sensed this was going to be a difficult night, all the more when you have to watch what you say since the girls' bedrooms were right upstairs. He also had to admit that Maria was a changed woman after the kidnapping. There was deep-seated anger that often flared up when Jorge asked her to do something for him. He had to be careful that his request didn't sound like a command. She certainly was a stronger woman having to manage the household while she struggled to learn English. Like many adults learning a new language, she was self-conscious speaking English, afraid that she would sound stupid. Her English instructor at the community college advised the students to speak English at home, especially around the dinner table with their children. Maria adapted this advice and found that she was finally gaining confidence in this new language.

After putting the salad bowls and glasses of sweet iced tea on the table, Maria announced that dinner was ready. Jorge went outside and called the girls in. Without having to be told, Julie and Paula washed their hands and then they each took their seats at the table. Julie bowed her head and said grace, thanking the Lord for the food they were about to eat. Starting with Jorge, Maria served each *Coccid Bogotano* and then passed the bread basket. As usual, Jorge asked the girls about their day at school. They took their turns telling him that Songfest was coming up in a few weeks and what songs their class was going to sing. Maria sat silently throughout the dinner. The girls noticed that their mother was unusually quiet and tried to draw her out with questions, but Maria merely nodded and said yes or no. When they had finished their flan for dessert, the girls and Jorge cleared the table. Julie put the dishes in the dishwasher while Maria packed the leftovers in storage containers. The girls chattered endlessly, but Jorge found Maria's silence deafening.

Once the kitchen was cleaned and everything in its place, Jorge asked the girls to bring him their homework so he could check it for accuracy. Six-year-old Paula was in first grade so she had math and reading worksheets while 11-year-old Julie had assignments in math, reading, spelling and social studies. Even if Jorge found mistakes, he told his daughters that they can learn from these. His mantra was: Repetition is the way people learn; that's why practice makes perfect. Both girls were good students and Jorge was proud of them.

With homework review complete, Jorge said good night to them. The next ritual was bath time. Maria supervised Paula who insisted on a bubble bath while Julie wanted to take a shower. Once Maria dried the girls' hair, they were ready to get into bed. Normally Maria read a bedtime story to each of them, but tonight she said she wasn't feeling very well. She would read to them the next night. The sisters passed knowing glances that something is wrong with Mama. Maria tucked Paula in her bed first, gave her a hug and a kiss, and said good night.

She turned on the night light and closed the door. She did the same with Julie and then went downstairs to join Jorge.

He was sitting on the couch staring at nothing in particular.

"Jorge," Maria said as she walked into the living room, "The girls are now in bed. It's time we talked."

Jorge stared at her. "It's a crazy idea to go back to Colombia. You're risking your life. And you'll lose your green card. Do you want us to move back to Colombia?"

"I hadn't thought of all of us going back. Paula and Julie have a better life here. And we're safe. If we all went, we could all be in danger. I was thinking I would go alone," Maria said as she touched his shoulder. "It's important that I go. It's important to my father. And it's important to me. I love him and I couldn't live with myself if I didn't go to him. How can I live with you if you deny me this? He's dying and he asked for me. How can I say no? I have to go, Jorge."

"I don't see how," Jorge said as he got up and paced the room.

Maria sat down on the love seat and looked up at Jorge. She rubbed her temples and said, "What if I had a disguise?"

"Now you're really crazy!" Jorge said, trying to keep his voice down.

"No, hear me out. Remember that movie we watched with the girls, 'Mrs. Doubtfire?'"

"No, refresh my memory," Jorge said, frowning.

"It was about an actor who went through a bitter divorce. He impersonated a female housekeeper so he could spend time with his children every day. Neither his children nor his ex knew it's him. It was terrific."

"But that was a movie!" Jorge just about shouted.

"I think it's possible. I could go as a nurse. I could wear a uniform, wig, glasses, and makeup, maybe something else to distort my looks further. I would be calling on my father as his nurse. It's perfect," Maria said, taking in a deep breath.

Jorge sensed Maria thought this crazy idea was logical. He had to take another tack. "Let's say the disguise works. What about the logistics of getting to Colombia and coming back? Sure, you can fly there. But you can't come back here without losing your green card. And that is out of the question. We need you here, Maria. I need you. Your children need you."

"What if I didn't fly to Colombia? My visa allows me to enter another country and come back. What if I fly to an island in the Caribbean? Then take a boat to Colombia? My father will pay all my expenses."

Jorge stopped, looked at Maria and shook his head. "You've had a lot of time to think about this, I see. It just may work. But it still is dangerous. There are a lot of details to work out. I don't know. I just can't see you going back and risking your life. We thought we lost you once. I just don't want to risk losing you again."

Maria got up and took Jorge's hand, leading him to sit down on the couch. "Sit down, Jorge. Maybe it's time we talked about my father. And you."

"What do you mean?"

"How do you feel about him?" Maria asked, her eyes searching his for the truth.

"I respect the man. He works hard."

"No, I mean on a personal level. How does he make you feel? Do you have affection for him?"

Jorge fell silent, put his elbows on his knees and rested his head in the palms of his hands. Maria waited for his answer. Jorge picked his head up and leaned back on the couch. Turning to Maria, he asked, "The truth?"

"Yes. Of course."

"I don't feel close to your father. I feel like an outsider. I'm not of white European blood like the rest of your family. I thought your father was disappointed in your choice of a husband."

"That's not true. You're making it a racial issue." Maria said.

"I am not. I'm speaking the truth. There are class barriers in Colombia and you know it. The native Colombians –Indians – are inferior to those that settled there from Europe. I'm of mixed race, mestizos –Indian and white – but because I got a good education, I was able to migrate to a middle-class rank."

Now Maria was quiet. She tucked her left leg under her knee and leaned back. "There was some discussion about your background, but my father knew my mind was made up. Besides, you had a good job and could provide for me and our future children. He really couldn't argue with that. And everyone in our family liked you right away. Especially my mother. That scored a lot of points."

Jorge smiled thinking about Mama. He knew she loved him like one of her own sons. And then he remembered her coming to him complaining about Don Pedro, how he wouldn't pay the ransom. She was so heartbroken about Maria's kidnapping that she wanted Don Pedro to do the impossible to get her back.

"Do you think my mother's anguish somehow caused the estrangement in the family with my father?"

"I don't know. It's possible. Everyone was so upset. We all wanted to know why you were kidnapped. Everyone in the family suspected you were set up. You even thought so yourself."

Maria looked up at the ceiling, thinking about who might have been the Judas. She was certain who it was but never said the person's name.

Jorge sensed she was thinking about the traitor. Now was the time to ask her. "Who do you think it was? It will be our secret."

Taking in a deep breath and exhaling slowly, Maria said, "I think Silvana is my traitor."

"Silvana? Why her? Why would she turn against you?" Jorge leaned forward wanting to know her reasons. His sister-in-law acted like Maria's best friend.

"Money is one motivator. I'm sure she got a nice payoff for her efforts. I think she was jealous of me. As the only daughter, I got a lot of attention from my father and mother. And then the attention doubled when we had Julie and Paula. Silvana doesn't have any children even though she wants them and has tried to get pregnant without success. Maybe this has made her bitter."

"I don't know. You know better how women think."

"It all makes sense to me. Silvana was with me the night I was kidnapped. She arranged the ride home that night after class. And the rebels left the keys in the ignition. How convenient. She is the one I have to watch out for."

"Now wait a minute. This isn't settled. You sound like we agreed you can go. We've been talking about a lot of things, but we made no agreement about it."

Maria reached for both his hands and held them tightly. "You know I have to go. I have to see my father before he dies. Time is running out and we have to work out a plan. I know I can do it and come back safely if I have you to help me work out the details. You're a smart man. Mama says so."

Jorge pulled her to him and hugged her. She's always had his heart.

Chapter 12

With the girls in school and Jorge at work, Maria had the house to herself. She poured herself a cup of coffee and then sat down at the table. She looked over her notes she made last night when Jorge and she devised a plan that would get her to Colombia and back to South Florida by passing Homeland Security. Since she had a green card and her Colombian passport, she could fly outside the US without restraint. The first step of the trip was to fly from Miami to Aruba, since the Caribbean island wasn't far from Colombia's coast. In Oranjestad, she would charter a sportfishing yacht to the Colombian seaport of Santa Marta. Next she would arrange transportation to the airport where a private jet would be waiting to take her to Bogotá, just an hour flight. They realized this strategy was feasible after Jorge called his boss Sal. Jorge knew Sal had often traveled to Aruba to go sportfishing and knew the island well. Sal recommended the Renaissance Marina in Oranjestad as the best place to charter a boat. Sal said Maria needed to pay a captain in cash if she wanted the best price. He suggested that she should have the captain wait for her in Santa Marta during her visit to Bogotá, guaranteeing her transportation back to Aruba. This would be an additional expense, but well worth it. Sal also said he would make the reservation for a private jet to fly Maria from Santa Marta to Bogotá. He would also arrange for a driver to pick her up at the airport unless Maria's father wanted to take care of that detail. The only thing left for Maria to do was to book a round-trip flight from Miami to Aruba. She would do that after she called her mother.

Maria punched in the telephone number and waited for her mother to answer. After just two rings, her mother said, "*Hola, Maria.*"

Her mother had caller ID.

"Mama, I have good news," Maria said. "I will come to see Papa."

"Maria, I'm so happy. We were hoping you'd find a way. Your father said not to worry about the money. He'll pay for it."

"Yes, you said that he would. And that's good, because it'll be expensive. We can't afford it ourselves," Maria said and explained the circuitous way she would get to Colombia and the reason for it.

When she finished, her mother asked how much money she would need. Maria itemized the approximate prices: $500 roundtrip airfare to Aruba, $28,000 for the roundtrip yacht charter to Santa Marta, $3,700 roundtrip private jet to Bogotá; total over $32,000. She asked if her father could wire the money into her checking account as she would need cash for the yacht charter.

"I'll have your father wire $35,000 into your account today, that's an extra three thousand just in case. It's better to have more than not enough. You're going to have to give me your bank's wire routing number and your checking account number."

"Is that the information that's printed on the bottom of the checks?" Maria asked.

"The checking account number is correct. The routing number on the check is not the one for wiring money. You'll have to call your bank for that," her mother said.

"All right. I'll do that and I'll also make the reservation for the flight to Aruba. Then I'll call you back after I make these phone calls. Tell Papa the good news."

"I will. I'll get him on the phone to talk to you when you call back," her mother said.

They said good-bye and Maria made her phone calls, first calling the bank and then American Airlines. Ten minutes later, she had her mother back on the phone. Maria recited the wire routing number and checking account number and asked her mother to read the numbers back to her so there would be no mistake.

"So when will you fly out?" Mama asked her.

"Tomorrow. I booked a flight out of Miami that leaves at 11:05 a.m. I get into Aruba at 1:50 p.m."

"Great. Can you be ready to leave by then?"

"It's going to be tight, because I have a lot to do today. But I think I can manage it. If there is any change, I'll let you know," Maria said.

"Good. I'll go get your father so you can talk to him for a minute."

"OK, Mama. But I have to warn you first. You can't tell anyone that I am coming. Remember we always thought there was a traitor who set me up to be kidnapped?"

"Yes. I remember that. You don't want me to let the family know?"

"I know it's hard, but you can't tell anyone," Maria said, her tone suddenly serious.

"But Maria, the family will see you when you get here,"

Maria hesitated, "They will and they won't. I know this is going to sound crazy to you, but I can't risk someone recognizing me and then informing the rebels. I was warned that I would be killed if they got their hands on me again. So I am not taking any chances. I'll be wearing a disguise."

"What?" Mama yelled.

"Mama, keep your voice down. Someone might hear you." Then as if Maria thought someone could hear what she was saying on Mama's end, she whispered, "I will come as a home healthcare nurse."

"But you're not a nurse."

"I know that, Mama. But the family is used to seeing nurses around Papa. You'll still have a real nurse to monitor Papa's vitals and whatever else he needs. You can say I'm a nursing intern shadowing the home healthcare nurse."

"My Lord, I hope it works," Mama said. She hesitated and then asked, "So who do you think was the traitor?"

Maria whispered, "Silvana."

"Silvana?" Mama asked. "You think she's the traitor? I don't believe it."

"I'm convinced of it. And I'll tell you why when I see you. Meanwhile, I'll call you from my cell phone after I arrive in Aruba and make arrangements with a charter fishing captain. That reminds me there's another thing I have to do today. I need to get an international calling card. So I better get going. Put Papa on the phone for me, please. I love you, Mama. I'll call you from Aruba after two o'clock tomorrow unless there is a delay. The flight number is 1162 if you want to see if it's on time."

Mama said good-bye and after a few seconds, handed the phone to her ex-husband.

"Maria, you make my heart glad. I know you're putting yourself at risk to come here, but I'm so happy. There is so much I want to say. You mean the world to me."

"Papa, I love you. I'm so sorry that you're sick. You should have told me long ago. I can't wait to see you," Maria said, her voice quivering. She was afraid she was going to cry so she took a deep breath and then swallowed. "I have to go now. There is a lot to do before I leave here tomorrow. I told Mama I will call when I get to Aruba."

"Yes, go and get what you need to get done. I can't wait to see you, too. I love you, Maria."

They said good-bye and Maria blinked back the tears. There just wasn't time for that now.

Maria sent a text message to Jorge about her airline reservation. She looked at her watch. It was already after ten o'clock. She would miss her English class at the community college, but she believed this mission was more important. She went on the family computer and used the Internet to find where she could shop for a nurse's uniform, white shoes, a wig, glasses and a padded bodysuit. The only difficulty was finding a store that sold a padded bodysuit. She'd have to improvise by buying a regular one that was too big and using fiberfill that she left over from making decorative pillows for the girls' rooms.

With the list of stores in hand, she grabbed her purse, a bottle of water, cell phone and her keys. She saw there was a text message from Jorge acknowledging her message and that he'd call her when he left work.

Her first stop at the mall was the lingerie store to find a bodysuit. She would have to buy an extra-large one for her purposes. When she went to cashier to pay for it, the woman looked up and down at her size-6 figure and asked, "Find your size all right, dear?"

"This is fine, but it's not for me. It's for my mother."

"Very good then," the woman replied with a smile.

Maria paid for the body suit with her credit card and left. She then went to the uniform store and bought several size 14 nurse's uniforms, white hosiery, and white shoes. Next stop was the wig store that catered to chemotherapy patients. After trying on many wigs, she settled on a short, curly style in auburn. The look was dramatically different from the days in Bogotá when she wore her hair long, parted on the side and clipped with a barrette. She would have to get used to the wig once she arrived in Colombia, because it felt like she was wearing a hat. And she hated hats.

Her last stop was at one of the chain stores that made eyeglasses for customers in an hour. She selected a very unattractive pair of black frames that were really too large for her face. She thought they were perfect and paid for them. The clerk did a double take when he looked at her selection and then her face. He asked her for her prescription and she told him she would take them as is. He raised his eyebrows and announced the price. After she paid him, he gave her the receipt, put the frames in an eyeglass case and handed it to her. The way he looked at her, she knew he thought her odd.

Maria turned and walked out the door to her car. She couldn't wait to get home and try on her disguise. She needed to make sure it would really fool people who knew her. She thought of greeting her daughters in the disguise when they got home from school, but pushed that thought back to wherever it came from. She would probably scare them out of their wits. Besides that, they didn't even know she was leaving town. She wondered if she should tell them the truth or tell them she was taking a short vacation without the family. Of course, then they would worry why their Daddy and they weren't going with her. That might make the situation worse. The truth seemed like the best plan.

She finally was back in her community and parked her car. It was another beautiful day in Florida. The cerulean sky was cloudless and there was a westerly breeze that ruffled through her hair as she walked to the townhouse, carrying her shopping bags. Once inside her home, she went into the master bedroom and undressed. She put on the bodysuit and looked at her reflection in the mirror. It was so big on her she couldn't help but smile. She went to the hall closet and got out the sewing box. She took the large bag of fiberfill to the bedroom, hoping it would be enough to fill out the suit. She stuffed it in the cups of the bra and around her abdomen and waistline so she would look thicker and matronly. She also put some around her back and realized she might have to encase this fiberfill with a lining so it wouldn't shift and irritate her skin. Once she was satisfied with the look of the added padding, she put on the uniform and shoes. She didn't bother with the hosiery for now. Then she put the wig on and the glasses. The look was almost right. She picked up a hand mirror and looked at her profile. Then she thought there was one other thing she could do besides putting on makeup. She went into the girls' bathroom and found the orthodontic wax in the medicine cabinet. It was what Julie used to protect her upper lip from being scraped by the metal prongs of her new braces.

Maria worked the wax under her upper lip and then looked in the mirror. She was amazed at how it transformed her appearance. It might interfere with her speech but so much the better. She wouldn't have to worry about anyone recognizing her voice. Tonight, after the girls went to bed, she would put on the disguise and show Jorge.

She needed to tell the girls she was going to Bogotá, but she would wait until after they did their homework. She'd reassure them that she would be back in a week. And she'd ask them to promise not to tell anyone about her plans, not even her aunts and uncles in Bogotá. They just might call with the sad news about Don Pedro's illness. If the girls let it slip that Maria went to see him, it could prove deadly for her.

Chapter 13

Jorge sat at the dining room table reviewing his daughters' homework while Maria finished cleaning up the kitchen after their dinner. She began to think about how she would explain her trip to Colombia to her children and she felt sadness grip her heart. It was going to be painful leaving them and Jorge, but she had a duty to her father. Everything was planned out. The funds that her father wired were now in their joint checking account. Her airline reservations were made. Jorge had been thoughtful to pick up an international calling card and extra batteries for her mobile phone. She still had to pack for her trip and get cash and traveler's checks.

"Good job, Julie," Jorge said. "You didn't make one mistake on your math homework. You keep this up; you'll be getting an A on your report card."

"I hope so," Julie said, smiling.

From the kitchen, Maria asked, "Are you finished checking their homework now?"

"Yes," Jorge said. He nodded, signaling Maria to come to the table.

She took off her apron and said, "There's something important I want to talk to you about."

The girls looked at each other with wide questioning eyes and shrugged their shoulders. They waited for her to continue.

Maria took her seat at the table and cleared her throat. "I have to go to Colombia for a few days. My father is sick, your grandpa, so I'll be leaving tomorrow. I want you to be good for Daddy."

"Can't we go with you?" Julie asked, her voice sounding like she was ready to cry. "We won't be any trouble."

"No, I'm sorry. I don't want to leave you, but I have to. Grandpa asked me to come. It'll just be a few days, a week at the most."

"Momma, don't go," Paula whined. She got up from her seat, ran over to Maria, and grabbed her arm. "Please take me with you."

"I'm sorry, Paula," Maria, said as she hugged her and kissed the top of her head. "You and Julie have school, and Daddy has to go to work. You'll be just fine here. I will call you every chance I get. Now don't worry. I'll be back soon."

Jorge smiled at Maria and said, "Your Momma's going to be fine. She'll be coming back."

"Of course I'm coming back," Maria nodded. "Come here, Julie." Maria pushed her chair back from the table to make room for her oldest daughter. "Both of you sit on my lap."

Julie got up and sat on Maria's left knee and Paula climbed up and sat on the right knee. The two girls looked at each other blinking back the tears. Maria put her arms around them and whispered,

"There is something you must promise me. If any of your uncles, aunts or cousins call here, don't tell them I'm coming to Colombia to see Grandpa. I want to surprise him. If you tell anyone, they'll tell your Grandpa. Then it won't be a surprise, will it?"

The girls shook their heads in agreement. They both studied their hands and frowned.

Maria continued, "After school, our neighbor Mrs. Goodman is going to take care of you until your Daddy picks you up after work. You'll do your homework with her daughter Lauren, and then you can play afterward."

"Okay, Momma," Julie said, her tears now streaming down her cheeks.

Now Paula was sobbing, too. Maria held them close to her and in a soothing tone, said, "You need to understand that I am leaving because it's important. You love your Daddy, right?"

The girls nodded. Julie wiped her tears with the back of her hand and took a deep breath.

Maria continued to comfort them. "Grandpa is my Daddy. I love him. He's sick so I need to see him and try to make him feel better. You'd do the same for your Daddy, if he was sick, right?"

Jorge came over to them offering a box of tissues. "Dry your eyes. Momma will only be gone for a short time. And when she comes back, she'll have a surprise for you."

Each girl pulled a tissue out of the box and blew her nose. Maria pulled out another tissue and wiped their eyes.

"What kind of surprise?" Julie asked.

"If I tell you now it won't be a surprise," Maria said with a smile.

"Momma," Julie whined.

"Jorge, I'd like you to get caller ID on our phones tomorrow. It's important for you to know when I am calling you, and who else might be calling here when I'm gone."

"I'll call the phone company tomorrow morning before I take you to the bank and the airport in the morning," Jorge replied.

Maria gave her daughters a squeeze and said, "It's best if you don't answer the telephone. Only Daddy answers it, okay?"

The girls nodded and then Julie pleaded, "Momma, I want to see Grandpa, too. Please, take us with you."

"I would if I could, but I can't," Maria said in a tone that she hoped would end the pleading. It was hard enough just to leave them. Seeing their tears broke her heart.

"It's time for you both to get ready for bed," Jorge said. "Julie, go run the bath water for your sister."

The girls eased off Maria's lap and turned their sad faces to her. "Come on, let's have a three-way hug," Maria said.

"Hey, what about me?" Jorge laughed.

"Come on, Daddy," Paula said.

He joined them into a four-way hug and the girls finally giggled. They broke their embrace and the girls went upstairs. Jorge and Maria were left alone. Maria looked up into Jorge's coal-colored eyes and said, "Thank you." There was more to say, but she couldn't speak. If she tried to say everything that was in her heart, she knew she would cry. She wanted to put on a strong front for her daughters because she didn't want them to be afraid for her or worry there was something wrong. She knew children were more intuitive than they were given credit for.

Jorge put his arms around her and kissed her softly. "Go get the girls ready for bed. We should probably turn in early tonight, don't you think? You've got a big day ahead of you."

"Yes, I do." Maria reluctantly broke from his arms and went to the girls' bathroom. Julie was shampooing Paula's hair, sculpting it into various art forms. Maria remembered her mother doing the same to her hair when she was a little girl. She had to smile. Were these rituals instinctive, she wondered. Maria picked up the hand mirror from the vanity and gave it to Paula so she could see herself. "Look at yourself, Paula."

"Cool," said Paula. "I wish I could go to school like this."

"You can't go to school in your birthday suit," Julie laughed.

"What do you mean? I'm not wearing a suit," Paula said.

Maria laughed. "Julie, she doesn't know what you mean by birthday suit."

"When you were born you had no clothes on. So being naked like you are now is called your birthday suit," Julie explained.

"I think that's silly," said Paula, clearly not understanding the little joke. "Anyway, I meant going to school with my hair like this. It looks cool."

Maria took the mirror back from Paula and returned it to the vanity. "Rinse your hair and finish washing up. Julie still needs her shower."

Paula took the soapy washcloth and washed herself. "Wash my back, please"

Julie took the washcloth from Paula and ran the washcloth in circles on Paula's back. After rinsing it out, she took the hand-held shower and sprayed the water over Paula's body. "All done. Here's a towel."

Paula squeezed the water from her dripping hair and wrapped herself in the towel. After she stepped out of the tub, Julie released the stopper to let the bathwater drain.

"Dry off, Paula. Put your jammies on and I'll dry your hair in your room," said Maria.

As they went into Paula's bedroom, Maria heard the bathroom door close and the sound of the shower. Maria sat on Paula's bed, waiting for her to get dressed. She looked around the room, a feminine girl's room with a mint green and apricot floral pattern comforter and a matching valance on the window. The walls were painted mint green, a most soothing color to calm an energetic little girl. A mobile hung from the ceiling near the window. She and the girls had handcrafted it last summer over several afternoons. Paper cranes were attached by fishing line to the arms of the mobile. Maria explained that the paper-folding technique they used to make the cranes was a Japanese art form called origami. They had made a duplicate for Julie's room as well. That summer she also taught them other arts and crafts. Maria believed it was a good way to teach children to follow instructions and it reinforced their reading skills. She liked to say, "If you can read and follow instructions, you can do just about anything: cook, sew a dress, and even build a house." The last example had sent them into gales of laughter.

Maria dried Paula's shoulder-length curly hair. Even though she always wore it in a ponytail to keep her hair out of her eyes, Maria let it hang loose to her shoulders when she went to bed. She looked just like a little doll in her pajamas.

"What story shall I read you tonight?" Maria asked.

Without hesitating, Paula said, "*The Runaway Bunny.*"

Maria pulled the book out from the bookcase while Paula got into bed. Maria sat on the bed by the headboard so that Paula could look at the pages while Maria read to her. Margaret Wise Brown's book was one of her favorites because the story expressed her sentiments as a mother: no matter where the little bunny ran to, his mother followed.

When she closed the book, Paula said, "Momma, can I go with you to Colombia?"

"No, sweet Paula. You stay here with Julie and Daddy. I'll be back before you know it. And I'll call you when I can. Now say your prayers," Maria said.

Paula recited the children's prayer and then Maria leaned down to kiss her goodnight. "Sweet dreams."

"Goodnight, Momma," Paula said, yawning.

Maria left the nightlight on and closed the door on her way out. Maria ran her hand over her forehead and cheek; the day's events had taken its toll on her. She took in a deep breath, exhaled and braced herself to say goodnight to Julie who was already in bed, her hair dry. When she saw her mother at the threshold, Julie turned off the MP3 player, removed the earphones and put them on the nightstand.

Maria sat down on the edge of the bed. Julie looked up at her with clear brown eyes that revealed her apprehension. Taking Julie's hands in her own, Maria said, "I'll be all right, you know. And so will you. Don't worry."

"But Mamma, what if?"

Not wanting to acknowledge the danger that faced her in Colombia, Maria didn't let her finish and said, "Julie, I know you don't want me to leave you, because it brings back bad memories. I'm only going back to see my father. He asked that I come to be with him. I can't say no to him, especially since he's sick. You understand that, don't you?"

Julie looked down at their hands. "I guess so. I just wish I could be going with you."

"I would take you if I could. Remember that surprise Daddy mentioned? I'm thinking we just might go on a trip during your summer vacation. Would you like that?"

Julie's eyes brightened. "Could we go to Disney World and Universal Studios?"

Maria smiled. "That is something your Daddy and I will consider. Now you must be a good girl. Do your homework. Help Daddy in the kitchen. Keep your room clean. And watch over your little sister." Then Maria remembered, "Please don't answer the phone. Leave it to Daddy, okay?"

"Okay, Momma. Will you call us tomorrow?"

"I promise I will." Maria said, leaning over to kiss Julie goodnight.

Julie reached up and put her arms around Maria's neck and hugged her close. "I love you, Momma."

"I love you, too." Maria got up and smiled at Julie. "Now say your prayers."

After reciting the prayer, she said, "Dear God, bless my Momma. She's going to see Grandpa. Please keep her safe and bring her back home to us. Amen."

Maria blinked back a tear and said, "Thank you for that, Julie." She leaned down and kissed her again. "Go to sleep now. I'll see you in the morning."

Maria turned, walked out of the bedroom and closed the door. She walked down the stairs and went into the kitchen to make a cup of herbal tea.

Jorge was sitting on the couch watching TV. "Do you want anything from the kitchen?"

"Sure. A cold beer. And thank you," he said.

After the tea had been brewed, she walked into the living room carrying the cup of tea and the bottle of beer. "Do you want a glass for the beer?"

"No, this is fine." He took the beer from her and took a long swallow. "That tastes good." He held the bottle in hand and studied it like he was seeing it for the first time.

"Jorge," Maria said after finishing her tea, "I'm so glad I have your support in this. It gives me the strength to go. I'm apprehensive, but I think the disguise will work. I'd like you to see it and tell me what you think."

"Of course. Go ahead and put it in. Let me know when you're ready and I'll come into our bedroom. Let's not take a chance Julie or Paula will come down and see you in it. It might confuse them and raise questions."

Maria went to the bedroom and got dressed in the disguise. She had taken the time to sew a lining in the bodysuit which secured the fiberfill in place. It also made the garment more comfortable. After she finished dressing, she remembered the orthodontic wax. Then she called for Jorge to come in.

Jorge looked at Maria from the doorway and his mouth dropped open. The transformation was amazing. There she stood wearing the curly auburn wig, oversized black-rimmed eyeglasses, white nurse's uniform, white hosiery and white lace-up leather nursing shoes. He looked closely at her face and said, "You look different. Your face. What did you do?"

"Julie's orthodontic wax," she said. "I put it under my upper lip. And I put on more makeup than I usually wear. So do you think anyone will recognize me?"

"No, but you may want to walk slower, since now you look heavy."

"That's a good point. I better take off these rings, too. Someone might remember them." Maria removed her wedding band and engagement ring from her left hand. She felt a pang in her heart. The only time she took them off was to clean the diamond. She saw a white mark on her finger where it had been. Maria didn't sunbath, but just being exposed to the South Florida sun on a daily basis tanned her skin. She thought it best to find another ring to wear. Rummaging through her jewelry box in the dresser drawer, she found a ring she had bought at a yard sale — an oval turquoise mounted in sterling silver. She put it on and admired it. She looked at her wedding rings with sadness and put them in the jewelry box for safekeeping.

Jorge asked, "When are you going to put on your disguise?"

"When I get to the airport in Bogotá. I can change in the ladies room."

"I'll leave you alone to pack your suitcase. Remember your passport and green card," Jorge said. "I'm going to watch TV."

Jorge left to return to the family room while Maria removed the disguise. She pulled the rolling carry-on suitcase from the top shelf of the closet. She had a checklist so she wouldn't forget a thing. Once she had everything packed, she took a shower in the master bathroom. She blew dry her hair and put on her blue nightgown. The color matched her eyes and Jorge remarked about it. When she returned to their bedroom she found Jorge already in their king-size bed smiling at her. The bedroom door was closed and the lamp cast a golden glow across the bed. Maria pulled the sheets and comforter back and lay down on the bed. Jorge reached for her and she turned toward him. They looked into each other's eyes with intensity. Jorge cradled her chin in his large hand and lifted her face up to him. He leaned down and kissed her tenderly. Maria always felt so safe in his arms. And when they made love, she felt not only passion but a spiritual connection to Jorge. She would cherish this time with him tonight. She prayed it wouldn't be the last.

Chapter 14

"Girls. It's time to leave. You don't want to miss the school bus," Maria said. "Get your backpacks."

Julie and Paula ran to Jorge to kiss him goodbye and then grabbed the handles of their rolling backpacks. "We're ready, Momma," Julie said.

"I'll take the car to drop you off at the bus stop this morning so give me a kiss goodbye now."

"But we always walk, Momma," Paula protested.

"I know, but I need to save time this morning. Come here." Maria kneeled down so she could embrace them at their level. They hugged and kissed. "Remember, I'll call you later. I love you both."

The telephone rang and Julie ran to pick it up.

"No, Julie. What did I tell you last night?" Maria asked in a louder voice than she intended.

Julie stopped and looked up at her mother with regret. "I'm sorry, Momma."

On the second ring, Jorge answered the phone. "Hello. Hi, Sal. Yes, sure." Jorge waved Maria to go.

Maria sighed with relief. She opened the door and the three of them walked to her car. Once they had their seat belts fastened, Maria started her car and drove to the bus stop. She knew she had to remain stoic so that there would be no tears. The girls sat in the backseat and were unusually quiet. Maria parked her car along the curb and let the girls out. They started to walk to the bus stop and Maria yelled, "Wait!"

She got out of the car and ran to Julie and Paula. "Just one more hug and kiss for Momma." First she hugged and kissed Paula. Then Julie. She closed her eyes and prayed that she would return safely to them. "Have a good day at school. I love you."

"Talk to you later, Momma," Julie said. "I love you, too."

"Me, too, Momma," Paula said.

Maria turned and walked back to her car, vowing not to cry. When she returned home, Jorge was just hanging up the phone. "That was the telephone company. We'll have Caller ID on the phones by the afternoon. And Sal called, he gave me the name of the charter jet company and the name of the pilot. I wrote it all down for you," Jorge said, handing her the sheet of note paper.

Maria took the paper from him and looked at it. "I'll put it in my money belt."

"So, are you ready to leave? It's almost seven-thirty. You're supposed to be at the airport two hours before you flight. And you still have to stop at the bank."

"Just give me a minute. My bag is packed. I need to get my purse," Maria said.

"All right. I'll get your suitcase and meet you in the car," Jorge said.

Maria went to each of her daughter's bedrooms and looked around. Then she went to the master bedroom and found the framed photo she wanted to take with her. It was a picture of Jorge with their daughters at Metro Zoo in Miami. Maria picked it up and put it in her purse. She put her arm through the straps of the brown leather shoulder bag and went to the kitchen to make sure no one left the stove on. She picked up her keys on the counter, looked around at her home and left, locking the door behind her. She prayed she would come home safely and be reunited with her dear Jorge and daughters.

They arrived at the Miami International Airport at nine o'clock. They made good time considering she stopped at the bank and they drove to Miami during the rush hour. After he parked along the curbside, Jorge got out of the car and retrieved Maria's rolling carry-on suitcase from the trunk. She met him there and reached to embrace him. Jorge hugged her and said, "Stay safe. Be very careful. And call me when you get to Aruba."

Maria looked into his dark glistening eyes. Am I crazy to leave, she thought. She dismissed her apprehension, and said, "I will. I love you, Jorge."

He smiled and mimed the words, I love you, too. She turned and steeled herself to go on into the airport alone, dragging her suitcase behind her. She went through airport security and then walked to her gate, stopping at a sundries store to buy a bottle of water, chewing gum, and a few magazines to occupy her mind while she waited. She took a seat and noticed that most passengers for this flight were couples, both young and seniors, and college students. She knew this from the t-shirt or caps that bore the university's logo. Everyone was dressed for comfort: shorts, capri pants, jeans, athletic shoes, and fleece jackets or sweatshirts in case the cabin was too cold for comfort. Maria dressed in a short-sleeve pink knit top over brown cargo pants and brown moccasins.

She looked through the broad expanse of glass and watched the airport workers load the jet with luggage and other cargo. It was another beautiful day in paradise: sunny skies with a few cotton ball clouds against cerulean blue. She remembered days like this at the beach with the girls. They would look up at the clouds and call out what they saw, a crow, a woman's face, a dog maybe. She had learned this from her father when he would take her, her brothers and her mother to the park. It wasn't too long before her brothers grew bored and wanted to play ball. Off they would go with her father while Maria and her mother stayed behind to play a game of cards.

Her daydreaming was interrupted with the announcement to board the plane. The flight attendant called passengers to board by seat numbers. Finally it was Maria's turn. She found her seat easily and put her bag in the overhead bin. She took the window seat and it appeared that she'd have the row to herself. She wasn't in the mood to have a conversation with anyone.

Once everyone was buckled in and the mandatory safety announcements had been made, the plane taxied down the runway. Maria got a stick of gum out of her bag to chew since it relieved the pressure in her ears when the plane gained altitude. She removed the wrapper, put the gum in her mouth and folded the paper into a ring. Not wanting to discard it in the seatback, she put it in her purse.

In a few minutes, the plane was airborne and Maria settled back into her seat. She thumbed through the airline's in-flight magazine and found a feature article to read about Aruba. She learned that it was a small island, just twenty miles long and six miles across. A Dutch-owned country, Aruba was a major fishing center and a port of call for the major cruise lines. Located only twenty miles north of Venezuela, it was a popular weekend retreat among Venezuelan and Colombians since it had beautiful beaches, casinos and nightlife.

She finished the article and then closed her eyes. A short nap would do her good since she hadn't slept well during the night.

The short nap turned out to be an hour and a half. In another hour the plane would land in Oranjestad, the capital of Aruba. Then it was up to her to find a charter boat captain to take her to the Colombian seaport of Santa Marta. Sal had reassured Jorge that Maria had nothing to worry about. These captains had families to support and they took all safety precautions when they took their clients out for half- or full-day fishing excursions. She had never been out in a boat before. She didn't know what to expect, but she was about to find out. She wondered if she made the right decision.

Chapter 15

As the jet made its approach to the Queen Beatrix International Airport, Maria gazed out the window looking down at Oranjestad, Aruba's capital city. She saw wide expanses of pristine white beaches and clear aquamarine water that surrounded the Dutch-owned Caribbean island. Most fascinating were the Dutch colonial buildings in colorful pastels such as pistachio, ocher, pink, and aqua trimmed in white gingerbread ornamentation. She couldn't wait to get a closer look once she was on the ground. She also saw a sleek cruise ship moored at its dock and beyond that, the Renaissance Marina, her immediate destination.

The flight arrived on time, 1:50 p.m. Maria retrieved her carry-on bag from the overhead bin and walked through the terminal to Aruba Immigration and Customs. After she cleared Customs, she went outside the terminal where taxis waited to take visitors wherever they wanted to go. Maria was greeted by a smiling taxi driver who opened the door to the back seat for her and put her bag in the trunk. She got in and secured her seat belt.

"*Bon bini*. Welcome to Aruba, madam," he said as he closed her door and then walked around to get into the driver's seat.

"Thank you. How much will you charge to take me to the Renaissance Marina?" Maria asked.

"Only eight dollars. But don't you mean the Renaissance Hotel?" he asked as he pulled out and drove away from the terminal.

"No, the marina. I'm going fishing. I'm meeting friends there. When we get back, I'll check into the hotel."

"Of course. This is the best place for big game fishing. You can catch sailfish, blue marlin, dolphin, kingfish, albacore, even barracuda."

"Yes, I'm looking forward to it," she said, knowing she wouldn't be doing any fishing or meeting any friends.

"Is this your first time to Aruba?" the driver asked.

"Yes, it is. I just love all the colors of the buildings," she said, as she looked out the window at the passing cityscape. "The pastel colors remind me of sherbet."

"I haven't heard that one before," he said, smiling at her remark.

"I guess I'm just hungry. I didn't have lunch. I was asleep on the plane when they served it."

"These charter boats are first class. Some of them are sport fishing yachts, actually. The captain will prepare lunch for you," the driver said.

Maria fell silent and enjoyed the passing scenery. Now that she was at street level, she could appreciate all the detailing on these two-story buildings including the white wrought-iron balconies. Many storefronts had colorful striped awnings in candy cotton pink and white or mint green and white to shield pedestrians from the sun.

It was just a ten-minute ride and the driver stopped along the curb at the Renaissance Marina. She pulled out $12 from her wallet which included a generous tip. The driver took the money from her, smiled, and thanked her. He retrieved her bag from the trunk and opened her door for her.

Smiling, she got out of the taxi and grabbed hold of the suitcase. "Thank you."

"Have a great time," the driver said before he returned to his car and drove away. Maria stood on the sidewalk looking out over the marina. The view was like one would see on a picture postcard. The sun sparkled over the calm surface of the harbor and there was a boardwalk lined with palm trees and lamp posts. She saw many sport fishing yachts with fly bridges as well as sailboats moored in slips along the piers. She wondered how she would know if these vessels were private or for charter, but as she walked down a pier and got closer to the vessels, she saw that charter boats had signs hanging from the back of the transom with the captain's name and a phone number. A private sport fishing boat lacked a sign.

As she walked down one pier, she saw a man hosing down the cockpit of a sport fishing yacht. He looked to be about 50 years old and wore a tan cap and dark aviator sunglasses. His skin was tanned like leather and he wore khaki shorts and a turquoise knit shirt with a logo embroidered on it. She saw the name of the boat was "Get Reel" and smiled at the double entendre.

Having turned the water off, the man was now standing on the pier coiling the hose over the water spigot. He turned when he heard the wheels of her suitcase bumping along the boards of the pier. "*Bon bini*. Welcome."

"Thank you," Maria said as she appraised him. "Are you the captain?"

"I sure am. I'm Captain Jack. Are you interested in a fishing charter?"

"Well, yes, uh — sort of."

"I don't understand," he said, his weathered face now in a frown.

"I'm interested in a special charter. I need to get to Colombia. You see, my father is sick and — I have to — I thought I could charter your boat." Maria said, feeling a knot growing in her stomach.

The captain looked at her and nodded. "Would you like to come aboard? We can sit in the salon where we have more privacy."

Maria nodded and Captain Jack took her rolling suitcase and set it down in the cockpit. He then got in the cockpit himself and then helped Maria aboard.

She grabbed the handles of the suitcase and they entered the salon. It was tastefully appointed with a large, taupe leather "L" shaped sofa positioned on the left side of the room along with a low-profile coffee table and two barrel chairs. There was a full galley with a large refrigerator forward of the sitting area and to the right a dining area with a high-gloss teak table and seating done in ostrich leather. Aft of the dining area there was a spiral staircase that led to the enclosed bridge. There were many large windows with teak blinds offering plenty of light and water views. Beige wall-to-wall carpeting coordinated all the colors of the décor.

"Go ahead and sit down," Captain Jack said. He adjusted the navy and gold throw pillows so she'd be comfortable and then he sat down in one of the navy blue and gold patterned barrel swivel chairs.

Maria sat down and said thank you and then was silent, gathering her thoughts.

"I would like to charter your boat to take me to Santa Marta. Do you know where that is?" Maria asked.

"Yes, and it will take some time to get there. Is this a one-way trip or do you want to come back here?" Captain Jack asked.

"Round trip. I'm thinking I'll stay in Colombia for a week to spend time with my father and family and then come back to Aruba. Is that something you'd be interested in?" Maria, asked, hoping he'd say yes. She already had a sense that she could trust this man.

"Yes, but it's going to cost you more than a regular charter since I'll be waiting for you in port for a week."

"I understand. That's not a problem. It's just very important that I get to Colombia as soon as possible. My father is sick. He needs a kidney transplant so I don't know how much longer he has — I'm sorry," Maria said, her eyes welling up with tears. "I need to get there. I have so much to tell him before he — ."

"Can I get you something to drink?" Captain Jack asked. Maria nodded and he went to the refrigerator and opened the door. "I have water, soda, beer, iced tea and juice. There's also wine and liquor if you want something stronger."

"Water is fine, thank you." Maria sighed. She pulled a tissue from her pants pocket and wiped her eyes. "What is your fee to take me?"

Captain Jack explained that his normal ten-hour day rate was $1,100 but since he needed to wait a week for her the charter would cost $14,000.

Maria remembered she budgeted double that amount, which was smart in case she extended her stay in Colombia beyond a week. "That's fair. Can we leave this afternoon?"

"Yes, I had a half-day charter this morning but I don't have any charters scheduled the rest of the week. I already gassed up so we can leave in an hour. I'll need payment now in cash or traveler's checks. I'll go make a deposit and call my first mate to join us. He'll bring the supplies. Will there be anyone else coming with you?"

"No. Just me."

"Do you have your passport?" Captain Jack asked as he got up and walked to the spiral staircase.

"Why do I need a passport?" Maria asked, swallowing hard. She thought she only needed a passport when going by air, not by boat.

"We'll be entering a foreign country and we must go through Customs and Immigration."

"That's going to be a problem," Maria said. She then explained that she had a Colombian passport, was granted political asylum by the United States, and carried a green card. She couldn't have her passport stamped by Colombian officials, because then she would be banned from returning to the U.S.

Captain Jack cupped his chin in his hand, thinking. "I see. So that's the reason you flew into Aruba and figured you get to Colombia from here. I can understand that. Especially if you want to see your father. I have my niece's passport on board since she crews with me when she wants to make extra money. I'll let you borrow it. When I go through Customs and Immigration in Santa Marta, I'll present the passports of all those on board and the crew list. They don't match up people to the passports so you don't have to worry about using her passport. But it'll appear strange for you to be a lone charter passenger. I'll see if one of my charter buddies will join us so you'll look like a couple. I think Captain Rick is having maintenance work done on his Bertram. Meanwhile, I'll go up on the fly bridge and look at my map. Then I'll let you know how long it will take to get to Santa Marta. Why don't you get your traveler's checks ready?"

Maria nodded. She felt very lucky to have found this kind man who was willing to smuggle her into Colombia. She took out $14,000 in traveler's checks from her money belt, signed them, and held them in her hand waiting for Captain Jack to return to the salon.

"By the way, what's your name?" Captain Jack asked when he returned to the salon.

"I'm sorry. I'm not thinking. My name is Maria Alvarez. I live in South Florida with my husband and two daughters. My father lives in Bogotá with the rest of my family."

"Pleased to know you," Captain Jack said. "It's 290 miles from here to Santa Marta. "I can get you there in sixteen hours."

"Sixteen hours? Can't we get there any faster?"

"If I go faster, we'll burn more fuel. And since we'll be cruising during the night, it's safer to go 18 knots to avoid any floating hazards. We'll leave here at three o'clock and arrive at Santa Marta tomorrow morning at seven."

Maria thought about it and agreed it was better to be safe. She then asked him if she would be able to use her cell phone out at sea. She knew she promised to call her daughters.

"No, Maria, at sea we are out of the range of cell towers. We have a radio on board that we use for official business. If you want to make any calls, do it now. Are those the checks?" Captain Jack asked, looking at Maria's hand.

Maria said, "I didn't fill in the 'payable to' line since I don't know your last name."

"It's Travis. Jack Travis. Make them out to Jack Travis Fishing Charters."

When she finished writing the checks, she handed them to Captain Jack. He took them from her, thanked her, and told her to expect Manual Ortiz, his first mate to come aboard in the next thirty minutes. He would make all the preparations to leave.

After Captain Jack left, Maria called her mother to let her know she was in Aruba and would arrive in Bogotá at nine o'clock in the morning. Her mother was so happy she started to cry. She said she would arrange for a driver to pick her up at the Private Jet Charter terminal. Maria asked to speak to her father, but he was taking a nap. Although she wanted to talk to her mother longer, she had more calls to make and excused herself. She pulled out the note paper Jorge had given her and then called Private Jet Charters and told the representative she would arrive at Santa Marta tomorrow at seven o'clock in the morning. The representative told her a driver would pick her up at the port and take her to Simon Bolivar Airport. Her jet would depart at eight o'clock and land at Eldorado International Airport in Bogotá at nine. By ten tomorrow morning she should arrive at her parent's home in the Santa Barbara neighborhood.

Maria took a long swallow of water and stood up. She walked out of the salon to the cockpit and looked around. Aruba was such a charming place. The weather was hot, but the trade winds kept it from being uncomfortable. She returned to the air-conditioned salon and called Jorge.

"Hello, Maria," Jorge said. "Are you in Aruba? Are you all right?"

"Yes, I'm in Aruba on a charter fishing boat. And I'm fine. I'm waiting for the captain, his first mate, and another captain to get here. We'll be leaving at three this afternoon, and we'll get to Santa Marta at seven tomorrow morning. I won't be able to use my cell phone at sea."

"Of course not. No towers," Jorge laughed. "I'll tell the girls you'll call them tomorrow. They'll understand that you can't get service."

"Remember they don't know about Aruba and this charter boat. They just know I'm going to Colombia."

Jorge reassured her and then continued, "What's the name of the captain and the boat? And what country is the boat registered?"

"The captain's name is Jack Travis and the boat is named 'Get Reel.' How would I know where the boat is registered?"

"Get Reel like R-E-E-L? Fishing reel. Cute. If you look at the name of the boat painted on the transom, you'll see the name of the country right below it."

"I'll go look," Maria said as she stepped into the cockpit. She leaned over the transom and read the lettering. "St. Vincent."

"That's a smart captain. St. Vincent is a neutral country. It's not far from Aruba either. No one with a political agenda should bother him."

Maria was amazed Jorge knew so much. Then she thought about Julie and Paula. "So are you going to be all right, taking care of the girls?"

"You know I will. Just make sure you call tomorrow morning. If you call before they leave for school, you can talk to them."

"Okay, I will as long as the boat gets there on time. I already miss you, Jorge."

"Me, too. Just be careful," Jorge said. "I'll wait to hear from you tomorrow."

"Okay. I'll talk to you tomorrow. Give my love to our daughters," Maria said before closing the cell phone.

Standing in the cockpit, she saw Captain Jack walking down the pier with another man, much shorter, stockier and younger. Then she saw Captain Jack board a boat moored at another slip and waved the shorter man to go on. Maria guessed he was calling on Captain Rick. She took the younger man to be Manual Ortiz, his first mate. He was carrying a box of supplies, probably groceries, she thought. When he was within a few feet of Get Reel, he said *"Hola."*

"Hola," Maria said, returning the Spanish greeting. She felt relieved that she could speak Spanish to him if she couldn't remember the right words in English when speaking to Captain Jack.

After he got into the cockpit, he introduced himself as the first mate, Manual Ortiz, just as Maria guessed. He had piercing dark eyes, a broad nose and straight black hair. He went into the galley and put the groceries and other supplies away. Maria followed him and was amazed how much storage space there was. She then returned to her seat on the sofa and finished her bottle of water. She left him to attend to his duties.

A few minutes later, she heard voices coming from the cockpit and looked to see Captain Jack boarding the boat with another man who was about forty years old. He wore a Greek fisherman's cap on his head and carried an army-green duffle bag. Captain Jack and the man entered the salon and smiled at Maria.

"Maria, this is Captain Rick. He'll be joining us on our trip. He's having some maintenance work done on his boat so he has some time on his hands."

"It's nice to meet you, Maria," Captain Rick said, lifting his hat. He had removed his sunglasses and looped them into the opening of the collar of his pale yellow knit shirt. There was an embroidered logo on his shirt with the name of his boat, "Bait's Motel."

Maria smiled at the name recalling the movie "Psycho." "It's nice to meet you, too. That's a clever name for a boat that takes people fishing."

"You have to have a clever name so fishermen will remember you," Captain Rick replied. He was several inches taller than Maria and had muscular arms, probably from hauling in swordfish or other large game fish. His hair was dark brown with gray around the temples. His eyes were turquoise, like the sea around Aruba. They held her gaze and then he looked at Captain Jack. "Did Captain Jack give you the tour?"

Captain Jack said, "No, I haven't, but why don't you show her around so I can get ready to leave."

"My pleasure," said Captain Rick. He pointed out the yacht's electrical panels concealed behind a large teak cabinet door. Beneath the panel was the satellite television controls and stereo amplifier. Also in this group of cabinets, he revealed an automatic ice maker. Then he led her up the spiral staircase to the fly bridge. Enclosed and air-conditioned, it offered unobstructed views all around. There was enough seating up here for eight adults. On the left side, an L-shaped settee had room for three adults with a small table to place drinks and snacks. There was also a black leather helm chair with a pair of black leather bench seats on either side. Maria noticed a small sink and a compact refrigerator/freezer. The engine controls were also up here, useful while fishing and for docking.

They went back down the stairs to continue the tour. Now he showed her the three staterooms. The master stateroom was situated midship and featured two cedar-lined closets, night stands and a credenza all in teak wood. Indirect lighting cast a soft glow. The color scheme followed the same as the salon with tan and navy blue and gold accents. For entertainment, there was a stereo, a flat screen TV and a DVD player. What Captain Rick referred to as the head looked more like a luxurious bathroom with a toilet, shower, linen closet, medicine cabinet, a granite-topped vanity with a sink and teak flooring. The effect was a spa at sea.

He also showed her the VIP stateroom situated forward. This was to be her place to sleep tonight since it afforded her the most privacy. It had the same luxuries as the master stateroom but instead of a king-size bed it had a queen-size.

Last on the tour was the third guest stateroom which was on the right side across from the master stateroom. It featured upper and lower berths. It, too, had a stereo, TV and DVD. Captain Rick explained that he and Manual would share this stateroom. Just aft of it was an adjacent head and shower. He explained this was the head they used during the day.

Making their way back to the salon, he pointed out all the amenities of the galley. It featured teak flooring, a dishwasher, four-burner stove and a large sink. Counter tops were pale gray granite and there was the full-size, side-by-side refrigerator and freezer. As if that wasn't enough, there was a trash compactor, toaster oven, and many slide-out drawers and cabinets. At the sink, there was a water pump indicator and a large window allowing for plenty of natural light.

After completing the tour, Captain Rick said, "I won't bore you with the electronics but this 61-foot Viking yacht is loaded. And Captain Jack is a stickler for maintenance so everything will run smoothly. I hope you'll enjoy your time aboard."

"I'm sure I will. The boat is really impressive."

Captain Rick continued. "Have you ever been on a boat before?"

"No. I never had the chance."

"Then you should know that when we give directions on a boat, we don't say left or right because it's confusing. Directions are oriented to the front of the boat which is the bow and the back of the boat is the stern. So we say port when we mean the left side facing the bow and starboard when we mean the right side facing the bow."

"I hope I can remember that."

"We typically use these terms when calling out a warning if there is a hazard in the water," Captain Rick said. "I can see by the look on your face you're wondering what kind of hazard. You've probably seen or heard about shipping containers. This is how most imported goods get to their destination. Every so often, one of these containers comes loose from the cables that secure it to the ship and it drops into the sea. Usually, it just sinks, but the insulated ones will be partially submerged, floating just under the surface. If you're not paying attention and your boat goes over it, it will take out the propeller. Then you're stuck in the water."

"Oh, my, that sounds dangerous," Maria said, putting her hand to her throat.

"The fly bridge gives us the advantage to see any hazard in the distance, giving Captain Jack or me time to avoid it. And I believe Jack has a scanning sonar system that allows him to see the sea floor ahead. It's great for detecting fast-moving schools of fish, but also for detecting shallow conditions and dangerous obstacles such as reefs and sunken wrecks."

Now that they were back in the salon, Maria noticed that someone had turned the stereo on. She smiled when she recognized the voice of Marcos Llumas singing a romantic Spanish ballad called "Vida."

Captain Rick asked Manual to take Maria's suitcase to the VIP stateroom. Now they were joined by Captain Jack who offered her lunch which she accepted with enthusiasm. He had prepared a Salad Niçoise for her, knowing that this was a favorite among his female guests. He took it out from the refrigerator and placed it on the dining table. Along with the entrée, he served her French bread, extra virgin olive oil for dipping, and iced tea with lemon. He and Captain Rick excused themselves so that they could get underway. Captain Jack went up the fly bridge while Manual and Captain Rick attended to the lines that secured the yacht to the slip.

Maria was left alone to enjoy her meal. It was delicious; all the ingredients were of the freshest quality. She heard the motor start up and the sound of the lines being taken in and coiled in their proper place. Captain Rick came into the salon and invited Maria to join them in the fly bridge when she finished her meal.

She thanked him and continued to eat. As she looked from the salon out the large windows, she saw Oranjestad from the waterfront in all of its glory. After the yacht cleared the "no wake zone," Maria felt the yacht accelerate. It was amazingly quiet in the salon. Soon she would be out in the deep waters of the Caribbean Sea. She had never been out on a boat before, much less a yacht, so it was an adventure for her. She was excited thinking that by tomorrow morning she would be in her homeland of Colombia and see her mother and father again. But she also remembered the threat of the rebels and it put fear in her heart. She hoped she would get there safe and sound and be able to return safely to Jorge and her daughters. With that thought, she began to pray.

Chapter 16

After Maria finished her lunch, she took the dishes to the sink. She thought about washing them, but she wondered if there was a water restriction so she left them.

She climbed the staircase to join the men in the fly bridge and took a seat on the sofa. Captain Jack sat in the black leather helm chair and the other men sat on the bench seats on either side of him. The view was as far as the eye could see, and by now Aruba was far off on the horizon. Now that she had settled down, Maria noticed the stereo was playing Latin jazz and there was a 15-inch flat screen TV. Manual took a bottle of water from the refrigerator and offered it to her. She signaled no with her hand and he opened the bottle and took a long drink.

Noticing the men were quiet, she smiled and said, "I hope I'm not interrupting anything."

"Of course not," said Captain Jack smiling at her. "Did you enjoy your lunch?"

"Yes, it was delicious. Thank you." Maria looked around and remarked. "This is much different up here than I expected. It's all very comfortable — air conditioning, tinted windows and with a roof over our heads; I won't even get sunburned."

She glanced over at all the electronics and said half joking, "Does this boat steer itself?"

Captain Jack answered, "Actually it does. Right now it's on autopilot, but I can turn it off anytime and take control manually. Everything here is designed to make navigation easy — there's a speed and depth gauge, a color radar, GPS and a plotter, a sonar scanning system and of course, a compass and VHF radio."

"That's just part of the electronics," Captain Rick added. "But the generator keeps everything running for well over two thousand hours."

Captain Jack nodded in agreement. Maria looked up, trying to do the math in her head. "That's like ninety-five days."

The radar held Captain Jack's attention. Although the auto pilot was on, Maria could see that his attention was on piloting the sport fishing yacht. Then a thought came to her. "You mentioned about the danger of submerged shipping containers. What about pirates?"

She saw the three men exchange glances. Captain Rick was the first to speak. "There are pirates, but we haven't encountered any. I've heard that pirates prey on sailing yachts. My guess is that they're slower moving. This beauty can haul ass — I mean — cruise at 31 knots, that's like 35 miles per hour. Of course, there are faster boats than this. In fact, they call them "go-fast boats" because they've been designed for speed. They can travel up to 80 knots in calm water, over 50 knots in choppy water and maintain 25 knots in five to seven foot seas like we get here in the Caribbean. It's what the drug runners use to smuggle cocaine from Colombia to Mexico and the states."

"Yes, it's really quite unsettling when you're out here at night," Captain Jack added. "If you're out on deck, you hear this really high-pitched whine on the water, but you can't see anything. The running lights are off so the speed boat can go undetected. You also see this dot on the radar screen so you know the boat is out there. It's something that we'll be watching out for tonight as we get closer to Colombia."

Maria's face twisted in worry, her brows knitting together. "Anything else you want to warn me about?"

"I think that about covers it," Captain Jack said. "Storms can come up fast, but I'm not concerned this time of year. Don't worry."

"You're in good hands," Captain Rick said, patting his friend's back. "Jack has been a sailor for more than thirty years and I've been in the business for twenty."

"You both have the experience. What about Manual?" Maria asked, noting that the first mate had been quiet during most of the discussion. He must be shy, she thought.

Upon hearing his name, Manual said, "About two years. I came from Venezuela. So many poor people. Aruba is much better. I always have a job with Captain Jack."

"That's right," Captain Jack agreed. Smiling, he looked at Manual and said, "I can always depend on you."

Maria felt comfortable with these three men who obviously had deep respect for one another. She knew about Venezuela and the problems in that country. Besides poverty, there was a high rate of violent crime, including homicides, robberies and kidnappings. She had several classmates in her Intensity English class who were from Venezuela. They, too, were granted political asylum to live in the United States because they feared they would be kidnapped and killed. Maria could certainly relate to them.

"Captain Jack, have you always been a charter boat captain?"

He looked at her and smiled. "Like father, like son. My father had this business, but has since retired. He wanted me to become a CPA or an attorney so I went to the University of Aruba and got a bachelor's degree in business. I considered being a CPA, but I love the sea. I guess I just have salt water running through my veins."

Maria laughed at the thought of that and said, "I want to be a CPA. I had been working toward that master's degree when I was at the university in Bogotá, but the credits didn't transfer to the universities in Florida. I plan on enrolling in college, but I have to be fluent in English. There's an English proficiency exam you have to take before you're accepted. But it makes sense. How can I expect to learn anything if I can't read and speak English?"

"In Aruba, most people speak Dutch and English. They'll also speak Spanish, especially if they deal with tourists. My two daughters are bilingual and are now enrolled at the university here. There's no chance they'll want to follow in my footsteps. The idea of putting bait on a hook or removing the hook from a billfish turns their stomachs."

"I'd have trouble with that, too," Maria said, nodding her head. "What are their plans?"

"They haven't decided as yet. At this point, they're studying and having fun." Changing the subject, Captain Jack asked, "So how are you getting to Bogotá?"

"I arranged for a charter jet to pick me up at the local airport in Santa Marta. It should get me into Bogotá in an hour. Be sure to give me your business card so I can call you when I'm coming back."

Captain Jack nodded yes and looked out over the horizon where he noted the position of several other boats out for an afternoon of leisure. "If you think you'll be staying longer than a week, please call me and let me know."

"I certainly will. And of course, I'll compensate you for waiting."

Taking out a pair of binoculars from the cabinet, Captain Jack peered through them and said, "There's a cabin cruiser to starboard with the "F" flag flying. That means he's disabled. We can stop and help, but if we do, we won't get you to Colombia on time to meet your schedule."

Maria took the binoculars from him and looked at the cabin cruiser in the distance. Tethered to its mast was the white flag with a yellow diamond in the center. "But maybe they're pirates using that as a ruse to get you to stop."

"That's a point. I'll call it in on the VHF radio so somebody else can help out if they want." Captain Jack picked up the radio receiver and reported the disabled vessel with the coordinates in his radar screen. Returning the receiver to its holder, he said, "That should do it."

"I feel terrible, but I'm glad we're not stopping. I just don't have a good feeling about it," Maria said. "Doesn't everyone out on the water have a radio like you do?

Nodding his head, Captain Jack said, "No, and it's too bad. But I wouldn't be on the water without it."

Maria was glad they were far from the disabled boat when they passed it. Feeling guilty, she didn't want to make eye contact with any of those onboard. She looked at her watch and was surprised to see that it was already five o'clock.

Captain Jack noticed Maria looking at the time and asked, "Maria, would you like to go below and rest for a while? At six, we'll serve drinks and appetizers and then at seven, we'll have dinner."

"I'm a little weary. I think I will," Maria said as she got up from the sofa. She went downstairs and made her way to her stateroom. She removed her shoes and stretched out on the bed. She laid there staring at the ceiling and thought about her daughters and Jorge. Her heart ached for them, but she longed to see her mother and father. She remembered the day Julie, Paula, Jorge and she left Colombia for the United States. Her parents had taken them to the airport. This was the first time she had seen her father cry. The only one with a dry eye was Jorge who she thought was trying to put up a strong front for the rest of them. She remembered how painful it was to leave her parents, but the fear of being recaptured by the FARC pushed her to make the decision. Maria never allowed herself to think about her parents dying. And now she had to face the fact that her father may not live much longer unless he found a donor in time. She wondered if she would be a match for him. She would have to find out as soon as she could.

Chapter 17

It was five-thirty in the morning when Maria heard Captain Jack knocking on her door to wake her. She went to the head and quickly got dressed and ready for the day. She was wearing the same outfit since she knew she would be changing once she got to the airport. She made her way to the galley where the men were having coffee and orange juice.

"Juice and coffee, Maria?" Captain Jack asked. Maria thanked him, took the glass of juice and watched him pour coffee into a mug.

"You are one terrific cook, Captain Jack," Maria said after she finished her juice and set the glass in the sink. "That pork tenderloin with that apple glaze you made for dinner last night was wonderful. That with the mashed potatoes and red cabbage — delicious."

Captain Jack smiled. "Thank you. It was nothing. Anyway, why don't you join me up in the fly bridge? You'll be able to see Santa Marta in the distance."

Maria took her mug of coffee and followed Captain Jack up the stairs. He told her Captain Rick was asleep because he took the night watch piloting the yacht. Manual was cleaning up the galley putting the clean dishes away in the cabinets.

Standing in the fly bridge, Maria looked straight ahead and could see the lights of Santa Marta. As the sun began to rise, the lights faded and soon the twin mountain peaks came into view. "Oh, look at that. What a sight."

"That's Sierra Nevada de Santa Marta. It's an isolated mountain system and the tallest coastal mountain range in the world. Now that the sun is up, you'll see Santa Marta and its beautiful white sand beaches. This is one of the most popular tourist hubs along the coast. It was founded in 1525, one of the first cities in Colombia. Also the last home of Simon Bolivar."

Maria remembered from history class that Simon Bolivar is regarded in Latin America as a hero, visionary, revolutionary, and liberator. During his short life, he led Bolivia, Colombia, Ecuador, Panama, Peru, and Venezuela to independence and laid the foundations of Latin American ideology on democracy. "So that's why the airport is named for him."

"Yes, that's right. He wasn't Colombian, though. He was born in Caracas, Venezuela."

Looking down at the wake, Maria said, "I thought I'd see dolphins out here."

"Not here. Over on the west coast of Colombia. But from July through September, we do get humpback whales that migrate here for the mating season. That's a sight to see."

"I bet," Maria said, thinking that Captain Jack was very knowledgeable. He made the trip very interesting for her.

As they got nearer to the port, Maria could see hotels, restaurants, and marinas with hundreds of boat slips. It was a beautiful sight with the sparkling aquamarine water edging the white expanse of beach. She regretted not bringing her camera.

Now that her coffee cooled, she drank it and thought about the day ahead. Soon she would see her mother and father. It had been two long years since they parted and she anxiously awaited their reunion. She glanced at her watch. It was 6:45 a.m., time to call her daughters and husband.

"Excuse me, Captain Jack. I'm going to get my cell phone and try to call my family."

"Go right ahead. You should get service by now. I'm going to radio immigration and get clearance to enter the port."

Maria descended the stairs and saw Manual out in the cockpit hoisting a yellow flag. She wondered what that was for. She went to her stateroom and picked up her cell phone. She turned it on and discovered it was still fully charged. She called her home, and after a few rings, Jorge answered, "Maria, how are you? Where are you? Is everything okay?"

Calming him, she answered, "I'm fine. I didn't even get seasick. I thought I might, but I'm fine. We're just about ready to dock in Santa Marta, and then I'll be on my way to the airport. I know I promised to call Julie and Paula. Can you put them on the extension?"

She heard Jorge yell to the girls to get on the other phone in the master bedroom.

"Hi Mommy," Julie said. Paula was next, "Hi Mommy, I love you."

"I love you, too. Both of you. Are you being good girls?"

"Yes," they said in unison. Then Julie said, "When are you coming home?"

Maria laughed. "Julie, I told you in a week. I've only been gone a day."

"I know," Julie said dragging out the last word. "I just miss you."

"I miss you, too. Now I bet you're still getting ready for school so let me talk to Daddy. Go ahead and hang up. I'll call you again in another day or so."

Maria heard the click of the extension and was free to talk to Jorge. "Are you doing all right on your own?"

"What do you think? I worry about you. Stay safe and let me hear from you."

Maria thought about telling him about donating a kidney to her father and then thought better of it. He would only worry. Besides, she still would have to be tested to see if she was a suitable match. Then she heard Jorge say, "Maria, are you still there?"

"Yes, I'm sorry. Just a little distracted."

"Yes, well, all right. Call me when you can. But only if it's safe and no one can hear you."

"I will. I'll try to call you tonight. I love you."

"I love you, too," Jorge said before closing the connection.

Maria turned her phone off and put it in her pants pocket. She heard a change in the sound of the engine. She looked out the porthole and saw the dock. Captain Jack and Manual were securing the ropes to the slip. Maria gathered her purse and suitcase and went to the salon to wait to disembark.

Suddenly the engine cut off, and Captain Jack entered the salon. He went to a drawer in the galley and gathered up four passports. There he found a box of business cards, pulled out one and handed it to Maria. "Here's my card so you can reach me. I'm going to the Customs and Immigration Office to get clearance. When I get back, I'll walk you over to the taxi stand. I'll just be a few minutes. If you're hungry, help yourself to a piece of fruit." Jack pointed to the basket of apples and bananas on the counter.

Then he opened the sliding glass door to the cockpit. He said a few words to Manual that she couldn't hear and then left the yacht. Manual came in and closed the door behind him. He smiled at her as he went to the galley for another cup of coffee. "Coffee?"

"No, thanks." Maria wondered where she left her mug. She was distracted and that wasn't a good thing. "I don't know where I put the mug."

"Probably in the fly bridge. I'll go see." A minute later he was back with the mug and showed it to her before putting it in the sink.

She smiled at him to show her thanks and then went out to the cockpit and sat down. She looked over the panorama and wished she had come here before. She lived in Colombia all those years and never had the pleasure to stay in this beautiful setting. There was a gentle breeze that ruffled her hair. She looked down the dock and saw Captain Jack approaching. When he saw her, he waved and gave the thumbs up.

When he reached his yacht, Jack stepped into the cockpit, opened the sliding door, and said, "We're cleared. Manual, take down the yellow quarantine flag and put up the Colombian flag." Looking over at Maria, he said, "Ready to go?"

Maria nodded, walked into the salon, and said goodbye to Manual. When she began to pull the suitcase, Captain Jack said, "I'll get it." Instead of rolling it across the carpet, he picked the suitcase by the handle and walked to the cockpit. There he lifted the suitcase and placed it on the dock. He stepped on the edge of the transom and onto the dock. Maria followed him and he helped her step out onto the dock. This was her last chance to have a good look. She stood there and turned around a full 360 degrees. Now she understood why Captain Jack said it was a tourist hub. It was spectacular. The morning air was cool and now she could smell breakfast cooking as she got closer to the marina's restaurant. It perked up her appetite, but her stomach would have to wait. She was sure she would be served breakfast on the private jet.

She and Jack continued to walk until they reached the taxi stand. She had told Jack along the way that the private jet company arranged for a driver to pick her up. Just as promised, there they saw a limousine with a driver leaning against the passenger door. The uniformed man waved to them as if expecting them. Captain Jack spoke to the driver and verified that he was to take Maria to Simon Bolivar Airport. Captain Jack opened the passenger door for her while the driver took the suitcase and put it in the trunk. Maria got in and looked up at Captain Jack. "Thank you for everything. I'll call you and let you know when I'm on my way back. Please say goodbye to Captain Rick for me"

"You're welcome. I hope it goes well with your father," Captain Jack said as he closed the passenger door. He turned and headed back to the dock.

Maria's eyes welled up with tears at the thought of her dying father and she tried to blink them away. The driver pulled away from the taxi stand and headed to the airport.

In a matter of minutes, she could see the airport control tower.

Maria could see he made this trip many times and in just a few minutes, he parked in front of a small building that was separated from the main terminal for commercial flights. She got out of the limousine and the driver met her with her suitcase. She was now ready for the next leg of the trip. She went into the terminal and looked around for the ladies room. *Damas* was clearly marked to the right and she went in there to change into her disguise. Since it was only 7:30 a.m., she had the room to herself. That made the transformation easier without having witnesses. She went into a stall and retracted the handle of the suitcase. Then she laid the protective paper cover over the toilet seat and balanced her suitcase on it. She unzipped the suitcase to get what she needed. The tight quarters of the stall made undressing difficult and she found herself hitting her elbow on the door and wall of the stall. She draped her clothes on the door hook and dressed in the nurse's uniform. The last things she put on were the wig and glasses. After packing her clothes in the suitcase, she went to the sink and looked at herself. Then she remembered the wax and got it out of the side pocket of the suitcase. She washed her hands and placed it under her upper lip. The transformation was complete. Now she was ready to check in for her charter flight. She wondered what the flight crew would think of a nurse chartering a private jet.

Chapter 18

Rolling her suitcase behind her, Maria approached the receptionist at the check-in counter. The name plate identified her as Lucy. The woman wore a tailored taupe suite, white blouse and taupe pumps. With her short brown hair cut in a classic bob, Maria thought she looked more like a flight attendant than receptionist. After Maria introduced herself, the receptionist checked her computer for Maria's name and confirmed her flight.

"Your reservation was made with a credit card" Lucy said as she focused on her monitor. "Do you want me to process your card for the airfare or do you want to pay another way?"

"Thank you for asking," said Maria. "I'd rather pay for the fare with my traveler's checks."

Lucy agreed and told her the amount due was $1,850. Maria took out the checks from her shoulder bag, signed them and handed them over. Lucy then gave her a receipt and confirmed the return flight. She said, "If you have a change in plans, please call. We can accommodate your schedule. Here's a business card. Now if you'll follow me, I'll escort you to your private jet."

Lucy came from behind the counter and seeing Maria's suitcase, took it from her. They went out the door to the tarmac and that's when Maria saw a Lear jet for the first time in her life. There were stairs to the entry way and Maria followed Lucy into the aircraft. The carpet, walls and headliner were cream colored, and the seating was upholstered in fawn leather. After she secured Maria's suitcase in a small walnut closet, Lucy led her to a choice of seven swivel chairs. She sat down in one chair facing forward that gave her a view out the window and into the jet's cockpit. There at the controls were the pilot and co-pilot dressed in traditional white shirts with gold braid epaulets and black slacks. Behind the cockpit were high-gloss walnut cabinets in the double galley and aft of that the lavatory and entertainment center.

"Mrs. Alvarez, may I get you breakfast? It's a short flight, only an hour, and I'll serve it to you once we're in the air," said Lucy who handed her a small menu.

Maria now realized that Lucy was also the flight attendant who did double-duty at the receptionist desk. It actually made sense since private charters flew when the paying client wanted to fly. No one would be coming in to check in once Maria's jet left for Bogotá.

"Yes, I would like breakfast," Maria said, looking at the selections. "I'll have the cereal with sliced banana and skim milk. And a cup of coffee. Thank you."

Lucy took the menu from her, went to talk to the pilot in the cockpit, and then returned to Maria.

"Please fasten your seatbelt. We're going to taxi out to the runway now." Lucy touched a control that automatically retracted the jet's staircase and secured the door. The effect shut out all outside noise much like a sound-proof booth. She then walked to the rear of the plane and took a seat.

Maria detected the faint whine of the engines and she sat up a little straighter. Sensing the aircraft moving, she looked to the cockpit and then out the window. The jet continued to taxi down the runway and finally came to a stop. She heard the pilot talking on the radio asking permission to take off. Then the Lear jet was speeding down the runway and it felt to Maria like it was going a million miles per hour. Suddenly the plane was airborne. It was so fast; Maria didn't even have time to think about saying a prayer. She did now. She wanted to land safely. She then realized she hadn't called her mother as she had promised.

As Lucy walked past her to go to the galley, Maria said, "Can I make a phone call? I promised to call my mother in Bogotá."

Lucy nodded yes, and retrieved the air phone from its holder. After she handed it over to Maria, she returned to the galley.

Maria held the phone and called her mother. She said hello when she heard her voice.

"Ah, Maria, I was beginning to worry about you. Where are you?"

"I'm in the air. In less than an hour we'll be landing in Bogotá. Did you schedule a driver to pick me up at the charter air jet terminal?"

"Yes, Sal is picking you up. He's familiar with that company."

"Did you tell him to look for a nurse?" Maria asked, wondering if her mother remembered the disguise.

"Yes, I did. We can trust Sal. You know that."

"Yes, he was helpful with the chartering the fishing boat and the Lear jet." Thinking of the purpose of the trip, Maria said, "How's Papa this morning?"

"His spirits are up. He's looking forward to seeing you. And so am I."

Lucy came with a breakfast tray and pulled out a walnut tray from the wall. She put it down and said, "If you need anything else, let me know."

Maria nodded and smiled at her. To her mother, she said, "Momma, I'll see you in a little while. I've just been served breakfast."

They said good-bye and Maria broke the connection. She held the phone up for Lucy to see that she was through with her phone call. Lucy took it from her and returned it to its holder.

The breakfast before her was inviting and Maria began to eat. She sipped her coffee — nothing like true Colombian coffee — and looked out the window at the landscape below her. She had a bird's eye view of the snow-capped mountains, sparkling rivers, and sprawling cities. She hadn't realized

Colombia was so dense with vegetation until now. Having lived in the capital city of Bogotá, it was just something she hadn't thought much about. She wondered what it was that she was looking at. Coffee plants? Banana trees? Avocado? Or perhaps growing there were the illegal coca crops that yielded 80 percent of the world's cocaine – the very stuff that financed FARC. From this altitude, it was anybody's guess. And then the image of walking through the forest with her captors flashed through Maria's mind. She wondered if there were others making the same trek through the woods even now. From all reports, FARC was still running amok.

Chapter 19

Maria followed Lucy across the tarmac to the jet charter's terminal at the Bogotá airport. When she stepped inside, Maria saw Sal waiting for her. She turned to Lucy and thanked her for her service and took her suitcase from her. She walked over to Sal and smiled at him. He seemed puzzled until he realized that he was looking at Maria. Then he smiled warmly.

"Maria, it's good to see you. I didn't recognize you, even though your mother told me to look for an overweight nurse," Sal said as he studied her face.

"So my disguise works?"

"Absolutely." Taking Maria's suitcase from her, Sal said, "Let's go. Your parents are waiting for you."

They walked to Sal's compact car. He opened the passenger door for her and Maria got in. After putting the suitcase in the trunk, Sal got in and started the engine. Maria thought he'd dressed as the owner of an international electronics firm should. He wore an Italian-tailored grey, worsted-wool suit with a pale blue shirt and grey striped silk tie. But rather than a traditional oxford shoe, Sal preferred soft Italian leather loafers.

He was clean shaven and his short brown hair was graying at the temples. At fifty-one, his light skin was beginning to show the signs of age, with laugh lines at the corner of his brown eyes and frown lines above his eyebrows, a reflection of his serious side for business and his lightheartedness with family and friends.

While Sal backed the car out of the space, Maria asked, "Have you seen my father?"

"No, not in a while," Sal answered as he put the car in drive. "But I know he is seriously ill. I'm glad you were able to come. I know that coming here puts you at great risk, but I think your disguise is convincing. You have to be cautious whenever you're around anyone other than your parents. You have my number stored in your cell phone. Just call me if you need me. You and Jorge are like second family."

"Thank you, Sal. I'm glad I can count on you. You helped make this trip possible. I do have one thing I'd like you to do. This afternoon, I'd like to be tested to see if I am a match for a kidney transplant for my father. Can you arrange that and call me later?"

"Yes, Maria. After I drop you off, I'll get in touch with your father's doctor. By the way, what name are you going by?"

"I thought I should use the name Marie Valdez. It's close to Maria. Just in case I get called by Maria and I answer. I can explain it away by saying I thought you said Marie."

"That's smart," Sal said as he watched the traffic around him. They were driving in morning rush hour and the roads were clogged with buses and yellow taxis. In the government's effort to reduce pollution, the citizens of Bogotá could only drive their car every other day. Consequently, public transit was a necessity.

"I didn't remember this much traffic when I lived here," Maria said. "I guess I'm used to living in the suburbs of South Florida."

As Sal drove through downtown Bogotá in stop and go traffic, Maria noticed the stark contrast between South Florida cities and Bogotá. Most of the streets in Bogotá were two way with a center island to separate them. Most of the major streets in South Florida were boulevards that were lushly landscaped with a variety of trees such as royal palm, tabebuia, jacaranda and other tropical foliage. There was always green grass and colorful flowers that softened the effect of asphalt. In Bogotá, the concrete medium featured an occasional spindly tree. The capital city also lacked a master plan so the buildings were painted in a rainbow of colors. City officials in South Florida had building codes and all commercial buildings had to abide by the rules. There were cases where the "golden arches" were not permitted because they didn't match the color codes permitted by the city. Bogotá was also plagued by graffiti. South Florida had its share, but buildings that were defaced quickly got a coat of Kilz® paint.

"I hear you have your share of traffic," Sal said.

"That's true, but it's really the main thoroughfares that get congested."

"Having never been to South Florida, I can't relate."

"Maybe you should plan on coming to Florida. Bring your wife. She'll love the shopping and the art galleries."

Sal laughed, "I'm sure she will."

Maria straightened up in her seat when she saw they were approaching the upscale, more modern part of Bogotá at the north end where she once lived with her family in Sante Barbara. It wouldn't be much longer when they would arrive at her family's apartment building.

"Are you nervous, Maria, I mean Marie?" Sal asked.

Maria smiled at Sal for correcting himself with her alias. "Yes. I'm so happy that I can see them, but I can't help but remember those awful months when I was held by the rebels. If they know I'm here, well, I really don't want to talk about it."

"I understand. If at any time you feel like you're in danger, call me. I'll get you right to the airport. That private jet charter company does a lot of business out of the airport so keep that in mind. They can accommodate you on short notice."

"Thanks, Sal. That does make me feel better," Maria said, putting her hand to her hair and stopped, remembering she was wearing a wig. She then realized that raking her hand through her hair was a nervous habit; one that she had to stop while she was in Bogotá.

"Keep in touch with me, Marie. I'll call you to let you know what time I'll pick you up this afternoon so you can get tested," Sal said as he changed lanes to the far right. The apartment building was just ahead.

"You're just going to drop me off in front, right?" Maria asked. She was thinking that if Silvana saw Sal in the building, she would think it odd that he brought a nurse here.

"Yes, no sense taking any chances. It would be odd that a family friend of Jorge's was bringing a nurse to your father."

"Exactly my thoughts." Maria turned to Sal and said, "Thank you again for everything you've done. We'll talk later."

Sal parked the car at the curb a few feet from the entrance and released the trunk. "Can you handle your suitcase?"

"Sure," Maria said as she got out of the car. She turned to Sal and smiled. "Drive carefully. I'll see you later."

Maria closed the passenger door and lifted the lid of the trunk. She removed the suitcase and wheeled the suitcase to the entrance to the building. She felt strange to be returning after two years, yet it was as if she never left. She entered the lobby and a mental picture of the day she was reunited with her family flashed into her mind. She remembered how Silvana stood back from the rest of the family and then reluctantly came to her and hugged her carefully as if she was afraid she might break. She wondered if she was here now or if she was at the boutique that she managed? She hoped their paths wouldn't cross. If they did, Maria knew that she had to keep her composure and play the part of the home healthcare nurse.

Maria looked around and all was quiet. She imagined her brothers were at work. She would have liked to be able to meet with them, but it was out of the question. She would have to carry on with this charade because her life depended on it. She took a deep breath and pushed the elevator button. When it opened, she wheeled the suitcase into the elevator and hit number 6 to take her to her parent's floor. The elevator ascended. It took a moment and the door opened. Maria looked around and stepped out. There was only one apartment on this floor, the penthouse. She took another deep breath and she knocked on the door. Every nerve was on edge and her heart was pounding in her chest. She wondered what toll the chronic kidney disease had taken on her father. She was about to find out.

Chapter 20

Suddenly feeling dizzy, Maria realized she was holding her breath while she waited for her mother to answer the door. She inhaled deeply and the lightheadedness disappeared.

The door opened and there stood her mother. Without saying a word, she smiled and grabbed Maria's wrist, leading her into the foyer. She closed the door softly and turned to Maria and began to cry. Maria wrapped her arms around her and kissed her cheek. "Mama, I'm so happy to be here."

They embraced each other and Maria could physically feel an emotional vibration course through her body. She let the tears flow without embarrassment. They now held each other at arm's length and appraised one another. Maria then realized what a toll her father's illness had taken on her mother. She had shed at least 15 pounds as her blue floral dress hung on her, camouflaging her once ample figure. Even though Mama wore makeup, Maria noticed the dark circles under her eyes, most likely from sleepless nights.

Drying her eyes, Mama tilted her head to one side and then walked around Maria looking her over. "Simply amazing. What a transformation. I was worried when you told me about this disguise, but I had no reason to. You're very convincing as a nurse."

Maria nodded, wiping her tears away. "We still have to be very careful. I'm anxious to see Papa, but let's get the details out of the way. Am I still going to stay in our old apartment?"

"Yes. You have it to yourself. In case someone happens to see you in the building, I've told the family that a student nurse is staying there to help care for your father while she completes her internship. You won't have to worry about meals. I stocked the refrigerator and pantry. I also changed the locks. Let me give you the key right now. Then I'll take you in to see your Papa."

Maria followed her mother into the kitchen where she opened a drawer and pulled out a small brown envelope. She handed it to Maria.

Opening the envelope, she saw the shiny brass key. "Thank you." Maria then slid the envelope into the side pocket of her white uniform.

"Come. Your Papa can't wait to see you," said Mama, taking Maria by the hand. They walked into the den where her father sat in a comfortable leather chair, his feet propped up on the ottoman. He was wearing an open-collared white shirt, a grey golf sweater over it and navy slacks. When he saw her, his eyebrows knitted together. Then he recognized her and smiled. He eased his feet off the ottoman and started to get up.

"Sit, Papa," Maria said as she rushed over and knelt down beside him. They hugged in a long embrace. Finally, they parted and looked at each other with tears flowing.

"Maria, can you take off the disguise so I can see you — my beautiful daughter?"

Maria looked at her mother, her eyes looking to the door. "Mama, are you expecting anyone? Is the door locked?"

"I'm not expecting anyone. The family knows to call before they visit. No drop-ins are allowed. And yes, the door is locked. Go ahead and take off the wig and glasses."

Maria removed the wig, glasses and wax from under her lip and laid them on the end table next to her father's chair. Knowing her own hair was matted to her head from the wig, she then ran her fingers through her hair to fluff it.

Papa clapped his hands and said, "That's my Maria! Still beautiful."

Maria looked for visual signs of the chronic kidney disease. She noticed that there were some bruises on his arms and his skin looked pale. He was also thinner than when she had last seen him. But other than that, there weren't any other visible signs.

"You look better than I thought you would, Papa, considering what you're going through."

"Now I'm getting what they call nocturnal dialysis treatments three times a week. I get hooked up at night. It takes, like, five hours. It's the best they can offer me now. A kidney transplant is what

I really need," he said as he lifted his glasses from his nose and wiped his eyes with a tissue.

Taking her father's hand in hers, Maria said, "I'm going to get tested this afternoon to see if I'm a match. Sal is making an appointment for me this afternoon."

Papa sighed and shook his head in dismay. "I didn't ask you to come here for that, Maria. That's a sacrifice I don't think you should make. I wanted you to come so we can clear up some things."

"I know, Papa. But I have two kidneys. If I'm a match, I would gladly donate one to you."

Mama came over to Maria and touched her shoulder. "I know you gave this a lot of thought. But you should know that there are a number of factors that have to match to be a successful donor. Don't feel like a failure if you aren't one. Not one of us in the family qualified to be a donor. So your Papa is on a waiting list."

Mama helped Maria up from her kneeling position on the floor. "Come, get up, Maria. Sit down on the couch and relax. I'll bring you coffee unless you'd rather have something else."

"Coffee is fine, Mama. Thank you."

Maria took a seat across from her father and looked around the room. It was just as she remembered it. There was a built-in wall unit in polished oak with open shelves for his books, glass-fronted cabinets for collectibles, and other cabinets to hold CDs, DVDs and the entertainment center. A large screen TV was hidden behind panels when not in use. There were palladium windows that took up another wall that bathed the room in natural light. The other walls had framed paintings, including one by Fernando Botero, Colombia's most famous artist and sculptor known for exaggerated portraits of obese figures. The one her father owned was titled "Man with Dog." She was always fascinated with the details. The fat man had a pencil-thin mustache, a shadow of a beard, and a black suit with a yellow-striped shirt and a tie. Propped on top of his head was a black fedora. She found the top of his hands and fingers disturbing since they sprouted hair, reminding her of a chimpanzee. She looked down at the floor and admired the Persian rug. She never really appreciated the luxuries her family enjoyed until she began living in the US and struggled to pay their bills. Her father worked hard and she didn't begrudge him any of these extravagancies, especially now that he may not have much more time to enjoy them.

"Papa, tell me how you're really feeling," Maria said, anxious to know the truth.

"Ah, Maria. Let's not talk about me. There's not much to say."

"Don't brush me off, Papa. I want to know. I *need* to know."

Don Pedro let out a loud sigh. "I don't have the energy I used to and my joints ache. I've lost my appetite. I had shortness of breath, but the dialysis has helped that. I don't sleep very well either."

Brightening, he said, "But I'm still alive and I have you here with me. That's what counts."

"I'm really glad I came. It's been too long since we sat and talked," Maria said looking him in the eyes.

"Yes, I've wanted to talk to — really talk to you for a long time. Somehow it just doesn't seem right to have a conversation like this on the telephone. I needed to see your face."

"I understand, Papa."

Both Maria and her father turned their heads to look at Mama as she entered the room carrying a tray. She set it down on the coffee table in front of Maria and served them small cups of strong black coffee. Maria saw there was also a plate of butter cookies that looked very tempting. Before leaving the room, Mama said, "Enjoy. I'll be in the kitchen if you need me."

Now that they were alone again, Maria felt anxious. She was acutely aware that the time she would spend with her father would probably be her last. The thought of her father dying was painful and Maria meshed her lips together. She didn't want to cry again so she looked upward, cleared her throat and swallowed.

Papa said, "I know this is hard on you. Somehow when one is the patient, you take each day as it comes. But the family, that's a different story. I know your mother worries if she will find me alive when she comes into the room. I hear her saying her 'Hail Marys' all the time."

"Yes, I know where I got that from. I do it all the time, too. It started for me—the praying I mean — when I was held captive. I still pray every day. Life is so uncertain. Somehow saying a prayer brings me hope that everything will work out just fine."

Her father took a sip of his coffee and said, "Hope. That's all we can do."

They both fell silent for a few minutes, drinking their coffee and thinking about what they wanted to say to each other.

Papa put his coffee cup down on the tray and took a deep breath. Exhaling slowly, he said, "I just want to clear things up about the ransom and the comments you heard. When you were kidnapped, I would have given all my money to FARC to get you back. But my bank accounts were frozen immediately once Jorge filed the missing person's report. We were only allowed enough money to pay the monthly bills and to keep my business running. I played the shrewd businessman negotiating back and forth with that nameless bastard so we could string them along while GAULA tried to find you. As it turned out, they got lucky. Believe me when I tell you, I would have traded places with you if I could.

"But there's another issue, one that your mother pointed out. That I was cold hearted to her, Jorge and the rest of the family. But it was the only way I could prevent myself from breaking down. I had a business to run. So I insulated myself the best way I could. I put on a front. So I'm sorry for the anguish I caused Jorge. He's a good man and I'm proud he's my son-in-law."

Maria began to cry. She was glad to hear her father apologize.

Papa cleared his throat and continued, "I couldn't buy your freedom, but I did do some other things that I hope you'll be happy about. I started a scholarship foundation for the officers' children at GAULA. Five percent of sales of Fino Foods will go to the scholarship fund every year. This way their children can go to college. It was the best way I knew to show my gratitude that they saved you."

"That's wonderful, Papa. I hope you publicize it in the supermarkets."

"Yes, there's signage in the stores. The fund has grown and in a few years the first students will be eligible to receive a scholarship. Several of the officers have children in high school."

"Are they academic scholarships or based on need?"

"Both. I think that is best, don't you?'

Maria nodded, "Yes. You know I am still taking English classes. Once I can pass the TOEFL test, I can enroll in college and get my degree."

"What's the toe-full test?"

"It's the Test of English as a Foreign Language to find out how proficient you are in English. All courses are taught in English in college and universities. They want to know that you'll be able to understand the coursework, otherwise you're wasting your money."

"Speaking of money, that's another issue we had. When you left for the United States, I didn't give you any money to start a new life. That was wrong of me. You see, I didn't want you to leave. I thought if I made it hard on you and Jorge financially, you would reconsider and stay. I just didn't realize how terrorized you really were."

"It was awful. We had the armored car. I was so afraid. I still am now. Those months with those stinking rebels don't fade away. I still have nightmares," Maria said with bitterness in her voice.

"I want to make it up to you, Maria. I made a new will. You'll get an equal share of my estate. I think it's an outdated custom that only the sons should inherit my money. I've already provided for your mother. I'm also appointing you to the Board of Directors of Fino Foods so you'll get a check every month. Meetings can be held through a teleconference. I am also giving you a gift of five hundred thousand dollars so you can buy a house and put money away for my two granddaughters' college expenses."

"Papa, I don't know what to say. I never thought— I never expected to hear anything like this." Maria got up from her seat and sat down on the ottoman in front of her father. She took his hands in hers and kissed his fingertips. When she looked up at him, she saw tears streaming down his cheeks. She leaned over and hugged him. "I love you, Papa. I can't bear to lose you. You're the world to me. I don't know what I'll do without you."

"There, there," Papa said, patting Maria's back to soothe her. "I'm not gone yet. I'm happy I got the chance to tell you these things. I love you. And I'm very proud of you. You're a fine person."

"Oh, Papa," Maria said, "It's just so hard. All this time. There was this invisible barrier. And now, I feel it's gone." Maria shook her head and sighed with relief.

"Yes. If there's anything else I can do for you, let me know."

Maria eyed the pack of chewing gum on the table next to her father. "How about a stick of gum?"

Papa laughed and handed her the gum. "That's not exactly what I meant. But here you are."

Maria unwrapped the gum, stuck it in her mouth, and began to chew. She absently folded the wrapper into a ring.

"Maria," Mama called. "I hear your cell phone ringing in your purse."

"I'm coming. It might be Sal," Maria said as she put the paper ring on the end table. "Excuse me, Papa. I'll be back in a minute."

Maria left the den and got her cell phone. She saw the caller was Sal. "Hello."

"Marie," Sal said, "your appointment is this afternoon at three o'clock. I'll pick you up around the corner from your building. If I get stuck in traffic, I'll call you."

"Okay, Sal. See you then." Maria ended the call and returned it to her purse. Then she turned to her mother and said, "Sal's picking me up at three. Hopefully I'll be a donor match."

"You're brave to even consider it," Mama said reaching out for Maria. They embraced once again. Maria thought it was so good to be home. No matter how old you get, you always need your parents. Somehow they always seemed to make things all right with the world. She now hoped she could make things right for them by extending her father's life with her donated kidney.

Chapter 21

A wave of nausea came over Silvana as she looked for a parking place in front of her apartment building and was relieved when she saw a car ready to pull out. She put her turn signal on indicating she was going to take the parking place so traffic could go around her. She hoped she wouldn't vomit in the car because she would be the one to clean it up. Roman was working in his family's business so he wasn't home to do it for her. Usually she could get him to do anything she wanted, even cleaning up after her.

With the parking space now open, Silvana paralleled parked at the curb. In the midst of the pedestrians, a white uniform caught her eye. There was a heavy-set nurse walking down the street. Suddenly, Silvana retched and opened the car door just in time to vomit out on the street. She hung her head down holding onto the car door for support and then she retched again. When she felt she wouldn't have another episode, she sat up and reached into her purse for a tissue to wipe her mouth. She looked at the sidewalk full of pedestrians and the nurse was gone. She wondered if she was one of the home healthcare nurses who were attending to her father-in-law. The way she was feeling she could use a nurse herself. She realized that she hadn't been feeling well since mid-afternoon. Was it something I ate? she thought. She left work early because of the nausea, but now felt a little better. Perhaps a cold glass of cola would soothe her stomach. She got out of the car, watching where she stepped, and opened the trunk of her car. She retrieved a shopping bag from the Montblanc Boutique. Inside was a gift Silvana picked out for Don Pedro. It was a black Montblanc cartridge fountain pen, with platinum-plated rings around the barrel and a clip on the cap set with a sapphire gemstone. She was advised that the gemstone was synthetic, but she didn't care. She thought it was the perfect gift for Don Pedro since he kept a journal. She wanted to ensure that she and Roman were in his good graces. She believed that her husband would get an equal share along with his brothers in inheriting Don Pedro's company, Fino Foods. And she didn't want him to change his will at the last minute. Silvana knew that of all Don Pedro's children, Maria was his favorite. But now that his daughter lived in the US, Silvana didn't give her much thought. She was glad to have her gone. Because when it came to Roman's parents, it was always Maria this and Maria that. She could do no wrong. And if it wasn't her, then it was the grandchildren, Paula and Julie. Silvana longed to have children and suffered two miscarriages that she kept secret. She still hoped to become pregnant. Then she could take her rightful place in the family.

Her in-laws doted on their grandchildren and missed them terribly. She had gone into her mother-in-law's bedroom and saw all the framed photos of her grandchildren displayed on the dresser. She wanted pictures there of her own children.

Silvana let herself into her apartment and went to the kitchen, dropping her purse and gift bag on the counter. She got a glass from the cabinet, added some ice from the freezer, and looked in the refrigerator for a can of cola. There in the back was one last can. She would have to remind Roman to get more on his way home from work. She poured the soda into the glass and took a sip. She took a deep breath and exhaled slowly hoping to ease her stomach. Perhaps if I lay down on the couch for a few minutes, she thought. And then she decided to call her mother-in-law, Anna Marie, to ask what time she could stop by to see Don Pedro and give him his gift. Maybe visiting with them would be a distraction to her nausea.

She picked up the phone and called Anna Marie to see if it was convenient to come over now. Her mother-in-law asked her to hold on while she asked Don Pedro if he was up for company. She heard a click and realized that the mute function was on so she couldn't hear her mother-in-law. She had never done that before, she noted. When Anna Marie returned, she told Silvana she could come over now, but don't stay long otherwise Don Pedro will get overtired.

She took another few swallows of the soda and then put the glass in the refrigerator. If the soda was still fizzy when she got back, she'd finish it then.

Silvana grabbed the gift bag and left her apartment, locking the door behind her.

She put her key in her jeans pocket and took the elevator up to her in-laws' suite. She smoothed her purple silk blouse over her hips and then flipped her long curly red hair behind one ear, revealing a large chandelier earring with amethyst crystals that dazzled in the light.

She stepped off the elevator and walked to the door. Before she had a chance to knock on the door, her mother-in-law opened the door wide and Silvana entered the foyer.

"Come in Silvana. My, you look pale. What's the matter?"

"Just nauseous. I got sick to my stomach when I was parking the car," Silvana explained.

"Is it something you ate?" Anna Marie asked.

"I don't think so. I just heated up what we had for dinner last night—*arroz con pollo.*"

Anna Marie looked at Silvana in the eyes and asked, "Are you pregnant?"

"Oh, stop. Let's not talk about that now," Silvana said, walking past her mother-in-law. "I want to see Don Pedro."

The two women walked into the den. Silvana said, "Don Pedro, I got you a little surprise."

"Now why did you go and do that? I don't need anything. Just your company is enough."

"No, I saw this and I thought how perfect it is for you," Silvana said, handing her father-in-law the gift bag.

He took it from her, reached into the bag and pulled out the wrapped gift box. He carefully removed the ribbon and paper and dropped it in his lap. He started to smile as he removed the lid and saw the Montblanc pen. The platinum rings around the black resin pen and the blue jewel sparkled as he held the pen and turned it around for Anne Marie to see. "Beautiful. Just beautiful. I'll think of you when I write in my journal. Thank you, Silvana."

Silvana bent over Don Pedro and kissed his cheek. "You're welcome." As she got up, she glanced over at the end table and spotted a paper ring. Where did that come from?

She wondered. She could see that it was made from a chewing gum wrapper, a lot like the one Maria made on the way home from class the night she was kidnapped. Did Don Pedro make it himself? She knew Don Pedro chewed a lot of gum since he quit smoking years ago. She just couldn't picture him making it. But maybe he did. Perhaps Maria had taught him.

"What's the matter, Maria?" Don Pedro asked, looking from the end table to Silvana. "You seem off in another world."

"It's nothing. I was remembering some things I have to do. I should go and get them done before Roman comes home."

"Stay. You just got here. Sit awhile," Don Pedro said, still admiring the pen.

"No, it's better that I go and leave you to rest – or write in your journal," Silvana said. She smiled at her father-in-law and turned to leave.

"All right then. Thank you again," Don Pedro said. He put the pen back into the box and sighed.

"I'll see you to the door," Anne Marie said as she followed Silvana to the foyer. "That was sweet of you to get Don Pedro the pen. He had a Montblanc pen years ago, but somehow it disappeared. We never could find it."

"He probably left it someplace. Or somebody picked it up without thinking."

"Who knows?" Anne Marie asked, raising her eyebrows.

"It doesn't matter now, does it?" Silvana answered gritting her teeth.

"No, it doesn't. You took care of that – the new pen. Thank you," Anne Marie replied, opening the door to let Silvana leave.

Silvana gave Anne Marie a quick kiss on the cheek and walked out the door. She was glad to leave because she didn't like the way Anne Marie looked at her just now. She felt like she was accusing her of taking the old Montblanc pen. So what if she did? Silvana took the elevator back down to her apartment and let herself in. She went to the kitchen and took the cola from the refrigerator. She finished what was left and put the glass in the sink.

What nagged at her now was not Anne Marie's attitude, but the chewing gum wrapper ring. It reminded her of Maria — Maria who could do no wrong. Did Anne Maria make the ring? She couldn't picture that. So who did make it and leave it on the end table? There had to be an explanation and she would find out, if it was the last thing she'd do.

Chapter 22

Maria sat in the doctor's waiting room. She found the pale green motif with moss green accents relaxing since she was anxious just being out in public. She admired the framed botanical prints that were artfully arranged on the walls and then studied the large floral arrangement of orchids on the large coffee table in the middle of the room. She was always amazed at the variety of orchids, each distinctly beautiful.

The receptionist sat behind a frosted glass window only to be seen when she opened it to retrieve the patient sign-in sheet from the countertop. Maria had signed in under her alias.

There were three other people waiting, an elderly couple sitting on the other side of the room, and a middle-aged man with a shaved head who sat a few seats away from her. Maria thought they should call these waiting rooms "reading rooms" since everyone was reading a book or a magazine. However, Maria was too anxious to read. She knew it was impossible for her to concentrate on the printed word so she simply sat there wondering if she were a suitable donor. She didn't know her blood type. It never seemed to be important, but now it was a major factor. She glanced at her watch. Her appointment was at three o'clock and it was now fifteen minutes after the hour. Just as she was about to get up to knock on the glass for the receptionist, the door to the inner office opened. A nurse similarly dressed as Maria called for Marie Valdez. When she saw Maria approach, she tilted her head back in surprise, obviously not expecting a nurse.

"Come this way, please, Marie," Maria followed the woman to a scale where she was weighed. The nurse put the secondary weight near the end of the scale and then had to adjust it for less weight. She knitted her brows together when she saw the weight at 125 pounds and gave Maria a quizzical look. Maria knew she looked much heavier because of the hidden padding.

Maria then was led to an examining room and told to get up on the examining table that was covered with paper. After Maria got comfortable, the nurse took her temperature with an ear thermometer and announced it was normal. She then took Maria's blood pressure. She recorded the readings inside the patient folder.

"The doctor will be with you in just a few minutes," the nurse said before she left the room. Maria looked around the small room. She thought when you've seen one examining room, you've seen them all. There was the table upon which she sat, a swivel stool on wheels for the doctor, and another arm chair against the wall, ostensibly for whoever accompanied the patient. Against one stark wall was a cabinet with a sink and a dispenser for paper towels and hand soap. A cabinet over the sink held whatever medical supplies the doctor needed, she assumed. Over on the opposite wall were the diplomas testifying that the man she was about to see was indeed a physician. There were no windows in the room; the only light source came from an overhead fluorescent light fixture.

Finally a man wearing a white lab coat over a grey dress shirt and maroon and grey paisley tie entered the room. He was tall with brown hair graying at the temples. He looked at her through gold wire-rimmed glasses and said, "Hello, Marie. I'm Doctor Manual Gonzalez."

"Nice to meet you, doctor," Maria said, feeling very nervous. She knew she was going to have to be truthful about her true identity once he started asking questions. She would have to assume her relationship with him was confidential.

"I understand you want to be tested to see if you are a suitable kidney donor," the doctor said as he looked at her patient folder.

"Yes, that's right," Maria said twisting her fingers together.

"The most likely suitable donor is a family member. Are you related to Don Pedro?"

"Before I answer that, I need to know that your patient files are kept confidential." Maria asked, feeling foolish to mention it, but she didn't want to have to worry about it later.

"Yes, your file is absolutely private. But now you have me curious. What is it that has you concerned? Do you want to explain yourself?"

Maria hesitated, and then decided she must tell him her secret "My name is Maria Alvarez and I am Don Pedro's only daughter. I left Bogotá two years ago when I was granted political asylum in the United States. I had been kidnapped by FARC and was rescued by GAULA after being held for four months. Perhaps you saw it on TV."

"Yes, I do remember that rescue. You were really lucky," the doctor said as he pulled the stool out and sat down. "So you came back because you father is gravely ill. I assume you were granted an emergency advance parole document so you can re-enter the United States."

Maria's eyes grew wide. "What do you mean emergency advance parole?"

Doctor Gonzalez cupped his chin in his hand. "That's a document the US issues if you want to return to your country of persecution for humanitarian reasons such as a grave illness or death in the family. Of course, you have to apply for it and that can take quite a bit of time. I know about it because in the case of a severe illness, the doctor has to send a letter testifying to the fact. From your question, I take it you didn't know about it."

Maria shook her head. "No, I didn't. All I know is that the US won't allow a political asylum refugee to re-enter if the person ever returns to their native land. Their reasoning is that if you go back you have nothing to fear anymore."

"That reasoning is valid. Are you planning to return to the US?"

"Yes, I am. I got here in a round-about way so my passport doesn't have a stamp for Colombia," Maria said dropping her hand and looking down at the pretzel she made of her fingers.

The doctor looked at Maria thoughtfully and noticed her hands working nervously. "Do you still feel your life is in danger?"

"Oh yes," Maria said, breaking down in tears. "That's why I had to know you wouldn't tell anyone. I'm wearing a disguise."

"I wondered about that. You look much heavier than the weight recorded in your medical file," Doctor Gonzalez said as he offered her a tissue.

Maria dabbed at her eyes under the glasses. She removed them and said, "I had no idea about the advance parole. But even if I did, I don't think there would be enough time to get it processed fast enough. My father is dying, I'm afraid."

"Then let's get back to the reason you're here. There are many tests that need to be done before a person can be considered a suitable donor. So let me explain. You must not have high blood pressure, cancer, kidney disease or heart disease and be between 18 and 60. Once your blood type is determined and it is compatible with Don Pedro's, I will review your medical history, the results from routine annual tests, and do a complete physical exam.

"After that, there is an EKG and a series of laboratory and X-ray tests to screen for kidney function, liver function, hepatitis, heart disease, lung disease and past exposure to a viral illness. Urine testing is also done to make sure your kidneys function normally. We will also do a CTA —a computerized tomography scan that determines if your urinary tract, kidneys and blood vessels leading to the kidneys are normal. That procedure is done in the hospital on an outpatient basis. During that scan, a contrast is injected into the blood stream through a vein in your arm while the CTA scan and X-rays are done. It takes about an hour and afterward you can resume your normal activities.

"You would also meet with a surgeon and a clinical social worker who will complete a psychosocial evaluation. After all that, a multidisciplinary committee reviews all the results and decides whether you able to safely proceed with the donation. Any questions?"

"What are the risks involved?" Maria asked feeling very overwhelmed with all of the information the doctor presented to her.

"The risks of donation are similar to those involved with any major surgery, such as bleeding and infection. Death resulting from kidney donation is extremely rare. According to current research, kidney donation doesn't change life expectancy or increase a donor's risk of developing kidney disease or other health problems. But first things first. I need to get a blood sample from you to determine if your blood is compatible with your father's. If it's not, there will be no further tests. I'll send the nurse in. All she does is prick your finger to draw a small sample. While you wait, we'll get the results. Then I'll come in and let you know. Are you ready, Maria?"

"Yes."

"Good. If you're a suitable donor, you can go through with the kidney transplant or you can change your mind. There is no pressure on you."

"But there is. My father needs a kidney."

The doctor looked at Maria and patted her twisted hands. "What you're doing is admirable. I'll send the nurse in."

The doctor left and a minute later the nurse entered with a lancet, a small vial and a packet holding an alcohol swab. She put everything down on the counter except for the packet which she tore open. "Please put out your hand, palm up, please," the nurse instructed.

Maria did as she asked. The nurse wiped her middle finger with the swab and discarded it. She then held Maria's middle finger steady while she used the lancet to draw blood. Once it began to flow, she suctioned the blood into the small vial. Then she wiped off Maria's finger and put a bandage on it. "All set. The doctor will be back in soon with your results. Are you okay?"

Maria took a deep breath. "Yes, I'm fine."

The nurse left the room and Maria was alone. She reached into her purse and pulled out her phone to see if there were any calls. She had it on vibrate so it wouldn't disturb the doctor. No calls. She would call Jorge and the girls after Sal took her back to the apartment. She wondered what Jorge would have to say about being a donor, if she was going to be donor, that is. Just as she put the phone away, the doctor came in with a card that bore the results from the test.

"Maria, your blood type is A. Your father is O which means your blood is not compatible with his. He needs someone with O blood to be a donor. I'm sorry. I know you wanted to help. Thank you for coming in. We won't need to do any more testing."

"I thought that O was the universal donor."

"Donor is right. Not recipient. He can give a blood transfusion to a person with any blood type but he can only receive O blood."

"I understand. Thank you anyway, doctor. I'm disappointed, but I'm glad that I came in to find out." Maria got off the examining table and made her way back to the waiting room where she called Sal to come pick her up. In one way she was relieved that she wasn't a suitable donor because Jorge would be upset about the surgery. On the other hand, she really wanted to save her father's life. And that just wasn't going to happen.

Chapter 23

Maria let herself into the apartment, locked the deadbolt and sat down on the couch. She took out her cell phone and noted the time. It was after five o'clock —a good time to call Jorge and talk to the girls. He normally didn't get home until six, but she had a feeling he might leave work earlier so he could pick the girls up and spend time with them in her absence.

She thought of the visit with the doctor and the business with the advance parole. Why hadn't she known about it? All she remembered was that returning to Colombia meant that she no longer feared persecution there so her asylum status would be revoked by the US. Thinking about it now, Maria believed there had to be humanitarian reasons to allow a refugee to return. But she thought if she had known about it before, by the time the advance parole was processed, her father would have died. What's done is done. The important thing is that she got to see her father, had a heart-to-heart talk with him and was tested to see if she was a suitable donor.

She called Jorge and was happy to hear his voice. She had left yesterday and she missed him terribly.

"Maria, how are you? How's your father?" Jorge asked.

"I'm fine. Just a headache. It must be the altitude. The elevation is much higher than Florida."

"Yes, considering Florida is at sea level, the change in altitude can give you a headache. Is it bad?" Jorge asked.

"Not too bad. I'll take something for it in a few minutes. My father is in good spirits, but I worry about him. I'll tell you more about him later. Are the girls with you?"

"Yes, I know they're not used to being with a sitter after school so I took off from work a little early. They're doing their homework at the table. I'll let you talk to them."

She heard Jorge say, "It's Mommy."

"Hi Mommy," said Julie. "I miss you."

"I miss you, too, Julie. How was school?"

"It was fine. My class is going on a field trip to the planetarium. My teacher wants to know if you can be a chaperone. Can you?" Julie said full of hope. Maria had chaperoned a class trip last year and it made Julie feel special that her mother was with her supervising her classmates.

"That sounds like fun. I'd love to go. When is it? Not this week, I hope."

"No, Mommy. Not this week. You can't be in two places at once. It's in two weeks. The teacher gave us the permission slip for our parent to sign," Julie said.

"Okay. You can have your Daddy sign the permission slip and you can tell your teacher I would be honored to chaperone your class trip," Maria said wishing she could give Julie a big hug. "How is your homework coming along? Do you have any projects your Daddy should know about?"

"No projects this week. But I bet we'll have to do something with the solar system since we're going to the planetarium," Julie predicted.

"You're probably right about that. Julie, let me talk to Paula now. Get back to your homework, and I'll try to call you again tomorrow. I love you, sweetie."

"I love you, too. I'll get Paula," Julie said.

Maria heard Julie say to Paula, "It's Mommy."

"Mommy, when are you coming home?" Paula asked with distress in her voice.

"Soon, Paula. Just a few more days and I'll be home. Are you being a good girl for Daddy?"

"I sure am. Daddy said he'll take us out for ice cream on the weekend if we keep our rooms clean and go to bed when he tells us to," Paula said now sounding very happy.

Maria thought that as much as she hated bribes, she knew they worked. A little reward for good behavior never hurt any child. "Good. That should be fun. What will you order, vanilla ice cream with sprinkles on top?"

"Yes, Mommy."

"The colored sprinkles or the chocolate ants?" Maria teased.

"No chocolate ants. Just the colored sprinkles," Paula laughed.

"Paula, I need to talk to Daddy now. Finish your homework, okay?"

"Okay, Mommy. I love you."

"I love you, too, Paula," Maria said picturing how great it will be when she returned home.

Paula said, "Mommy wants to talk to you."

After a pause, Jorge said, "So tell me about your father."

"He's doing as well as can be expected. He's on dialysis three times a week. He's on a strict diet and he looks pale. I haven't seen him walk, but I think he must be weak. We know the best thing for him is a new kidney. That's why I got tested today to see if I'm a suitable donor."

"You what?" Jorge asked, practically screaming into the phone.

"Don't get excited. It turns out I can't be a donor. I am not the right blood type."

"I can't believe you did that without even asking me first. Do you know what the risks are? You could die."

"Now stop. I'm sorry I didn't mention it to you first, but now that's over. I am not a donor. But if I was, I wouldn't die."

"Don't be so naïve. Any time a person goes under general anesthesia, she could go into a coma or die on the table from a stroke or heart attack. There's also the risk of infection. So you could die," Jorge said trying to keep his voice down.

"I'm sorry I upset you. Please calm down. Understand that I wanted to help my father. It just wasn't meant to be. I'm not a match," Maria said, feeling emotionally exhausted.

"All right. You're my world, Maria. I almost lost you once. The thought of losing you again is just too much for me. Please be very careful. Did Sal take you to the doctor?"

"Yes, he did," Maria said hoping she wouldn't get Sal in trouble.

"Well, he's going to hear from me," Jorge threatened.

"You'll do nothing of the kind. Sal is a good friend and has helped us put this trip together. We couldn't have done it without him. Just drop the whole thing, will you?" Maria asked hoping he would calm down. "Maybe you should see how the girls are coming with their homework."

Jorge took a deep breath and exhaled loudly into the phone. "Okay. So are you seeing your parents again tonight?"

"Yes, I'm going to have dinner with them so I can tell them—" Maria stopped herself from continuing not wanting to bring up the donor issue again.

"Tell them what?" Jorge asked.

"Nothing. Listen, before we hang up, has anyone called for me?" Maria asked, quick to change the subject. She didn't want Jorge to get upset all over again.

"No. I'll let you know if you do, especially if someone in your family calls."

"All right then. I love you, and I'm happy I have you to worry about me. I'll try to call tomorrow," Maria said.

"I'll talk to you then. Be careful," Jorge said before hanging up.

She closed her cell phone and put it back in her purse. Then she took a naproxen tablet from the bottle and went to the kitchen for a glass of water. She swallowed the pill and then went into the bedroom to lie down until it was time to join her parents for dinner. She knew they would be disappointed with her news, but at least they'd know she tried to help.

Chapter 24

Maria checked the hallway before leaving the apartment to go to her parent's penthouse. She didn't even have to knock on the door when she arrived there because her mother stood at the threshold waiting for her. After Maria stepped into the foyer, her mother closed the door and turned the deadbolt. They faced each other with a smile and embraced.

"I just love having you here, Maria. Come on. Let's go join your father. Dinner will be ready in thirty minutes. Would you like something to drink?" Anne Marie asked as she led her daughter into the den.

"Yes, thank you. I'd like a glass of wine, if you have it," Maria answered following her mother. She drank wine only on social occasions, but tonight she really felt it would help relax her.

"White wine? We're having fish tonight — *fillet of sole à la meunière.*"

"Sounds wonderful. I've ordered it when we've gone out for dinner, but I never cooked it myself," Maria said.

"It's very easy. It only takes a few minutes," Anne Marie said. "But now, go sit down, and I'll bring you the wine."

Maria walked over to her father and bent down to kiss him. "Hi, Papa."

Don Pedro reached up to Maria and hugged her. "I'm so glad you're back."

Maria looked at him and remarked, "You look tired. Did you have a nap?"

"Yes, I'm tired, but that's the normal now. I take a short nap otherwise I lay awake at night."

Maria took a seat on the couch just as her mother entered the den carrying two glasses of wine. She handed one to Maria and held the other as she sat down next to Maria. "Aren't you having any, Papa?"

"No, not allowed. I'm just sipping on a glass of water," Don Pedro said.

"Here's to you just the same," Maria said raising her glass to toast him and then took a sip. She put the glass down.

Anne Marie raised her glass and said, "Yes, here's to you, Don Pedro." She sipped her wine and leaned back against the throw pillows on the couch.

"Thank you, ladies." Don Pedro looked at Maria and with a smile on his face said,

"Can you flip your wig now, Maria?"

Maria looked at her father and getting his joke, laughed as she removed her wig. "I suppose this can go, too," she said as she took off her glasses and removed the orthodontic wax from her mouth. She stashed both in her purse and then fluffed her hair with her fingers.

"So tell us about your doctor's appointment," Anne Marie urged.

Maria cast her eyes down, took a breath, and then looked at her father. "I wish I had good news, but I am not your blood type. I'm A and you're O. Only a donor with—" Maria stopped herself. "Sorry. I'm sure you know all this by now."

Don Pedro sighed. "Yes. Thank you for getting checked, Maria. I appreciate it." He looked off at the Botero painting of the man and the dog.

Noticing the gift bag on the ottoman, Maria said, "What's the occasion for the gift? Did I forget something?"

"Oh, this," Don Pedro said indicating the gift bag that lay by his feet on the ottoman. "Silvana came by this afternoon."

"Really?" Maria leaned forward and said, "This is from her? What is it?"

Don Pedro handed Maria the gift bag. "See for yourself."

Maria put her hand in the bag and pulled out the gift box. She opened it, already knowing it was a Montblanc pen by the shape of the box and the signature gift bag. "It's beautiful. I thought you had a Montblanc pen."

"Yes, but it disappeared. I never could find it."

"Did Silvana give a reason for the gift?" Maria asked putting the pen back in the box and dropping it in the gift bag.

"Just that she was thinking of me."

"That was nice," Maria said thinking that Silvana must have a motive.

Maria and Anne Marie exchanged knowing glances and resumed drinking their wine.

"How is Silvana doing these days? I don't talk to her much," Maria said.

"She's all right, although she was sick this afternoon. She's still managing that fancy designer boutique uptown. She has a flair for fashion as they say," Anne Marie said. "I think she dresses a little too trendy, but what do I know? Look at me? Grey slacks and a grey sweater. I can't get more conservative than that."

"Yes, but it goes so pretty with your silver hair, Mama," Maria said.

"And your pretty blue eyes," Don Pedro added, winking at Anne Marie.

Maria noticed her father was actually flirting with her mother. She wondered if the two of them had reconciled. Her mother was certainly taking good care of him.

"Stop it you two. You're making me blush," Anne Marie said, casting her eyes down and then looking up at Don Pedro with a smile.

A timer sounded from the kitchen and Anne Marie said, "Excuse me while I go take the rice off the burner. I'll be right back."

Anne Marie left the room and Don Pedro smiled at Maria. "I don't know what I'd do without her. She's been a real trooper during this ordeal."

"That's Mama. She has a good heart. She's always been there for all of us."

Anne Marie came back and said, "You better not be talking about me."

Don Pedro said, "Only good things."

Maria smiled. "How are my brothers?"

Don Pedro frowned and said, "They're all working hard filling in for me. But it's good for them. It's a good transition for them to take on more duties and decisions while I am still here to give them advice if they need it. Roman has taken over marketing, Fernando is in our research and development department, and Salvador is in charge of customer relations."

"So they have clearly defined roles now. Didn't you have them rotating through departments before?" Maria asked.

"That's right. I think that's the best way to learn the business so you really understand all aspects of it. It was also a way for them to see what their passion was. Now with you, it was all about math. You knew you loved it early on."

"Thanks to your help, Papa," Maria smiled and took another drink of her wine.

"I really miss the big family dinners we had when we were young."

Anne Marie stood up quickly. "That reminds me. I'm going in to the kitchen and dinner will be on the table in just a few minutes. I'll let you know when it's time to come to the table."

"Do you need any help, Mama?" Maria called after her.

"No, sit."

"What happened to Mama's cook?" Maria asked.

"Your Mama wants to be sure that I follow the diet. There are a lot of restrictions with chronic kidney disease and for patients on dialysis. So your mother doesn't trust her old cook anymore. She met with a dietician and plans a menu with foods that I'm allowed to eat. She's done a great job."

"What kind of restrictions?" Maria wanted to know.

"Salt, protein, fluids, potassium, and phosphorous."

"I can understand the salt and fluids, but the other stuff?"

"Now that I'm on dialysis, protein isn't such an issue. I can have fish, chicken, meat, and eggs. But I can't have avocados, bananas and kiwis because of the potassium. I can have limited amounts of potatoes if they've been soaked in water before cooking. And I can have small portions of oranges and melons."

"What happens if you eat bananas?" Maria asked. She loved bananas with her morning cereal and they were grown in Colombia.

"The high level of potassium can cause abnormal heart rhythms."

"Oh. That would definitely be a problem. What about phosphorous?"

"The restriction on that mineral is to protect my bones. So I am not supposed to eat beans, peanut butter, cola and dairy products like milk and cheese. But I'm allowed a half cup of milk a day so I can have my cereal for breakfast."

"It sounds like there's a lot to know. I can see why Mama is doing the cooking herself. She doesn't want anyone to forget and give you a banana by mistake."

"You're right about that," Don Pedro said. He looked to the doorway where Anne Marie stood. "Are you ready for us now?"

"Yes, dinner's ready," Anne Marie said as she went to Don Pedro to help him out of his chair.

He stood up and took a deep breath. Maria watched as he took painful steps to the dining room. "Are you all right, Papa?"

"Just a little achy, that's all. I'll be fine."

Anne Marie looked at Maria and nodded with shared knowledge that Don Pedro was minimizing his real discomfort.

They took their places at the dining room table, with Don Pedro sitting at the head. Maria and Anne Marie sat across from one another. Maria was impressed with the beautiful table her mother had set. There was a white damask tablecloth with matching napkins at each place. She had put out her fine bone china rimmed with platinum and her sterling silver flatware gleamed in the candlelight. Crystal wine glasses were at each place as well as crystal goblets of water. There was also a floral arrangement of bright pink roses in a silver bowl in the center of the table.

"The table looks exquisite, Mama. You make me feel so special. And the dinner looks delicious."

"Thank you, Maria," Anne Marie said with a smile. "May I serve you?"

"Serve Papa first." Maria said, reaching out and patting her father's hand.

Don Pedro smiled at Maria and then handed his dinner plate to Anne Marie. She served him the fillet of sole that was garnished with chopped parsley and lemon wedges and then added rice pilaf and a couple of broccoli spears that were fragrant with garlic and olive oil. She then passed the plate back to him.

"Thank you, Anne Marie. It looks splendid," Don Pedro said as he took the plate from her.

Anne Marie then served Maria and herself. Out of habit, they bowed their heads and listened as Anne Marie said grace over the food. When she was finished, they said in unison, "Amen."

Anne Marie held the bottle of wine and smiled at Maria.

Maria took her wine glass and held it out to Anne Marie so she could serve her. "Thank you. I know I'll enjoy this wine with your gourmet dinner."

Anne Marie poured wine into her glass, held it up, and then said, "Here's to good health."

Don Pedro lifted his water goblet and said, "I'll drink to that."

They all drank from their glasses and began to eat their meal. Maria noticed soft piano music playing undoubtedly from her mother's vast CD collection.

"You know I came here in disguise because I still fear FARC," said Maria. "Are they still the terrorists that I knew?"

"Yes, *Fuerzas Armadas Revolucionarias de Colombia*. They have had a terrible hold on this country. They claim to be fighting for political, social and economic justice in Colombia, but that's nonsense. What they did is build a drug empire with cocaine. And how? Target the 85 percent of rural Colombians who live in poverty and pay them more than they could earn growing crops like coffee. Did you know that Colombia produces 90 percent of the cocaine sold in the US? I couldn't believe it when I heard it on the news."

"I had no idea it was that much. Didn't I hear that President Clinton increased funding to Colombia in the form of military aid?" asked Maria.

"That's right. Five million dollars' worth over five years. That makes our country the third largest recipient of US military aid, behind Israel and Egypt. The goal is to reduce the coca crop in half in five years."

"So what are they doing with the money — the military?" Maria asked.

"From what I know, most of the aid is earmarked for massive aerial fumigation of coca. The hope being that the reduced crop would undercut the funding that the guerillas earn. But our government did these fumigations up until 1998. It's not new."

"What about the coca farmers?"

"Good question. More than likely they're displaced and move on to find someplace more remote to plant the coca. There's a government program to give these farmers a thousand dollars to start with new crops, but they're distrustful of the government."

"Maybe that's why those farm houses I stayed in were vacant and the fields were barren. There was nothing but dried up stalks and leaves," Maria said, the picture of those places still vivid in her mind.

"I'm sure a lot more goes on than we know about. I hear our military is trying to gain control of the areas that were seized by FARC."

"It never seems to end, this civil war," Maria said.

"And let's not get into the paramilitaries. That would take up the rest of the night," Don Pedro said, taking a sip of water.

Anne Marie cleared her throat and asked, "Can't we talk about something more pleasant?"

"Of course. We can talk about you," Don Pedro said smiling.

"You're impossible."

Maria smiled at her parents. She was happy to see that they now had a good relationship. It made her feel better knowing that her father was well taken care of and that her mother was kind to him, even loving.

They finished up the dinner with small talk and finally Anne Marie and Maria cleared the table.

"I'll help you with the dishes, Mama."

"Just stack them in the dishwasher. I'll put out some fruit and cheese in the den if you want something more," Anne Marie said.

Don Pedro pushed his chair back from the table and Anne Marie helped him to his feet. The two of them walked to the den. "Do you want to watch TV while we clean up the dishes?" Anne Marie asked.

"That's fine," said Don Pedro as he sat down in the easy chair and propped his feet up on the ottoman.

Anne Marie turned on the TV and left the remote on the end table. "See you in a few minutes."

Maria was busy stacking the dishwasher when Anne Marie came in and said, "Just put the dishes in the dishwasher. We can hand wash the silverware and the crystal. I'm afraid the silverware will get spots and the glasses will break."

"I was just going to suggest that. You've had these beautiful things for so many years. No sense taking any chances."

After the dishes were in the dishwasher, Maria washed each goblet carefully and put them in the drain rack. The silverware was next and Anne Marie took each piece and dried it off.

"So Mama, I can't help but notice that things have improved between you and Papa."

"You did, did you? Yes, when I found out about his poor health and his remorse over you, I realized

I needed to forgive him. I now have a better understanding of what really happened, of what he was going through. Besides, life is short. I need to make the best of every day. There's only so much time. I don't want to have regrets when —," Anne Marie stopped before she could finish. "I am so glad you came here to be with your father. It's a gift."

Maria looked at her mother and could see her eyes were wet with tears. She turned to her, dried her hands hastily on her apron and hugged her. "Yes. I had to come. And I'm glad I did. I just need to stay out of sight of Silvana. I just feel she would inform FARC if she knew I was here."

"Don't worry. Your disguise is good, when you have it on." Anne Marie and Maria laughed. "Tell me why you feel Silvana was the traitor. Or do you want to discuss this in front of your father?"

"I think it's important you both know how I feel," Maria said taking off her apron and putting it in a drawer.

"Come, then. The glasses will drain dry. I'll put them away later."

They walked into the den and sat down on the couch. Seeing the expressions on Maria's and Anne Marie's face, Don Pedro turned off the TV.

"Maria wants to tell us something. Let's listen," Anne Marie said to Don Pedro.

Maria looked at her father and then at her mother. She hesitated and then began, "I've mentioned this to Mama, but not to you. I always felt there was a traitor in the family that fed information to FARC so I would be kidnapped. I believe it's Silvana."

"Silvana? Why *her*?" Don Pedro asked, looking at Maria intently.

"Look at the circumstances the night of the abduction. Jorge was home sick so he couldn't pick me up from class. Silvana arranged a ride with Roberto, who's a stranger to me. She was very quiet when we left class. Normally she is a nonstop talker. I was the only one abducted. They were put in the trunk, but conveniently the keys were left in the ignition. There were no fingerprints on Roberto's car. Jorge said Silvana seemed very reserved when she got back, not panic-stricken. Like she knew she was safe the whole time."

Don Pedro put his elbow on the arm of the easy chair and put his hand under his chin, a sign Maria knew he was processing her theory. "But what's her motive? It can't be money, can it?"

"I think it's jealousy," Maria said. She saw that her father was ready to interrupt. "Wait. Here me out. Silvana is jealous because I have children. She is childless. She wants the attention that children bring to this family. She is also jealous because I'm the only daughter in the family and that makes me special. She sees how you act toward me, Papa. I think she wants the same attention from you."

"Ah, the Montblanc pen," Don Pedro said. "You may have something here. By having you kidnapped, then you're out of the picture and she somehow thinks I will devote more attention to her.

But it just didn't work. I was crazy thinking about you. I couldn't focus on anyone else but you. Just ask your mother."

Anne Marie nodded in agreement.

"What about her own father? Isn't that enough to have his attention? After all, she is an only child," Don Pedro asked.

"I don't know about him. But I know what I see and I know what I feel. I think Silvana is the traitor. I felt it when I returned after my rescue. Everyone rushed to greet me. Not her. Guilt kept her away. Of course, for appearances, she finally hugged me, but I could feel stiffness."

"Silvana. What kind of woman would do a thing like that to her family? How could she turn you in as a target for FARC knowing that you might even be killed? That's despicable. How can she face us knowing she is a traitor? The nerve of her!" Don Pedro said, his voice rising as his anger flared. Then he paused, inhaled deeply to calm himself and said, "We'll be extra careful in making sure Silvana doesn't know you're here. That's a promise."

"I know you will. If she did suspect I'm here, I'm sure she would call whoever it was that arranged for my abduction," Maria said, her face now contorting with worry.

"We'll keep you safe, Maria. And if at any time we think you might be in danger, we'll get you out of the country. Now try not to worry. Let's enjoy the time we have together," Don Pedro said. "Come here. Give me a hug."

Maria got up, knelt by him and wrapped her arms around her father. He returned the hug and kissed her cheek. Maria always felt at peace whenever her father hugged her. He helped her to put away her worries as only he could do.

Chapter 25

"Alfredo? It's Silvana."

With his voice barely above a whisper, Alfredo said, "You should know not to call me at work. I'll call you later on your cell phone."

The line was disconnected and Silvana sat there staring at the phone bewildered. What kind of reaction was that? Silvana thought. Alfredo was her paramour of about two years, though the intensity of their relationship seemed to have cooled. She wondered if there was someone younger or prettier than her who was getting his attention now. She knew she tended to be obsessive about her figure and face. She was only 31, was five foot seven in bare feet and wore a size eight. She worked out three times a week and liked to wear clothes that showed her figure off at its best. She put her phone down on the coffee table and went to the bathroom mirror. She glanced at herself and turned around abruptly. She refused to obsess about her appearance. Alfredo would call her back as soon as the bank closed at 4:30 p.m. She checked the time on her cell phone: only thirty minutes.

She remembered how she met Alfredo. It was about two years ago and she was already managing her parents' store, Silvana's Collection, and taking night classes at the university to finish her degree in fashion merchandising. Roman had settled down into his cozy routine of married life and Silvana missed the excitement of nightclubbing. She loved the ritual of shopping for a new outfit, getting dressed, fixing her hair and applying makeup. More than that, she glowed in the attention she got when she was on the dance floor. She tried to get Roman to take her out many times, but the most he wanted to do was go out to dinner or a movie. He complained he was too tired to go dancing. So what could she do? No respectable married woman went out to clubs alone. So she was stuck at home, but she still craved the attention from other men.

One day she was in Banco de Colombia to deposit the day's receipts. She was filling out a deposit slip when she looked to the glass-walled office of the vice president of the bank. He happened to look up just then and their eyes met. He smiled at her and she glanced away. When she looked back at him, he was still smiling at her with a knowing look. She smiled, pushed her red curly hair behind her ear and that was all the invitation he needed. He got up from his desk and took long strides over to her.

"Can I help you *senora*?" the handsome banker asked.

"Just filling out the deposit slip for my business receipts," Silvana said mesmerized by his brown eyes with long lashes, dark hair and a perfect smile. She could smell his cologne and it was intoxicating.

She thought this man was handsome enough to be on the big screen as the stereotypical Latin lover. He was impeccably dressed in a navy three-piece suit tailored to fit his trim physique. He was tall since he towered over Silvana and she was wearing four-inch black Prada heels.

"What business would that be?" the banker inquired holding her eyes with his.

"A women's clothing boutique called Silvana's Collection," Silvana answered, still smiling. She was wearing a fitted black jacket over a tweed pencil skirt. She toyed with the collar on her royal blue silk blouse.

"I'm Alfredo Caltado, vice president of this bank. I'm the one to see if you ever need a commercial loan. And your name?" the banker asked as he handed her his business card.

Taking the card from him, Silvana said, "Silvana Perez. Thank you. I just might take you up on it."

Silvana heard his cell phone ring. Reaching into the breast pocket of his suit, he took out his cell phone. He looked at the screen and put his finger up. "I'm sorry. I have to take this call." Alfredo Caltado then walked back to his office.

Silvana looked at the business card and put it in her purse. She walked up to the bank teller and made her deposit, still thinking about the vice president who had left his office to meet her. She made up her mind right then that she would make an appointment to see him about a business loan. She really didn't need a business loan since her parents owned Silvana's Collection plus three more stores, one in Barranquilla, one in Santa Marta and another in Medellin. But she'd think of something.

Two days later, she called Alfredo Caltado for an appointment. He was very happy to hear from her and said he'd like to take her to lunch to discuss her loan. At noon the same day, Alfredo picked her up in front of Silvana's Collection and took her to the Royal Bogotá Hotel. When they walked into the lobby with its crystal chandelier, white marble floors, and sweeping staircase, she understood why this place was so highly rated. Alfredo escorted her to the restaurant where they had a leisurely lunch and a bottle of pinot grigio. They had an appetizer of clams on the half shell and then enjoyed a mixed green salad with grilled shrimp. Alfredo didn't wait for the wine steward to refill their wine glasses. He kept an eye on Silvana's glass and replenished it often. She declined dessert and finished the meal with coffee.

Alfredo never talked to her about the commercial loan during lunch, but wanted to know all about her and her family. She told him that her parents owned four women's clothing stores and they were, in fact, named after her. She saw him looking at her wedding ring, but he didn't ask about her husband. She looked for a wedding ring on his hand but didn't see one. She knew that he could still be married because some married men were opposed to wearing a ring.

Finally Silvana was able to ask him a few questions and found out he was forty years old. He had a master's degree in finance and accounting and worked for a few other major banks before settling at Banco de Colombia to become vice president of commercial loans. He dropped names of society's elite which did impress her. He said he was married and he had two sons who were attending the university. When the bill came, he signed for it instead of putting down a credit card or cash. Silvana thought it was odd until he said he wanted to show her his suite at the hotel. So he has an account here, she thought. She looked at her watch and it was just one o'clock. She had closed the store for lunch and had to reopen the store at two so she was in no hurry. Besides she was enjoying this charming man who was not only handsome but powerful.

They took the elevator to the penthouse and when he opened the door, she saw not an ordinary hotel room, but a suite with a living room, a kitchen and through the double doors, a bedroom. Silvana walked over to the window to admire the view over the city. She heard the door close and then romantic music. She felt his hands on her shoulders and he turned her around to face him. He looked into her eyes and then he kissed her softly. Silvana was surprised that the gentle kiss stirred such passion in her. She kissed him back passionately. She remembered him beginning to undress her and she protested that they were in front of the window. He led her to the bedroom where he finished removing her clothes. What amazed her was that no time during their lovemaking, did she think of Roman. She felt like she was under Alfredo's spell.

As they lay there on the rumpled sheets, Alfredo asked about the loan that she wanted to talk to him about. She said she was hoping to expand the store to include designer shoes and handbags. She already carried some accessories in Silvana's Collection so why not dress the whole woman? she speculated.

Alfredo advised her to write a business plan because she would need to submit one with her application. And then he told her something that got her mind working. He said that he had connections that could make her rich if she had important information to give in return. Of course, she wanted to know what was considered important information. He revealed that this group would pay for surveillance information on individuals that could command high ransoms. He admitted that he had access to the banking and investment accounts of Bogotá's wealthiest customers and knew their approximate net worth. He didn't probe her further but told Silvana to think about it. Is there someone you know whose family would pay a lot of money for their relative's release? he asked her. If you do, there's money in it for you.

Silvana returned to the store after their tryst and thought it surprising that Alfredo spoke so openly about his shady business dealings, but she believed that he must trust her. She then considered his proposal the rest of the day — and every day thereafter until he called her at the store. He asked how her business plan was coming and she told him she was working on it. He said he wanted to see her so she agreed to meet him for lunch the next day. Worried that someone she knew might see her with him, she drove her own car to the hotel and went directly to the penthouse. This was the beginning of the long affair and the time when the seed was planted to betray her sister-in-law.

It took several weeks and several trysts before Silvana finally agreed to the business arrangement, but she was gleeful when she did. Silvana gave Alfredo a photograph of Maria and said she would let him know when the abduction should take place. Maria would be out of the picture, maybe for good, she thought. She knew kidnappings by FARC were commonplace, since the nightly television news carried the stories. Alfredo told her that she could give him just a few hours' notice. This rebel group was mobilized and ready to act quickly. And that's exactly what happened. One afternoon, Maria called Silvana to ask for a ride home from her night class at the university. She explained Jorge was sick and confined to bed. Silvana called her classmate Roberto who agreed to take them home. Finally Silvana called Alfredo with the news. That very night, Maria was kidnapped when Roberto was driving them home from class. Roberto never knew about the set-up and she had a hard time not laughing about it when he was amazed that the keys were left in his car's ignition. Silvana knew beforehand that she and Roberto would be locked in the trunk of his car. Alfredo had told her how to get themselves out of the trunk. She remembered she found it hard to act afraid when she faced Don Pedro and Anne Marie let alone Jorge. And the trip to GAULA's office annoyed her since she hated getting up so early. But in the end, it was worth it. She received $50,000 and Maria was out of the picture.

And now Silvana sat waiting for Alfredo to call her back. She had to tell him she thought Maria was here. And what if she was? What would they do? Alfredo said that if Maria ever returned to Colombia, FARC would make it their mission to kill her. Would Maria risk her life returning to Bogotá?

Silvana got up and paced the living room. She looked around and thought the place looked shabby. She'd have to talk to Roman about hiring an interior designer to replace the bachelor pad furniture. There was a brown leather recliner, an overstuffed upholstered couch in drab green, and a coffee table in rustic pine that had a stack of magazines on it. A brass floor lamp was in one corner, and there was an end table with a blown glass lamp by the recliner. The gleaming hardwood floors gave the room potential along with the floor to ceiling windows.

Just as she was about to sit down on the couch, her cell phone rang. She picked it up off the coffee table and saw that it was Alfredo. "Hello Alfredo. I'm sorry I bothered you before."

"It's all right. What's the matter Silvana?" Alfredo asked.

"You're going to think this is crazy, but I think my sister-in-law is here in Bogotá."

"You're right. It would be crazy. What makes you think she's here? Did you see her?" Alfredo asked.

"No, I haven't seen her. But when I was with Don Pedro this afternoon, I saw this paper ring made out of a gum wrapper on his end table. Maria used to make them."

"Silvana, it's probably an old one. He was probably going through old stuff, remembering. You said he's sick and dying.It's natural for him to reminisce."

"I suppose so, but I just have this feeling. I don't know. Maybe it's nothing."

"Well, just keep your eyes open. If she is here, you can be sure she'll be visiting her father. Do you think she'll stay in the apartment building?" Alfredo asked.

"I don't know. If I were her, I wouldn't. It'd be too easy for me to spot her," Silvana said.

"If you do see her, let me know. I promised my contact I'd alert him. He wasn't happy that they never got the ransom money for Maria. They'll want to go after her again."

"Okay. So when can I see you? How about tomorrow for lunch? Same time, same place?" Silvana said in her most seductive voice.

"I'll have to let you know in the morning. I'm supposed to have lunch with a potential client, but it has to be confirmed," Alfredo said.

"You'll have more fun with me," Silvana teased.

"True, but it's my job," Alfredo said. "I'll talk to you later."

Silvana held the phone to her ear knowing that he had hung up and said, "You'll cancel that lunch date. I know you will."

She then closed the phone, put it back on the table, and saw her hand tremble. "Damn you, Alfredo."

Chapter 26

Don Pedro sat in his easy chair with his feet propped up on the ottoman. On his lap lay the family photo album, and he smiled as he looked at each page. Next to his feet was a memory box that held arts and craft items that his children had made in school. On the floor was another box filled with glazed clay sculptures that Maria created in an art class in high school. Maria knelt down on the floor and picked up one of a cat holding a fish. She remembered feeling proud of these pieces at the time, but today she thought they looked amateurish. She was amazed that her parents still had them. But then again, hadn't she kept so many of things Julie and Paula had made in school? She realized that's what loving parents do. She replaced the sculpture and picked up the memory box. She placed it on the couch so she could sit there and look through the treasure trove. There were many drawings and cards that her brothers and she had made. She saw a Popsicle stick trivet and a toy snake made of linked tongue depressors. There was a handmade doll Maria remembered making in home economics class. Since everything was hand sewn, she thought it would be a good project for her daughters to do during summer vacation.

She looked up at Don Pedro. "Are you feeling all right, Papa?"

Don Pedro looked at her and said, "Just a little tired."

"Do you want to take a nap?"

"No, I don't want to miss a minute with you," Don Pedro said, taking a sip of water.

"Whatever you say, Papa," Maria said. She picked up the handkerchief parachute with a clothespin man as the jumper. "Who made this?"

Don Pedro looked up. "I believe it was Salvador. There should be more than one in the box because he and Fernando would compete with each other to see which parachute landed last."

"No, I only see one. Oh, what's this?" Maria asked pulling out what looked like two disposable plastic dinner plates that were secured together with ribbon. Tiny bells were tied on the ends.

Don Pedro laughed. "That, my dear Maria, is a tambourine."

"You're kidding," Maria said and then tapped the tambourine with her fingertips.

"Bravo, bravo," Don Pedro shouted and clapped his hands.

Anne Marie suddenly appeared at the doorway and said, "What's the commotion?"

"Didn't you know your daughter is a born percussionist?" Don Pedro teased.

Maria stopped playing the toy tambourine. "What fun to be a kid again! This box is filled with great stuff."

"Yes, Maria, your mother didn't believe in letting her children watch too much television. She preferred that they spent their time doing homework, participating in sports or doing something creative."

"I guess that's where I get it from. I always like to have Paula and Julie doing creative things. I recently taught them origami."

Don Pedro looked at the end table and held up the paper ring made from a gum wrapper. "I guess this is your handiwork."

Maria's eyes grew wide looking at the ring. "Did I leave that here the other day?"

Don Pedro nodded. "I'm afraid so."

"Do you think Silvana saw it when she gave you the Montblanc pen?"

"I honestly don't know. She didn't say anything about it. You look worried. What are you thinking?"

Maria said, "If Silvana saw it, she'll know I was here. I remember making one like that the night I was abducted. I gave it to her. She told me I was crafty."

"Maria, just think for a minute. This ring could have been made a long time ago. Look in the box. I bet there are other origami projects in there including a ring or two," Don Pedro said. He leaned forward watching Maria as she looked in the memory box. She pulled out an origami crane and one ring made from a different brand of chewing gum.

"You're right, Papa. Hand me the one you have. I'll put it in this box, just in case she comes to visit again. Or maybe I should just throw it away."

Don Pedro held out his hand and Maria got up to get the ring from him. She stared at it and shook her head. Finally she put it in the box and collapsed on the couch.

Anne Marie sat down next to Maria and hugged her. "You're shaking. Would you like a soothing cup of tea?"

"No thank you, Mama," Maria said hugging her back.

"Hey, you two. Where's my hug?" Don Pedro asked sounding like a child.

Anne Marie and Maria looked at each other and smiled. They got up and went to Don Pedro. They knelt down at his chair and reached up to hug him in a loving embrace. "That's better," he said with broad smile.

The telephone rang, distracting Anne Marie. "Excuse me," she said getting up and walking to the kitchen. "Let me see who that is."

Maria returned to her place on the couch. "When I think about my childhood, I remember Roman, but not a lot about Fernando and Salvador."

"That's because they were already in school when you were born. So there is a big age difference. You didn't share in the same interests or friends because of that," Don Pedro explained.

"That's right. And by the time I was in high school, they were already married and having children. I just wanted to be with my friends."

"It's a good thing we had those family dinners every Sunday so you got to know them," Don Pedro laughed.

Maria smoothed the skirt of her white uniform and said, "Otherwise we'd be strangers. Now that I live in Florida, I miss those times with the whole family. It's just awful that I was kidnapped. If it hadn't happened, we'd still be living here with you."

"We can't undo the past, Maria. I, too, have regrets, as you now know. I wish I had arranged to visit you in Florida, but I didn't. Let's make the most of the time we have together."

Maria looked at her father and blinked away her tears. "I know, Papa. It's just hard. I still see a counselor every week to get over the trauma. I still have nightmares. You know they dug a grave for me. I was terrified. That's when I was forced to write another letter to you."

"That's the one I never got," Don Pedro said exhaling deeply.

Maria looked at him and realized that the conversation was distressing him. She decided to change the subject.

"Let me see what Mama is doing," Maria said, getting up from the couch. "Can I get you anything while I'm up?"

"Not right now, thank you."

A few minutes later, Maria and Anne Marie returned to the den taking their places on the couch.

"Who called?" Don Pedro asked.

"That was the nurse letting me know that she would be a half-hour late," Anne Marie said.

"That was considerate of her," Don Pedro said as he closed the photo album. "Do you want to look through the album, Maria?"

"Sure," Maria said as she got up and took the album from him. She sat back down and said to her mother, "Do you want to look with me, Mama?"

Anne Marie smiled and slid closer to Maria on the couch. Maria opened the album and said, "It's been ages since I've seen these pictures. These were taken at the park. I remember when the weather was nice we used to go there on a Saturday or Sunday and take a picnic lunch. Look at this picture of me on the swing. How I loved the swings. I actually thought I might fly off into the blue sky if I could only go higher."

"Yes, you would yell to me, 'higher, Papa, higher!' And then you'd get scared and say, 'not so high, Papa, no so high, I'm scared.' I got such a kick out of you," Don Pedro sighed.

"How old am I here, about six, Mama?" Maria asked.

Anne Marie nodded, put her arm around Maria's shoulder and said. "We had such fun at the park, didn't we Don Pedro?"

"We certainly did. I have an idea. Why don't we go to the park tomorrow?" Don Pedro suggested. "The weather has been nice."

Maria and Anne Marie exchanged glances. "Do you think you're up for it?" Anne Marie said.

"Sure, we'll go for an hour or so. If I get tired, I'll let you know, and we'll come home. It will be like old times."

Maria saw her mother looking at her for her reaction. "It's fine with me, but I will have to wear my full disguise. I can't risk running into Silvana."

"That's fine. I think it will be fun. It will be good to get out of the house," Don Pedro said. He smiled at his wife and daughter. "And I'll be with the prettiest women in all of Bogotá!"

"I thought it was 'in the entire world.' Now it's just Bogotá?" Anne Marie teased.

"Please forgive me, I meant to say 'in the entire world.' So it's a date then? Let's go at eleven-thirty tomorrow morning, shall we? We'll have a picnic lunch," Don Pedro said and waited for a response.

"Okay, Don Pedro. But if I see that it's too much for you, we'll be coming right home," said Anne Marie.

Maria saw that her mother looked concerned but wanted to please him. As she stood up, she said, "I think it's going to be fun. Like old times. Now if you'll excuse me. I'm going to go back to my apartment so you can take a nap, Papa. I'll come back for dinner and this time I'll help you cook, Mama."

Don Pedro yawned and covered his mouth to be polite, "You don't have to go."

"I know, but I am," Maria said. She went to her father and kissed him on the cheek.

Anne Marie stood up and said, "I'll see you to the door."

When the two women were in the foyer, Anne Marie said, "When you first arrived, your father seemed renewed. But now he seems to be getting weak again."

"Then perhaps we should forget about the park," Maria said, touching her mother's arm.

"No, I don't want to disappoint him. He might feel better tomorrow morning. Tonight he's gets his dialysis treatment. The nurse is coming after dinner tonight to hook him up to the machine."

"All right, then, Mama," Maria said as she put her arms around her mother. "I'll come back at five-thirty to help you make dinner."

Anne Marie hugged her daughter and said, "I love you, Maria. I'm so glad you're here."

"I know, Mama. I'm glad I came," Maria said as she broke the embrace. She opened her purse and pulled out the wig, eyeglasses and orthodontic wax. She put them on and looked at her mother and shrugged. "I'm ready now."

Anne Marie smiled at Maria as she opened the door. Maria stepped out in the hallway and heard the door close quietly behind her. She said a silent prayer asking for the Lord's blessing for her parents. And for herself, she asked that Silvana wouldn't see her.

Chapter 27

Reaching into her purse, Maria took the photo of Jorge and her daughters and looked at it. The picture was taken on their first visit to Miami Metro Zoo and she wasn't prepared for all the walking they had to do. When she picked up the zoo's brochure she learned that the park covered 740 acres with 300 acres set aside for animal exhibits in a cage-free environment. It was hot and humid with not a cloud in the cerulean sky. Thankfully there were many shady spots to stop and rest and there were machines that sprayed a fine mist that temporarily cooled the skin. As they strolled along the path, they discovered that the animals were grouped by their natural geographic territory, Asia, Africa and Australia. Animals that lived peacefully together were put in one exhibit while other animals were separated by a moat. The first exhibit they saw upon entering Metro Zoo were the rare white Bengal tigers in the Asia section. There were two of them with white fur and brown stripes. The picture had been taken in front of that exhibit.

Now she felt homesick. She wanted to call home and talk to the girls and Jorge. She reached in her purse to find her cell phone just as it rang. She looked at the caller ID on the screen and saw it was Jorge calling.

"Hello, I was just getting ready to call you. I miss you," Maria said.

"I miss you, too, Maria," Jorge said, sounding concerned. "I thought you should know that Silvana called. She wanted to speak to you."

"What did you tell her?" Maria asked, her stomach rising to her throat.

"I told her that you were out shopping— a good excuse since it's Saturday—and that you would call her back."

Maria inhaled and exhaled slowly, trying to calm down. "Did she have anything else to say?"

"No, not at all. You can call her from your cell phone. Then you won't have to worry about it. She won't know where you're calling from," Jorge said.

Suddenly feeling nauseous, Maria paused and then said, "I'm not prepared to talk to her."

"You'll do fine. Just act like you're here. Not there."

"That's not easy. I'm not a good liar."

"What do you think you'd be lying about? She doesn't know you're in Bogotá," Jorge said.

"I don't know. I have a bad feeling. Something's up. I just don't know what it is. Silvana rarely calls," Maria said, rubbing the back of her neck. She could feel her neck and shoulder muscles tensing up.

"Go. Call her," Jorge urged.

"All right. But first let me talk to Julie and Paula," Maria said, feeling unsettled.

"They're at the playground. Why don't you make your call to Silvana and I'll go get them. Call me back in about fifteen to twenty minutes. You can talk to them then," Jorge said.

"Okay. I'll call you back," Maria said.

"Talk to you later," Jorge said, ending the connection.

Maria stared at her phone mustering up the courage to call Silvana. She wondered why Silvana called. Did she see the paper ring she had left on the end table in her father's den? She knew she had to relax before she spoke to Silvana. She didn't want to sound nervous, because that would prompt Silvana into asking all kinds of questions.

Maria sat up straight on the couch, closed her eyes, and did a series of deep cleansing breaths, the type she learned in yoga class. After a few minutes she felt ready to call Silvana.

She selected Silvana's number from her cell phone's contacts list and touched the send button. Just when she thought the call was going to voice mail, she heard Silvana say hello.

"Silvana, it's Maria. Jorge said you called."

"I see you're calling from your cell phone. You're not at home?" Silvana probed.

"That's right. I'm out shopping. Jorge thought I should call you back right away since we don't hear from you very often. I thought you might have important news. What's going on with you?" Maria said, leading the conversation back to Silvana.

"Nothing much. I just happened to think of you. I was visiting Don Pedro yesterday and I saw a ring made out of a gum wrapper, just like the one you made for me when we were driving back from class. I haven't seen anything like it in two years."

Maria swallowed hard. "I had forgotten about that. Maybe Don Pedro was looking through those memory boxes, the ones that have all the craft projects and cards from when we were children. He might have looked at it and put it aside. Or you know what? He chews a lot of gum since he quit smoking. Maybe he made it himself."

"I can't see Don Pedro making a paper ring," Silvana said.

Maria realized that she better not offer any more information. She didn't want to sound defensive and rouse Silvana's suspicions.

"I don't know, Silvana. Why don't you ask him?" Maria said, wanting to change the subject.

"It's not important. But it's too bad you can't be here. You know your father is seriously ill. He needs a kidney transplant. It's too bad no one in the family is a match. Of course, we don't know about you. If you were here, you could be tested. Wouldn't it be something if you could save his life?" Silvana asked.

"Yes, it would be wonderful. But I can't come back to Bogotá. You know that," Maria said, feeling a tinge of guilt knowing she was lying. "My father is on the donor list of patients needing a kidney. Hopefully he'll get one soon. How does he look?"

Silvana hesitated and then said, "He looks fine. But he doesn't have much energy."

"I guess that's expected," Maria said, not knowing what else to say. Then she added, "How's business with the store?"

"Great, in fact. It was a smart move adding a line of shoes, purses and accessories to the designer clothes. My sales have doubled. I hired a young fashion merchandising intern who loves waiting on customers and coordinating their whole outfit. Once a woman sees herself in the mirror, she has to buy it all. I think that's where the department stores go wrong. They make the customer do all the work, going from one end of the store to the other. Now I have a data base of wealthy customers. I know their taste and when I get a new shipment in that I think they'll like, I call them or send a postcard."

"Is your mother still doing all the buying?" Maria asked, hoping Silvana now forgot about the paper ring.

"Yes, but now I am going with her on her buying trips. It's great fun going to the fashion houses in Paris and Milan."

I'll bet, Maria thought. "And how are you and Roman doing?"

"Fine. He's quite content going to work, coming home for dinner, and watching soccer on TV."

"I think you could say that about a lot of men," Maria said.

"How are Jorge and your little girls?" Silvana asked. "It was rude of me not to ask about them sooner."

Maria was surprised she even thought to ask. "They're well. Has Anne Marie shown you the pictures that I sent?"

"Are you kidding? Of course. And you wouldn't believe how many framed pictures of your daughters sit on her dresser. It's amazing."

Maria sighed, "I wish my father were well enough that he and my mother could come to Florida and stay with us for a while. Phone calls just aren't enough."

"Yes, but that's the way it goes. You left," Silvana said.

Maria didn't like Silvana's tone of voice. "If you remember I didn't have much choice. I lived in fear that FARC would recapture me and kill me. They're known to do that—to set an example. We had to buy a bullet-proof car, for God's sake."

Maria stopped speaking realizing she was losing her temper. Silvana remained silent. Finally she said, "I guess it was a good thing you left. They probably would kill you if you were here."

Maria felt a chill go up her spine. It wasn't just the words. It was the way Silvana said it. Maria didn't think she could remain civil to Silvana any longer. Maria touched the volume button on her cell phone prompting a beep.

"What was that?" Silvana asked.

"I think I've got another call coming in. Let me take the call. We can talk later," Maria lied.

"Go ahead. Take the call. I'll talk to you again soon."

Maria pushed the end button on her phone to disconnect the call. She closed her eyes and sighed. She couldn't stand Silvana. She might even hate her. But she had to watch out for her. The tone of Silvana's voice sent a message loud and clear. This woman was capable of arranging her death if she had the chance. Maria was determined not to let that happen.

Chapter 28

When Maria woke up Sunday morning she was disorientated. Then she realized she was not in Pembroke Pines with Jorge, but in their former apartment in Bogotá. It was left furnished but was stripped of accessories and decorator touches that make a place feel like a home. All of her personal belongings had been removed when they moved out of the apartment years ago. For a couple of months after Maria's fateful rescue, her family lived in fear that Maria would be abducted once again and only this time, murdered. Eventually the decision was made that Jorge, Maria and their daughters should move out of the family's apartment building. Jorge's boss, Sal, was instrumental in finding them a safe place to live. Shortly after that, Jorge and Maria didn't feel safe there or anywhere in Bogotá so they applied for political asylum at the US Embassy in Bogotá.

Despite the lack of paintings on the walls, throw pillows on the couch and knick knacks here and there, the apartment was still comfortable. There were three bedrooms, two baths, a well-appointed kitchen, a formal dining room, and a spacious living room. Large floor-to-ceiling windows in the living room made the room bright and airy during the day, but at night Maria took care to draw the drapes so no one outside could see her.

Maria sat up in bed and looked at the time. She had a couple of hours left before their scheduled outing at the park. As her mind cleared, she recalled her telephone conversation with Silvana regarding the paper ring. She was so upset when she called Jorge that she started to cry as soon as she heard his voice. Jorge calmed her down and advised her to leave Bogotá if she was so nervous. He reminded her that she could change her reservations and return to the US at anytime. No one was forcing her to stay.

She decided to dismiss her fears and not let them rule her. Although she would remain cautious, she would enjoy the time she had with her parents. They were going to Simon Bolivar Metropolitan Park, a place that she remembered fondly for its shimmering lake with paddleboats, a winding path through woods and manicured lawns, a Victorian-style gazebo and the beautiful Botanical Gardens. Maria got out of bed and looked out of the window. The skies were clear so it would be a perfect day. She wished that she could forego the disguise, but that was foolish. She was unaware of what her brothers and their families' plans were for Sunday. It was unfortunate that she couldn't meet with them. Maybe sometime in the near future her brothers would come to Florida and visit with her. She had suggested it to them in their telephone conversations, but the trip would be needlessly expensive for them since they would have to stay in a hotel. Maria's townhouse wasn't big enough to accommodate them. But now that her father promised her $500,000, she could pay cash in full or use some of the money for a substantial down payment on a single-family home. She had visited the home of Lucy, one of the students in her English class who owned a five-bedroom home with three and a half baths. She remembered thinking the house was enormous, but Lucy said she needed a large home so her family could visit for extended stays. She had admitted to Maria that she was also a political refugee. She had told her mother about her in their last conversation. Lucy said they were tipped off that her husband was going to be kidnapped, so they fled Venezuela with their two children that same day. Maria assumed they were wealthy Venezuelans considering the price of such a home. It was just then she realized she hadn't told Jorge anything about the money her father was giving her. It was just as well. She would tell him everything once she was home.

After making her bed, Maria went to the kitchen and brewed a small pot of coffee. With her cup of coffee in hand, she sat at the white table and looked around the room. The country-style kitchen was as she left it: White cabinetry with leaded glass fronts, white quartz countertops and a white tile backsplash with a floral design. It held so many memories for her because the kitchen was the heart of her home. She looked at the white refrigerator and remembered how it had been plastered with pictures her daughters had drawn sitting at this very table. Now it was just a refrigerator. The room felt very empty and so did Maria. She missed her daughters. She knew she had to call them. She got her cell phone from the bedroom and called Jorge's cell phone. She was disappointed that the call went right to voice mail. She left a message and told him she was going to the park with her parents. She then dialed her home phone. After three rings, she heard Jorge's voice on the answering machine. She left the same message and then hung up. She wondered why he didn't answer the phone. Perhaps he took the girls out for breakfast and Jorge left his phone in his car or at home. She knew there was nothing to worry about, but she did anyway. Taking her phone with her, she returned to the kitchen and finished her coffee. She didn't have an appetite so she washed the cup and put it on the drain board. There wasn't anything else to do but take a shower and get dressed.

Thirty minutes later, Maria was ready for their excursion so she called her mother.

"Mama, shall I come up now and help you make lunch?" Maria asked.

Her mother had agreed and was waiting for her with the door open when Maria got off the elevator. She quickly went inside and Anne Marie closed the door behind her. Maria heard the deadbolt click.

"How's Papa this morning?" Maria asked as she hugged her mother.

Anne Marie gave her daughter a kiss on the cheek and said, "He's much better this morning. Thank goodness for dialysis. Without that—I don't want to think about it."

Maria followed her mother into her kitchen. "I always liked this kitchen. It's so homey. I was looking at the kitchen in the apartment downstairs and I realized I copied a lot of the look from yours. White makes everything look clean. Just as a kitchen should be."

Anne Marie laughed, "Yes, because with white you can't hide the dirt. But you'll notice I don't have white tile floors. Hardwood floors don't show every speck of dust. "

"I have white tile floors in Florida and it's awful. It's murder on my back when I'm preparing meals or doing dishes. Plus I have to mop every day." Maria smiled and said "Is Papa in the den?"

"Yes, go see him. I'll finish up here, and then we'll be ready to go in a few minutes."

Maria walked straight to her father who was sitting in his favorite chair in the den and gave him a hug. "Good morning, Papa. How are you?"

"Much better today. I'm really looking forward to the park. It will be like old times. And did you take a look outside? It's a perfect day for a picnic."

Maria agreed that her father looked remarkably better than he did yesterday. It gave her renewed hope that he would have some good days ahead as long as he maintained the dialysis treatments. Just as she was about to sit down, Maria heard her mother call them that she was ready to leave. "Let me help you, Papa."

Maria helped her father get up from the chair. She walked along side of him in case he faltered, but he seemed stronger today.

Anne Maria said, "I'll take the picnic cooler. We can take the elevator down. I'll let you off at the lobby and I'll go down to the garage level. Then I'll get the car and drive it around to the front of the building and pick you up there."

"Do you need help carrying the cooler?" Maria asked.

"Not at all," Anne Marie said as she hoisted the strap of the insulated cooler onto her shoulder. She grabbed her purse with her other hand. All set? Don Pedro, do you have your pager?"

Don Pedro patted the pager that was hooked onto his belt. "I wouldn't dream of leaving home without it. Do you have your cell phone?"

Maria and Anne Maria both said yes in unison and laughed. They left the apartment and Maria pushed the button to summon the elevator. Once they entered the elevator, Maria asked, "Is that pager to let you know if there is a donor?"

"Yes. I keep it with me at all times. Just in case."

The elevator stopped at the lobby and Maria and Don Pedro got off. The elevator door closed behind them and they began walking slowly across the marble floor to the street exit. Maria caught a glimpse of herself in the gilt-framed mirror on the wall and didn't recognize herself. She hoped no one else would either. She held the door open for Don Pedro while he walked outside. Maria followed and switched her shoulder bag to the other arm so she could support her father if she had to.

The street was quiet since there was light traffic with a few bicyclists wearing racing helmets whizzing by. Maria put on her sunglasses and looked around. She wished her mother would hurry up with the car. She glanced at the front door and then turned to face the street. She saw her mother's Volvo approaching and she was relieved. Finally, her mother parked the car in the space marked loading zone and got out of the car. She went to the front passenger door and opened it for Don Pedro. Maria and her father walked to the car. Maria got into the back seat while Anne Marie helped Don Pedro into the car.

"Don Pedro. Anne Marie. Wait!" Silvana called from the lobby door. She ran over to the car. "Where are you going? I'm surprised to see you going out."

Don Pedro answered through the open door, "We're going to the park. I'm tired of being cooped up inside all the time. I need fresh air and some sunshine. Today couldn't be a better day. Look, no rain in sight. And it's not hot. Just cool enough for a sweater."

Maria wanted to hide, but she knew she had to play the part of the home healthcare nurse. Anne Marie stood in front of Silvana blocking her view of Maria.

Silvana took a couple of steps to the left of Anne Marie to peer into the back seat and said, "Who is that in the back? Is that a nurse?"

Anne Marie said, "That's right. I thought it best to have her go with us. She's on duty anyway." Anne Marie glanced at Don Pedro.

Maria thought Anne Marie must have relayed a signal because Don Pedro said with authority, "Let's get going. Take care, Silvana. Have a great day." He then reached out and pulled the door closed.

"All right, then. See you later. Have fun," Silvana said.

Maria saw Silvana staring at her, her eyebrows pinched together in thought. She hoped Silvana didn't recognize her. Since she was sitting in the shadows of the back seat perhaps Silvana didn't get a clear look at her.

Walking quickly to the driver's side of the car, Anne Marie said, "See you later, Silvana. Take care of my son."

"I always do, Anne Marie," Silvana said adamantly.

Anne Marie got in and put the car in drive. No one said a word until they were a few blocks away from the apartment building.

Maria exhaled heavily. "That was a close call. Do you think she recognized me?"

"I don't think so. You were already in the car by the time she was on the sidewalk."

"I hope you're right," Maria said. "But who knows how long she was inside the lobby looking out at us."

Watching the passing scenery, Maria remained silent during the thirty-minute drive to the park. Her parents chatted, but Maria didn't hear their conversation. She was too absorbed in her own thoughts. She worried about Silvana recognizing her and alerting FARC. And when she remembered that she had not yet heard from Jorge, a wave of nausea overcame her. She would try calling him again once they got to the park.

"Maria, didn't you hear me?" Anne Marie asked.

"I'm sorry, Mama. I'm just thinking. What did you say?" Maria looked at her mother in the driver's seat.

"Do you want to have lunch in the picnic area where we can get a table or do you want to go sit by the lake?"

"I think the picnic area will be crowded on a Sunday. Let's take our chance and go by the lake. We can sit on one of the park benches or spread out a blanket on the grass, just like we used to do. Is that all right with you, Papa?" Maria asked, touching her father's shoulder.

"I think a bench would be best," Don Pedro said as he patted her hand. "Once I get down on the ground, I might have some trouble getting up again."

"We got an early start. It's not even noon yet so I shouldn't have trouble finding a place to park near the lake," Anne Marie said. "Most people are still in church."

With that thought, Maria realized that Jorge had taken the girls to Sunday school. Knowing she should be able to reach him sometime after noon, she felt relieved.

Anne Marie drove through the park entrance and ten minutes later she parked the car in a lot. There weren't many people in the park, just a few joggers running along the path.

Everyone got out of the car and Marie helped her father get up. Anne Marie already had her purse and a blanket tucked under one arm; the insulated cooler hung from her other shoulder. Under protests from her mother, Maria took the cooler from her and carried it. As they started to walk toward the lake, Maria could already feel a cool breeze. The tall stands of trees rustled in the wind. Her feet crunched on twigs and dead leaves as they strolled to the walkway that circled the lake. She looked at her parents who were walking hand in hand, and her heart filled with love. She felt blessed that she was their daughter, and she was glad she had made the dangerous trip to see them.

"What is it, Maria?" Anne Marie asked.

"Nothing important. I'm just glad to be here with you two. That's all," Maria said.

"You know we're thankful that you came," Don Pedro said. He pulled his sunglasses from his shirt pocket and put them on. "Look at the lake. It's just spectacular the way it sparkles in the sunlight. When I see this, it affirms my belief in God."

"It is a beautiful sight," Maria agreed. "There's a bench over there. Shall we sit there?"

"*Si*," Don Pedro answered.

Anne Marie spread the blanket out and instructed Maria to put the cooler on it. Then they took a seat on the bench. It was peaceful being in the park, with the melodious songs of birds replacing the blare of traffic. At one side of the lake, Maria saw a pavilion and small pier where dozens of paddle boats were tethered.

"If you're up to it, we can rent a paddle boat after lunch," Maria suggested.

"Only if you and your mother pedal. My knees can't take it," Don Pedro said.

Suddenly all three of them stared at each other wide eyed as they heard a loud buzz. Don Pedro grabbed his pager and looked at it. He pushed the button to silence the alarm, his mouth hanging open. He said to Anne Marie, handing her the pager, "Here, call the transplant team. Then we're going to have to leave."

"Oh my Lord, I can't believe it," said Anne Marie, taking the pager from him and pulling her cell phone out of her purse. She called the number and said, "This is Anne Marie, Don Pedro's wife. The pager just went off."

Maria watched her mother as she listened to the member of the transplant team. She could hardly believe that the call came through. She clutched her father's hand as they listened to Anne Marie's end of the conversation. "We're at the park. No, he hasn't had lunch yet. He had breakfast at six. Okay, no food. Yes, I have a suitcase packed in the trunk, just like we were instructed. All right. We'll leave now and come directly to the hospital. Yes. Thank you so much. I'm so happy. Okay. I will." Finally she closed the phone.

"Don Pedro, Maria, they have a kidney," Anne Marie said in a rush. "We must leave now and get to the hospital." She knelt before Don Pedro, wrapped her arms around him and kissed him on the cheek. When she leaned back, Maria could see tears streaming down her mother's face.

Maria felt numb, unable to cry or speak. She hadn't expected a donor to be available at all, much less when she was right here with her father. It was a miracle. She looked at her father and he turned to her. "It's just what I've been praying for, Maria. To have this happen when you are here to witness it. God answered my prayers. I just hope the surgery goes well."

"Papa, I am so happy for you," Maria said as she hugged him tightly.

"Okay, my ladies. We can't waste another minute. Let's get to the hospital where my team waits," Don Pedro said.

"Mama, are you going to be able to drive because I can?" Maria asked concerned that her mother may be distracted by the alert.

"I think that's a very good idea. Let's gather up everything and get to the car."

Don Pedro got up from the bench and said, "As I said, this a great day. Picnic or no picnic."

Maria grabbed the blanket and cooler. Her mother handed her the car keys and said, "Be careful."

Maria knew she would drive as carefully as she could. She wanted to be sure her father got to the hospital safe and sound. He was about to receive the gift of life.

Chapter 29

Silvana watched Anne Marie drive away and wondered about the nurse who sat in the back seat. She couldn't identify the woman because of the glare of the sun on the window, but her intuition made her think it could have been Maria.

Silvana was in the lobby of the apartment building when she saw her father-in-law, mother-in-law, and the nurse standing on the sidewalk. The nurse had her back to her and looked much heavier than Maria, but something about the woman nagged Silvana. She had run out to the sidewalk because she was curious where the threesome were going. Now she knew they were going to the park so that was nothing unusual.

Silvana stood there wondering what to do. She debated whether to call Alfredo. He might not want to talk to her since it was Sunday and he was with his wife and family. But she longed for him. She found herself thinking of him even when she was with Roman. She wondered if the baby she was carrying was Roman's or Alfredo's. The day after she had gotten sick to her stomach, she took a home pregnancy test and it was positive. She began fantasizing that Alfredo would divorce his wife and she would divorce Roman. Then the two of them would be free to marry each other. Since Alfredo had never talked about his wife, Silvana felt sure that Alfredo loved her. Why else would he meet with her several times a week for lunch in his hotel suite? Perhaps she should call him. Wasn't the fact that the nurse could be Maria important enough to alert him?

Silvana pulled her phone out of her jeans pocket and punched in Alfredo's cell phone number. After she began her affair with Alfredo, she routinely deleted the log of all incoming and outgoing calls on her cell phone. She had heard that many suspicious spouses looked at the calls on their mate's cell phones. She didn't want to get caught.

She heard the phone ring twice before Alfredo said in a whisper, "Why are you calling me? I can't talk to you now."

Before he could hang up, Silvana said, "I think I saw Maria."

"What do you mean *you think* you saw her?"

"She was in the back of my mother-in-law's car. At least, I think it's her."

"You're not sure?"

"No, I'm not positive."

"When you're positive, then call me."

The line went dead. Silvana realized that calling him was a big mistake. His tone of voice was like ice, all business and no tenderness. She worried about losing him. She would have to make sure she saw the nurse again so she could be positive it was

Maria. She knew Alfredo wouldn't send out a FARC rebel for a nurse.

Silvana suddenly felt exhausted. Instead of going to the gym as planned, she returned to her apartment and found a note for her from Roman. He wrote that he was joining his bicycle club for a Sunday ride. She had forgotten all about it. It was just as well. It would give her time to sort out her feelings. She went to the living room and lay down on the couch. She closed her eyes and many thoughts bombarded her mind. She wondered what she should do about the pregnancy. She always wanted to have a baby but wasn't so sure she wanted to stay married to Roman. She could tell Alfredo and wait for his reaction. Maybe he would want to marry her and then again, he might tell her to get an abortion. Or he could insist the baby was Roman's and go ahead and have it. She didn't know what to do so she did nothing.

Silvana was just about to doze off when her cell phone rang. She retrieved it from her pocket and saw the caller was Anne Marie.

"Hello."

"Silvana, I'm in the hospital with Don Pedro. We got the call from the transplant team. They have a kidney for him," Anne Marie said, quite out of breath.

"Thank God. That's wonderful. Shall I come to the hospital now?"

"Oh no. They're running some tests first and then they'll prep him for surgery. It will be a long time.

I'll let you know when to come. It makes no sense to have you sitting around the hospital waiting."

"Is there anything I can do?"

"No, Silvana. Just be sure to tell Roman when he gets home from his bike ride. I'm going to call his brothers now to give them the good news."

"Do you want me to call Maria?"

"Maria? No, dear. I already called her. But thank you just the same. Take care, Silvana. I'll keep you posted," Anne Marie said before closing the connection.

Silvana stared at the phone. That was some news. She wondered if the nurse went to the hospital with her in-laws or if they dropped her off somewhere on the way. There was only one way to find out.

Chapter 30

Anne Marie drove up to the front entrance of the hospital, turned off the engine, and put the keys in her purse. She released the trunk and then got out of the car.

Opening the door for Don Pedro, she said, "You and I will go to Admitting while Maria parks the car."

Maria got out of the back seat and stood by her parents. Anne Marie handed her a single key, the valet key, she presumed. "Okay, I'll just be a few minutes. Do you want to take the cooler in now?"

"No, that can wait. Let's get settled first. You or I can get it later. And we should since I made ceviche. It only keeps a couple of hours so we'll want to eat it soon." Anne Marie took the suitcase out of the trunk and rolled it in front of her as she and Don Pedro paused in front of the automatic doors to the hospital. "Here we are. Our prayers have been answered."

Don Pedro took Anne Marie's hand as they walked into the hospital. Maria watched as the door closed behind them and then she got in the car. She silently said a prayer to the Virgin Mary to bless her father.

Maria drove to the visitor's parking garage and easily found a place to park. She grabbed her purse and was about to put the valet key in there but thought she'd never find it again. She slipped it into the pocket of her uniform which also held the apartment key.

As she walked to the entrance to the hospital, she thought she should call Jorge once her father was given a room. On the way to the hospital, Anne Marie said that her father would be staying in a suite. However, right after the surgery, he would be in Surgical ICU for a day or two.

Maria went into the lobby and found her parents at the admitting desk. Her father was already wearing the hospital's ID bracelet and her mother sported a photo ID on her left chest that was printed from her driver's license.

"Marie, since you forgot your driver's license, you'll have to have your picture taken for the ID badge," Anne Marie said, making a point to use Maria's alias. "Sign your name on this sheet so she can finish up."

Maria took the clipboard from her mother and wrote Marie Valdez on the next blank line. She handed the clipboard back to the security guard. She stood in place for the camera and in a minute, the photo ID printed out. Maria took it from the guard, peeled the backing off and pressed it down on the fabric of her uniform over her left breast. When she looked up, she noticed an orderly pushing an empty wheelchair toward them. He was wearing light blue surgical garb and blue clogs to match.

Don Pedro?" the orderly asked.

Don Pedro said yes. The orderly checked Don Pedro's bracelet and said, "Have a seat, sir and I'll take you to your room."

"I can walk."

"I can see that, sir, but hospital regulations require that I take you. Please sit down."

Don Pedro sat down with a sigh. Maria figured his knees were aching.

Maria and Anne Marie followed the orderly as he pushed the wheelchair down the hall to the bank of elevators. The young man pushed the call button and waited for the elevator to descend. Maria felt self-conscious in her uniform knowing she didn't merit wearing it so she remained quiet. There was time to talk when they got to the hospital suite.

Maria looked up and down the hall and noticed the stream of nurses, doctors, and other medical personnel all on a mission to take care of the hundreds of patients in the hospital. She knew this hospital was ranked in the top three in Bogotá and were up to date in all that technology offered.

They got in the elevator and went to the fifth floor. This floor seemed more like a hotel than a hospital with a carpeted hallway, painted cornflower blue walls accented with a white chair rail, and framed reproductions of Bogotá's famous artists on the walls. She recognized one by Botero immediately.

Don Pedro's suite was at the end of the hallway, affording the most privacy. Maria looked around the room and found the color scheme in shades of grey and blue most inviting. Of course, there was a hospital bed with its crisp white linens and blanket, but it was flanked on either side by built-in nightstands and a wardrobe in a rich cherry wood. A soffit over the bed had recessed lighting. There also was a recliner, a love seat and a couch for guests to sit and visit the patient. In front of the couch was a cherry wood coffee table with a variety of popular magazines. There also was a private bathroom with a sink, bathtub, and shower. On the wall opposite the bed was a TV. There was also a wet bar with a sink and small refrigerator like the ones found in hotels.

The orderly put the brake on the wheelchair and helped Don Pedro get up. "Thank you, sir."

"Your doctors will be coming in shortly. Sit down and relax." The orderly left the room with the wheelchair closing the door behind him.

Maria went over to the wet bar and opened the refrigerator. She found bottled mineral water and a variety of juices. She closed the door and turned to face her parents. "No champagne."

"There will be time for that later," Anne Marie said.

"I'll drink to that," Don Pedro said.

There was a knock at the door.

"Come in," Don Pedro said.

The doctors walked in wearing slacks, a dress shirt with a tie and a white lab coat over it. Their names were embroidered on the coats, but Maria was too far away to read them. They both were clean shaven and wore their hair short. One doctor appeared to be in his early sixties as he had grey hair and wore bifocals. The younger doctor, who was in his forties, had grey hair at the temples and his face was deeply tanned. His laugh lines appeared white at the corners of his eyes. She guessed he was the outdoor type, maybe he played tennis or golf on his days off.

"I'm Doctor Juan Garcia and this is Doctor Hector Perez. We are part of your transplant team and we will be doing your surgery today."

"I'm honored to meet you, doctors,' Don Pedro said. "I've been praying for this day to come. This is my wife, Anne Marie, and this is Marie."

Anne Marie and Maria smiled at the doctors.

"We're very happy that you're here, and it won't be long before we take you in for surgery. You already have been through an extensive battery of tests that evaluated you to determine that you would benefit from a transplant, but we will draw blood now to run a profile, just to make sure everything is normal, and you don't have an infection. Besides that, we thought you'd like to know what the procedure is for transplant surgery," Doctor Garcia said, the senior physician.

"Yes, doctor."

"We will not remove your kidneys but place the donor kidney in the lower right side of your abdomen where we will surgically connect it to nearby blood vessels and your bladder. The surgery takes three to four hours and then you will be in ICU. After that you'll come back to your suite and stay for four or five days."

Doctor Perez continued, "Now we need to start an IV in your arm and you'll be given antibiotics as a precaution against infection. You also get prepped for surgery. While that is being done, you ladies may want to visit the coffee shop for thirty minutes."

Anne Marie and Maria looked at each other wondering what prepping involved.

Doctor Garcia said, "After surgery, you'll have a catheter for several days to drain the urine and there will be a drain near the incision which will be removed five to ten days from today. Do you have any questions?"

Don Pedro said, "Yes, I know I will have to take immunosuppressant medicines for the rest of my life to prevent rejection of the donor kidney, but what about dialysis?"

"That's a good question," Doctor Garcia said. "We'll keep you on dialysis until we know the new kidney has taken over—usually in one to two weeks. Then you'll be off dialysis and be able to resume a normal life and a more normal fluid intake."

"I thought there wouldn't be a need for dialysis," Don Pedro said.

"There isn't when the donor is living. The kidney functions immediately. In this case, dialysis is called for," Doctor Garcia said.

"I understand," Don Pedro said.

Maria could see the impact that this fact had on Don Pedro. Someone died and now Don Pedro had the gift of the kidney. She looked at Anne Marie and saw the same grim expression.

"Oh, just a couple of more things. You will have a liquid diet after surgery and then within two to three days, you'll be back on a normal diet."

"That sounds good," Don Pedro said.

"All right then. Someone will be in here to draw your blood. You'll want to change into a hospital gown which you'll find in a drawer over there. Other than that, we'll see you soon in the OR."

Doctor Perez asked, "Any more questions before we go?"

Maria saw her father look at her mother urging her to ask the question.

Anne Marie said, "What about the survival rate?"

"Excellent. Survival rates are in the high nineties one year after and remain in the nineties after three years. Like any surgery, the risks are the same—infection, bleeding, breathing problems. But we take extra care to avoid any complications. We think you're a good candidate."

"Then when can I go back to work?" Don Pedro asked.

Anne Marie rolled her eyes and said, "I don't believe you're even thinking about work."

"That's quite all right. Usually in three to six weeks you can resume all of your normal activities, including returning to work."

Doctor Garcia said, "When Don Pedro goes in for surgery, you can go home if you like, and we'll call you when he's out. Or you can stay here in this room or go to the cafeteria, coffee shop or the chapel."

"I'd rather stay," Anne Marie said. "I don't see any point in driving home."

Maria didn't know if she should stay or not. She wanted to stay with her mother to offer her support but worried about Silvana showing up.

"All right. There's a call button by the bed if you need anything. It will bring a nurse in to see you," said Doctor Perez.

"Thank you again, doctors," Don Pedro said.

Both doctors smiled, turned, and left the room, closing the door behind them.

No sooner had the door closed, it opened again with a nurse wheeling a cart that held the sterile supplies she needed to prep Don Pedro.

"Hello, Don Pedro. I'm here to get you ready for surgery. You'll need to change into a hospital gown. Why don't you do that now? "I'll pull the privacy curtain around the bed so you can change there."

Anne Marie said, "We'll go to the coffee shop. I'd like to talk to him before he's taken to surgery. Shall we come back in twenty minutes?"

The nurse said, "That should be fine."

Anne Marie and Maria went over to Don Pedro and kissed him goodbye. Anne Marie squeezed his hand and said, "Wait for me. I'll be back soon."

"Of course.

"See you later, Pa--," Maria caught herself ready to say Papa. "Don Pedro."

The two women left the suite, closing the door behind them.

"I almost blew it," said Maria.

"What do you mean?" asked Anne Marie.

"I'm almost said Papa."

"I didn't notice."

"That's good."

A few minutes later, they were seated at a table sipping coffee. Maria looked at her mother whose forehead was furrowed with worry.

"Mama, everything is going to be fine. Papa has come this far, and now he's going to have a new life. It's a blessing."

"I know Maria. I'm sad someone had to die to give your father his kidney."

"I am, too, but organ donation is a real gift, the gift of life."

They sat quietly for a few minutes drinking their coffee, both absorbed in their own thoughts.

"Have you told your husband the good news?"

"No, in fact I should try calling him now. I wasn't able to reach him earlier this morning."

"I'll go back to the room now and give you some privacy to talk," Anne Marie said as she got up from her chair. "When you get off the phone, come up, and we'll send your father off to surgery with our best wishes. Then you can go to the car and get the cooler."

"OK, Mama. I'll just be a few minutes." Maria watched her mother leave the coffee shop and shared in her concern. There were always risks in surgery, but if her father made it through without a problem, his life would be greatly improved.

She took out her cell phone from her shoulder bag and called Jorge. She waited as the phone rang hoping he would pick up. Then the line went dead. She looked at the screen. It read "Signal lost." She got up from her chair and went out into the hallway. She tried the number again. This time the screen said "searching for signal."

Maria closed the phone and decided to join her parents in the suite. She didn't want to keep them waiting for the biggest event in their lives.

Chapter 31

Silvana drove to the hospital in hopes of seeing the nurse and determining if it was Maria. She would peek in Don Pedro's suite to see if her sister-in-law was there. She would remain out of sight because Anne Marie explicitly told her not to come to the hospital until she called her.

As she was driving into the parking garage, she saw the nurse walking to the entrance of the hospital carrying a cooler. Silvana surmised that was the cooler that they had taken for the picnic in the park. Even though the nurse was heavy set, there was something about her walk that made her think of Maria.

Silvana found a parking space and sat there a minute collecting her thoughts. If the nurse was no more than a home healthcare nurse, there would be no reason for her to wait during Don Pedro's surgery. However, if the nurse was Maria in disguise, she would more than likely want to be there when Don Pedro came out of the OR.

Silvana got out of the car and walked to the hospital. She checked at the information desk to find out which room Don Pedro was in and secured a photo ID badge.

When she got to the suite, she waited outside and looked up and down the hall to see if anyone was approaching. Then she opened the door to the suite a crack so that she had a view into the room without being spotted. She saw Anne Marie sitting on the couch talking to the nurse who was opening the cooler on the coffee table. Perhaps they were going to have their lunch now.

Silvana quietly closed the door and walked quickly to the elevator. She walked out of the hospital and back to her car in the parking garage. The wind had picked up and she wondered if it might rain even though it was not in the forecast.

She slid onto the seat and pulled out her cell phone from her jeans pocket. She dialed the number for Alfredo and waited for him to answer.

"So, what's the verdict?" asked Alfredo.

Silvana found his tone of voice strictly business. She wondered if anyone else around him was in ear shot of the conversation.

"Yes, the nurse is Maria. She's in the hospital suite with my mother-in-law. They're waiting there while my father-in-law is in surgery."

"What are you talking about, *surgery*?" asked Alfredo.

"I'm sorry. After I spoke to you earlier today, my mother-in-law called to tell me they were taking my father-in-law into the hospital. They have a suitable kidney for him so he's having a transplant now. Maria is disguised as a nurse and she's in the room now."

"Are you sure it's her?"

Silvana lied and said, "Yes, I'm sure the nurse is Maria."

"Tell me the hospital and room number," Alfredo said.

Silvana recited the information and then said, "Alfredo, I'm not going to be at the hospital when it happens. I don't want to be connected to it. I'm going home."

"Fine. And thank you. This is going to work out well for me. I'll get right on this right away."

Silvana knew Alfredo meant he would benefit financially by turning Maria over to FARC. Now she wondered if she should tell him she's pregnant. She dismissed the idea when she heard a woman's voice call, "Alfredo, come here for a minute, please."

"I've got to go now. Talk to you soon," Alfredo said before hanging up.

Silvana stared at the phone. She wondered what he meant by "soon." Now her life was more complicated than she wanted it to be. She was in love with a married man and she believed she was pregnant with his child. She also just gave Alfredo the signal to have her sister-in-law abducted and murdered. She hoped it was Maria. And what if the woman wasn't her? If the woman was lucky, a rebel would check to see if she had on a disguise before killing her.

Chapter 32

When Maria entered her father's hospital suite, she found her mother pacing the floor. She put the cooler down on the coffee table. She opened the lid and said, "You made enough food for an army, Mama."

"I know. I can't seem to get out of the habit of cooking for a big family now that I'm an empty nester. That's what they call old people like me in the US, right?"

"That's right, Mama, but you're not old. An empty nester just means that your children are adults and live independently."

Maria heard the door latch release and looked at the door. It opened a few inches and quickly closed again. Maria looked at her mother. "Did you see that?"

"Yes. That was odd. Maybe someone realized they had the wrong room."

Maria walked to the door, opened it and stepped out into the hallway to see who had been at the door. No one was there. She looked toward the elevators and saw the doors close. Maria returned to the room and said, "Whoever was there is gone now. I don't like it. I wonder who peered in."

Anne Maria walked to the doorway and put her arm around Maria. "Come, sit down. Let's have lunch."

"All right," Maria said as she let her mother lead her to the couch. "You can serve me some ceviche but don't give me much. Did you also bring arepas?"

"Yes, would you like one?"

"Maybe after I eat the ceviche. I don't know how much of an appetite I have."

Anne Marie served them a portion of the ceviche in the plastic bowls she had packed in the cooler. "I know what you mean. I feel anxious, too. But we should try to eat."

After eating a few forkfuls, Maria said, "It's as delicious as always. What kind of fish do you use?"

"I like to use corvine but any firm-flesh fish will do. The trick is to make sure you let the fish marinate in the lime juice long enough. The acid of the juice effectively cooks the fish."

"How long do you let it marinate?"

Anne Marie took another forkful of the ceviche. "Usually eight hours. Then you drain off the lime juice and add the other ingredients, you know, chopped tomatoes, onions, cilantro, parsley, Worcestershire Sauce, Tabasco, tomato juice, more lime juice. Did I leave anything out?"

"Salt and pepper?" Maria asked as she put her bowl down on the coffee table.

"Of course," Anne Marie said as she took a bottle of orange drink out of the cooler and offered it to Maria.

Reaching for the bottle, Maria said, "Thank you. I haven't had one of these drinks in a long time." Maria twisted the cap off the bottle and took a long swallow.

Looking at Maria's bowl of ceviche, Anne Marie asked, "Have you had enough to eat?"

"I'm afraid so. I'm worried about Papa's surgery and about Silvana knowing I'm here. But I am happy to say that when I went to the garage to get the cooler, I was able to get a signal so I called Jorge. I told him the good news. He said he'd say his prayers for Don Pedro."

"Yes, prayers help. "You look very nervous, Maria. Are you sure you want to stay in the hospital. You might feel more comfortable waiting in the apartment. I can call you when your father gets out of surgery."

"I don't know. I really don't want to leave you alone." Maria said as tears came to her eyes.

"I know. I'll call Sal and see if he can come over. Then if you want to leave at any time, he can take you," Anne Marie said.

Maria brushed the tear from her cheek and said, "All right, Mama. Call Sal. Maybe Vivian can come too."

Anne Marie reached into her purse and pulled out her cell phone. She found Sal's listing in the phone's directory and pushed the send button.

When she heard Sal say hello, Anne Marie said, "Sal, I wanted you to know that we're at the San Ignacio University Hospital. Don Pedro was called in for surgery for his kidney transplant. He's in the OR now." Anne Marie paused to listen to Sal's reaction. "Yes, it is wonderful. But I have a favor to ask. Could you come over to the hospital and wait with us? Maria is nervous and I think she'd feel more at ease if you were here. If she needs to leave in a hurry, you'd be here to drive her."

Maria watched her mother listening to Sal. She prayed Sal would be available to help her escape if necessary.

"All right, then. We'll see you soon. I'm sorry Vivian can't make it right now. We'll see her tonight," Anne Marie said as she closed her cell phone. She turned to Maria. "Sal is leaving now. Vivian is visiting her aunt in the nursing home and won't be able to come to visit until tonight.

Maria sat back on the couch and closed her eyes as she let the tears flow down her cheeks. She was so happy that her father was getting the kidney and a chance for a longer life, but the door opening and closing to the room gave her a premonition that Silvana had been the one who had spied on them. If so, her life was in danger. She hoped Sal would arrive soon. Her life may depend on it.

Chapter 33

"I need to stretch my legs, Mama. I'll go down to the nurse's station and check to see if they have anything to report on Papa," Maria said as she walked to the door.

"You can just call them, you know," Anne Marie advised.

"I know. Like I said, I need to walk. I'm fidgety," Marie said, opening the door and closing it behind her. She looked down the hallway to see if there was any sign of Silvana and there was not. She only saw nurses entering or leaving hospital suites.

As she walked down the hallway, she passed patient rooms, a janitorial closet, and a chapel. She remembered the doctor mentioning the chapel and she wondered if anyone went in there to pray. Finally, she saw the nurse's station where only one nurse was busy watching the bank of patient monitors. She imagined the other nurses who worked this shift must be attending to patients, checking their vital signs, and recording the information into computers.

When Maria reached the nurse's station, the nurse asked, "May I help you?"

"I was wondering if you had any word about Don Pedro's surgery."

"No, your doctors will come to see you when the patient is in recovery and give you a report. We don't get updates."

"I see. I'm sorry for the interruption."

"No problem. If you don't want to wait in the patient's suite, you can sit in the chapel. You passed it on your way here."

"Thank you, but I'll probably go sit in the room and wait," Maria said as she turned to return to the room.

She looked down the hallway and saw a man open the door to her father's suite. She drew in her breath when she realized that the man was one of the FARC gang that abducted her from the car that awful night. What was he doing here? She saw him withdraw his head from the room and start walking down the hall towards her. Maria didn't think he'd recognize her in her nurse's disguise, but she couldn't take a chance. She walked as quickly as she could to the chapel, quietly opened the door and closed it behind her. She knew she had to hide, but where? The chapel was about the size of a hospital suite. She looked straight ahead to see a crucifix on the wall. In front of it were tiered banks of votive candles that may be lighted to say a prayer for a loved one. The coin box was attached to the legs of the stand. On either side of her were five rows of pews in polished oak. The floor was carpeted just like the hallway. The chapel was dimly lit with indirect lighting. She looked for a light switch. She found it on the wall to her left and turned the lights off. As her eyes got used to the dark, she felt her way along the center aisle and found the edge of a pew. She got down on her hands and knees and crawled along the carpet. She then lay flat on the floor and slid under the pew. She felt her cell phone dig into her hip and adjusted it in her pocket. She waited and held her breath, wondering if the FARC rebel was looking for her. He had to be, she thought. It was probably Silvana who spied on her earlier and alerted the rebel. She exhaled slowly trying to calm herself, but it was no use. The adrenaline was flowing. Then she heard the door of the chapel open and saw a beam of light from the hallway stream in. She heard the rebel mumbling curses under his breath. Suddenly the lights in the chapel were on. He had found the light switch. Maria heard the door close with a click. She heard a scuffing sound along the carpet. She closed her eyes tightly hoping he would leave.

Suddenly his hands were around her ankles as he pulled her out from under the pew. She tried to scream, but one hand covered her mouth while his other hand held a syringe which he plunged into her neck. She felt groggy and was unable to move. Her eyelids felt like weights and she tried to keep them open. She was aware of being dragged along the floor to the doorway, but she was helpless to do anything about it. She heard him open the door and close it behind him. Maria wondered where he went. The door suddenly opened again and the man pushed a wheelchair into the room. After he closed the door, he lifted her off the floor and put her in the wheelchair. Maria continued to fight falling sleep. She realized sunglasses were being put over her glasses. She couldn't move and she wished she could scream. She then sensed the motion of the wheelchair being pushed out of the room, down the hallway, and to the elevators. She heard the doors open and the wheelchair was pushed in. Maria dozed off and when she tried to open her eyes again, she realized the man was lifting her from the wheelchair and placing her on the floor of a van. The smell was foul and smelled of sweat. She tried to open her eyes and she tried to speak. Then her body went limp and she was unconscious.

Maria then heard two voices and realized that she was still in the van. She didn't know where she was or how much time had passed. Her hands were free and so were her legs. The rebels must have believed that they gave her enough of the drug to keep her unconscious for a long time. But now she was fully awake and she must escape. If she didn't, it was just a matter of time until they executed her. She had to keep her eyes closed and let them think that she was still unconscious.

She listened to them talking and heard one of them say, "Yes, the banker's girlfriend gave her up. I never thought we'd see her again. But she really doesn't look the same. I just hope he's right."

Maria heard the van pull into a parking garage and when she squinted to look out through the back window of the van, she realized she was right. The driver parked the van but left the engine running. Maria wondered if she was being transferred to another vehicle. This would be her chance to escape. She found the two keys in her pocket and placed each one between her forefinger and middle finger of her right hand and made a fist.

She heard the back door of the van open and waited until the rebel got close to her. As he reached for her thighs to drag her out of the van, Maria sprung up and thrust the keys into his eyes. The rebel screamed in agony as he fell to the ground grabbing at his eyes, cursing her. Maria scrambled out of the van, and then she saw the other rebel running toward her. She waited and just as he was about to grab her by the arms, she kicked her foot high and caught him hard between the legs. He howled in pain and dropped to his knees. Maria then ran to the driver's side and hopped in the van. She backed out of the space and drove out of the parking garage. When she looked at the rear view mirror, she saw both rebels still on the ground. She pulled out onto the street and tried to get her bearings. As she drove along the street, she realized they were in the south area of Bogotá, a terrible place to be. She made a U-turn and headed the other way. As soon as she was a safe distance from the parking garage, she would call Sal. She would have to ditch the van and get out of Bogotá fast.

Chapter 34

"Sal, Sal, you have to help me," Maria gasped while she was driving the van. She glanced nervously at the rear-view mirror to see if she was being tailed.

"Where are you? Your mother and I are worried sick about you," Sal said. "I'm at the hospital with your mother. You simply disappeared."

Maria could hear her mother's tearful voice in the background.

"I've got to get out of here now! A FARC rebel grabbed me. He knocked me out. I felt a needle in my neck. I came to in a van. When they were going to take me out of the van, I escaped. I'll tell you everything when I see you. Meet me in the parking garage of our apartment building. Ask Anna Marie to give you my purse. All of my documents and visa are in there," Maria said as she noticed a few buses among the light traffic on both sides of the street.

"All right, Maria. I'll leave the hospital now and meet you in the parking garage. Your mother wants to talk to you. I'll have her call your cell phone so I can hang up and leave. Are you hurt?"

"Not really. My neck is sore and I'm hung over," Maria said. "Sal, come now, please!"

"All right. I'm leaving now. I'll get there as soon as I can," Sal said before closing the phone.

Maria saw a bus parked at the bus stop. She pulled up behind it and parked the van. She got out, slammed the door, and ran to see the route number posted on the side of bus. She was in luck. It would take her to her neighborhood. When she got on the bus, she realized she didn't have a token. She explained to the bus driver that she had been mugged. He nodded and waved her on. Maria thanked the driver and moved to the back of the bus and sat down. She looked out the rear window to see if anyone was following the bus. She noticed cars passing the bus with none following it. She peered into the cars as they drove by, but she didn't see anyone resembling her abductors.

Suddenly her phone rang, startling her. She pulled it out of her pocket and saw from the caller ID that it was her mother.

"Maria, where are you? Are you all right?" Anna Marie said through her tears. "I didn't know what happened to you. You disappeared!"

"Mama, I'm all right now," Maria said lowering her voice to a whisper. "I saw one of the rebels in the hallway at the hospital so I hid in the chapel. He came in and found me. He knocked me out with an injection. Later I woke up in a van, but I pretended to still be out. When they were about to transfer me to another car, I escaped. I took their van."

Interrupting, Anne Marie said, "Are you still driving it?"

"No, I ditched it and got on a bus. I should be home in another few minutes. Do you have any word about Papa?" Maria could hear her mother sniffling. She felt terrible that she couldn't be there for her. Her mother was all alone, but Maria had no choice. She had to leave Bogotá immediately.

"No, he's still in surgery. It should be another two hours or so."

"I'll say my prayers again for him, Mama. I'm sorry I can't be with you. But I have to leave now. I'll have Sal take me to the airport. When I hang up with you, I'll call the charter company to get the plane ready for take-off."

"What if they don't have a plane ready?"

"Mama, I have cash. They'll get a plane ready. I'm sorry to have to get off the phone with you, but I need to call them. I'll call you later when I'm on the plane."

"Yes, I need to know that you got there safely. My dear Maria. I'm sorry this happened to you. You knew it was dangerous to come and you did it anyway. We put your life in danger."

"Mama, stop. Don't talk like that. Nobody forced me. I just need to get out of here as fast as I can. I'm sure those bastards will be sending others after me. I heard the rebels say the banker's girlfriend gave me up. I think they were talking about Silvana. She must be having an affair. Be on your guard, please, Mama"

"I will. I won't keep you. I love you. Be careful. Call me as soon as you can," Anne Marie said, her voice trembling with emotion.

"Goodbye Mama. Try not to worry. I love you and I'll call you in a little while," Maria said and then pushed the end button. She found the number for the charter airline and called them. When the receptionist answered the phone, she explained she had an emergency and needed to leave immediately. She also told Maria she was lucky that the aircraft was available since Sunday was a slow day. The woman took her information, confirmed her reservation, and said a jet would be ready to take off in thirty minutes. Maria thanked her and told her she would be at the airport as soon as possible.

Maria sighed with relief as she closed the phone. Seeing that her bus stop was just a block away, she got up from her seat, and walked to the front of the bus. After the bus stopped, Maria looked at the traffic and exited. When she was standing on the sidewalk she looked around. Traffic was light just as it had been in the morning. At the next corner, she crossed the street and walked briskly down a side street. At the next avenue, she turned right, and headed north. The apartment was only another two blocks. She wanted to run, but she didn't want to draw attention to herself. Wearing a white nurse's uniform was enough. She wondered if she should change her clothes.

When she arrived in front of the apartment building, she was afraid she might see Silvana. She opened the front door and found the lobby was deserted. Maria ran to the elevator, went to her floor and let herself in the apartment. She looked at the key and thought she detected blood on it. She shivered at the thought and closed the door behind her. She went into the bathroom, washed her face and hands, and smoothed the wig. She looked at her watch and figured Sal should be in the garage by now. She packed her suitcase and was ready to go. She opened the door slowly and checked the hallway. She stepped out, locked the door and rushed to the elevator dragging her suitcase. She held her breath praying Silvana wouldn't be on the elevator. The door opened and she stepped inside. She pushed the button for the garage and watched the numbers descend on the lighted panel hoping that Sal would be waiting for her. Just as the door opened, a car pulled up. She didn't recognize it. Her heart leaped to her throat. Then the passenger window lowered and she saw that it was Sal.

"You gave me a real scare. This isn't the car you usually drive," Maria said as she threw her suitcase in the back seat and slammed the door. She opened the front passenger door and got in.

"I'm sorry to scare you, Maria. This is Vivian's car," Sal said as he drove out of the garage and headed to the airport. "Your purse is on the floor by your feet."

Maria looked down and pulled the purse to her lap. "Thank goodness."

Maria rummaged through it and found all her valuables were intact. She took a deep breath and let out a sigh. She looked at the side-view mirror and then turned her head to look out the back window. She wondered when the stinking bastards would show up. She hoped she'd never see them again, but she knew they wouldn't give up until she was dead. She shuddered at the thought.

Sal said, "Maria, you're very lucky you made it. I hate to think of what could have happened."

"I'm scared, Sal. I just hope I get out of here alive."

"Tell me what happened. From the beginning," Sal prompted.

Maria told him the story and when she was finished, Sal was parking the car at the charter jet building. Sal took Maria's suitcase out of the car and waited as she got out of the car. He put his arms around her and hugged her. "Good luck. Call your mother when you get on the jet and let her know you're safe. I told her to keep me posted about you. Come on. I'll walk you into the terminal."

"All right, but I'm going to slip into the ladies room and get out of this disguise."

A few minutes later, Maria walked toward Sal wearing a pair of navy slacks and a white cardigan set. Gone were the wig, nurse's uniform, orthodontic wax, and oversized glasses.

"What a transformation! The beautiful Maria I remember," said Sal smiling broadly at her.

"Thank you, Sal. Now I'm ready to check in."

When they arrived at the check-in counter, Maria introduced herself to Natalia, the flight attendant who noted in her computer that Maria checked in to return to Santa Marta. After paying the fare, she turned to Sal and motioned for him to follow her away from the counter. "Thank you, Sal. You saved my life. Now it's best that I leave while I still have a chance."

Their eyes met and they both knew that Maria was right. Sal shook his head and said, "Go. May God be with you."

Maria forced a smile and turned to go. She turned around before heading out the door to the jet. Sal was still standing there, but now there were tears rolling down his cheeks. Maria felt her heart go out to him, and her eyes filled with tears as well. She waved to him and turned, dragging the suitcase behind her.

Natalia said, "Here, let me take that for you." She took the suitcase from Maria and led the way.

Maria followed the woman and boarded the jet. Now she would have to call Jorge to let him know she was on her way home. Or at least she hoped she was. She still had to make the long boat trip back to Aruba. She wondered when and where the FARC bastards would show up. She was lucky so far. But it was just a matter of time. She hoped her luck wouldn't run out before she got home to Jorge and her little girls.

Chapter 35

Maria quickly boarded the jet and sat down with a sigh. As she pulled the seat belt strap across her chest and attempted to snap it into the clip, she noticed a tremor in her hands. She took a deep breath, exhaled slowly, and strapped herself in.

She asked Natalia how long it would be before takeoff and was told less than five minutes. Maria looked out the window for any sign of trouble. All she saw were mechanics and airport workers going about the duties. She figured FARC rebels had already organized a gang to pursue her.

She dreaded calling Jorge because she knew she would upset him, but she pulled out her cell phone and did it anyway. He answered the call on the first ring.

"Hello, Maria. How are you?"

"I don't have much time to talk Jorge, because the jet is going to take off in a few minutes. I'm coming home now. I'm flying back to Santa Marta, and then I'll take the yacht back to Aruba. I'll need to call the captain when I get off the phone with you so he can be ready to leave immediately," Maria said, speaking quickly before the plane took off.

"What happened, Maria? What's going on? Are you all right? I thought you were at the hospital. Isn't your father in surgery?"

"Yes, he is, and Sal is going back to the hospital to stay with my mother. I didn't want to leave, but I had no choice."

"Tell me, what happened!" Jorge yelled.

"Right now, I'm safe," Maria said in a soothing tone in an effort to reassure her husband. "When I was in the hallway of the hospital, I saw a FARC rebel look into my father's hospital room. I ducked into the chapel and hid under a pew. But he found me anyway and drugged me."

Jorge interrupted, "Drugged you? Are you all right? Did he hurt you? I don't believe this!"

"Jorge, let me finish. I'm all right now. He put me in a van. I woke up when he was about to transfer me to another vehicle. That's when I gouged his eyes with my keys. I got away. I took off in the van."

"This rebel was alone?"

"No. I kicked the other one between his legs. He collapsed on the ground."

"Dammit, Maria. I almost lost you again. Why did I ever let you go? I was a stupid fool to agree to your crazy plan. It's just *loco*. You're still in danger. The rebels will track you down. They'll stop at nothing to get to you."

"I know that, Jorge. Pray that I get home safely. I'll call you again when I'm on the yacht. Tell our girls that I love them. But I must go now so I can call the captain before the jet takes off."

Jorge sighed. "I love you, Maria. Make sure you come home to us, you hear me? I can't stand the thought of losing you."

"I will. I love you. I'll talk to you the minute I step aboard the yacht." Maria ended the call and phoned Captain Jack. She hoped he was still waiting at the dock and not cruising along the coast.

"Hi, Maria. I'm surprised to hear from you. I thought I wouldn't get a call from you for another few days."

"Something came up, and I need to leave Colombia immediately. I'll explain everything to you when I see you. My jet is about to take off so I'll be in Santa Marta in about an hour. How soon can you be ready to leave? I need to get back to Aruba right away."

"I can be ready in an hour. I just have to refuel and restock some food and water. Are you all right?" Captain Jack asked.

"Yes," Maria lied. "We'll talk when I see you. Good-bye"

Maria ended the call and put her phone in her pants pocket. Natalia announced to her that the pilot was ready for takeoff and Maria nodded. She closed her eyes and thought of her narrow escape from the rebels. She was lucky to be alive. She wondered about Silvana. What was her sister-in-law up to? The rebels said the banker's girlfriend gave her up. Maria didn't know of any woman who would give her up except Silvana. Was her sister-in-law having an affair with a banker? Maria remembered hearing about corrupt bankers and internal revenue service employees selling information to the FARC. That's how they found out which wealthy families to target for kidnapping. She wondered what motivated Silvana to sell her out. She never thought it was money since Roman provided for her and Silvana also had a good income from the boutique. Silvana's own parents were wealthy. She was still convinced Silvana was jealous of her. Perhaps Silvana even hated her. It was a powerful emotion that drove Silvana to betray her own sister-in-law.

Maria knew that the leftist rebels would kill her and they were probably in hot pursuit. She remembered that they communicated by radio and cell phones so they could reach their comrades all over Colombia. She wondered if they were smart enough to figure out her plan to escape. If so, she may not make it out alive. They could be waiting for her at the Santa Marta airport. Or at the dock, just lying in wait to kill her. She was lucky the injection hadn't killed her. Maybe they had intended to kill her with it, but didn't get the right dose. Or maybe her would-be captors had planned a tortuous death after the drug wore off. She shivered at the thought.

Maria knew she was making herself more upset thinking about the risk she had taken. She still had to get home. Until she arrived in Miami and walked into the waiting arms of Jorge and her daughters, she had to be on guard. She hoped her luck would hold out. She opened her eyes and looked down to see Colombia from the air. She was leaving her parents once again, and she hadn't said any proper goodbyes. She wondered how her father was. He should be coming out of surgery in another hour. She knew the hospital had a good reputation, but there were always risks in surgery, especially with general anesthesia. She said her prayers again for her father and her mother. And then she prayed that the Lord would help her get back to her family safely. She closed her eyes once again and fell asleep.

Chapter 36

Maria felt a hand on her shoulder and awoke with a start to see Natalia at her side.

"I'm sorry to startle you, but we are going to land in a few minutes," the flight attendant advised.

"Thank you. I'm all right." Maria yawned and ran her fingers through her hair so it wouldn't look like she just got out of bed. Remembering her dream about the FARC rebels storming into the airport terminal, Maria asked, "Do you log out of your computer when you leave the desk to board the jet?"

"Not usually, although I suppose I should. I just leave it on for my replacement. Why do you ask?" Natalia stood before her looking sheepish.

"Does the monitor have the latest transaction on it?" Maria asked looking up at Natalia hoping the answer was no.

Natalia hesitated then said, "Yes. The customer's name, departure date and time and estimated arrival at the destination. And, of course, the method of payment."

"Oh, I see." Maria suddenly felt like she was going to be sick.

"You look pale. Are you going to be all right? Do you want a sick bag?" Natalia said.

Maria put her hands on her cheeks and thought about the FARC rebels. If they had actually entered the charter jet terminal and looked at Natalia's computer screen, they would learn that the airplane was headed for Santa Clara and would arrive an hour after departure. She realized it was only a dream, but it was possible that the rebels stopped at each of the charter jet terminals in the Bogotá airport looking for her. If they found a lone passenger going to Santa Clara, wouldn't they radio their comrades along the coast to wait for her? Surely there were FARC rebels along the Colombian coast. They were the ones who ran the drugs in the "go fast boats."

Suddenly Maria heard the captain say, "Natalia, take your seat and buckle up. We're cleared to land."

"Excuse me while I take my seat," Natalia said leaving Maria to her tortured thoughts.

Maria looked out the window wondering if the FARC rebels were already in Santa Clara waiting for her. She put her forefinger to her mouth and started chewing on her nail. She saw the runway rising up to meet her and she closed her eyes as the jet touched down. She wondered if Captain Jack would have a car waiting for her. She had forgotten to ask. She hoped that he did, but what if a FARC rebel was posing as a taxi driver? She couldn't stay on the plane, because she had to get to the dock. She continued to stare out the window as the jet taxied to the terminal. It would just be another few minutes before the stairway would be lowered so she could exit the plane. She now wished she had a weapon in her purse. She should have thought about it before. Perhaps Sal could have gotten a gun for her. But it was too late for that. She craned her neck trying to get a better look at who may out there waiting for her. She cupped her chin in her hand and then bit her knuckle. She let out a heavy sigh just as Natalia got up and opened the door to let the stairway descend to the tarmac. Maria pulled out her cell phone and looked at the screen. It was already five o'clock. She certainly lost track of the hours, probably from the drug.

Natalia reached for Maria's suitcase in the storage compartment and said, "I take your suitcase in to the terminal for you. Come on. Follow me."

Maria unbuckled her seat belt and stood up, smoothing her purple knit top over her charcoal gray slacks. She grabbed her purse and followed Natalia down the stairs holding onto the handrail. She looked around, but she didn't see anyone who posed a threat. It would be another couple of hours until sundown and right now the glare from the sun in the horizon was blinding. As she followed Natalia who click-clacked in her stiletto heels across the pavement, Maria looked down at her comfortable loafers. Not stylish she admitted but certainly more practical for walking on the concrete. When Natalia reached the door to the terminal building, she opened it and held it for Maria. Maria froze.

"Is there something wrong?" Natalia asked.

Maria peered inside. She scanned the room and saw an attendant behind the desk. Other than him, the room was vacant. She noticed the travel posters on the walls and comfortable leather seating in the center of the room. There were a few potted areca palms placed near the chairs. Other than that, Maria found the room minimally decorated. She walked in and Natalia followed her.

"We're here in Santa Clara. I hope you enjoyed the flight," Natalia said smiling.

"I did get some needed rest. Thank you. Take care." Maria took her suitcase and thought she'd better visit the ladies room before venturing out to look for a taxi to take her to the dock. She found it unsettling that the terminal was so quiet. But then Maria reminded herself that it was Sunday. Private air charters catered to businessmen who typically enjoyed a leisurely weekend with their families, not flying to appointments.

Of course, the FARC rebels were another matter. They did business on demand and because of this she was scared.

Maria walked into the ladies room and found it vacant. She entered a stall, latched the door and heard the main door open. She held her breath until she heard the familiar click clack of Natalia's heels on the tile floor. When she was finished, she left the stall, and glanced under the other bathroom stalls. She was relieved when she recognized Natalia's navy leather pumps. Maria went to the sink, washed her hands, and looked in the mirror.

Well, this is it, she thought. You've got to go outside and find a taxi, like it or not. She took a deep breath, exhaled slowly and did an about face, wheeling her suitcase behind her. She opened the door just a crack and peered outside. Not seeing anyone other than the male attendant at the counter, she walked out and found the door to the parking lot. She looked out the door window and saw a taxi parked along the curb. A man was in the driver's seat wearing a baseball cap and dark sunglasses. Maria wondered if he was the driver requested by Captain Jack or a FARC rebel. There was just one way to find out.

Chapter 37

Standing by the door of the charter jet terminal, Maria pulled her cell phone from her pocket and called Captain Jack. She held her breath waiting for him to answer.

"Hello."

"Captain Jack, it's Maria. Did you send a taxi for me? There's one outside the charter terminal and I just wanted to make sure you sent it," Maria said.

"Yes, I did send a taxi from Beachside Resort Limousine Service. The logo is on the door. Do you see it?"

Maria looked out the window once again and verified the company was, in fact, Beachside Resort Limousine Service. "Yes, I see it. All right, then. I'm on my way. See you in a few minutes."

"Great. We're ready to leave as soon as you get to the dock," Captain Jack said before ending the call.

Maria pocketed her cell phone. She opened the door and pulled her suitcase behind her. She saw the taxi's trunk open, and the driver got out of the car. He was no taller than Maria with a slim build. He wore jeans and a yellow polo-style shirt with the taxi company logo embroidered on it. She noticed the yellow baseball cap he was wearing also had the same logo. For some reason seeing these logos assured her. "Hello. Did Captain Jack send you?"

"*Si senora.*" The driver walked toward her with a bounce in his feet and took her suitcase from her and put it into the trunk of the car. Then he opened the car door so she could slide into the back seat.

Maria wiped her sweaty palms on her slacks and got into the car. The driver closed the door for her and got into the driver's seat. He told her his name was Paulo and that Captain Jack already paid him his fare, including his tip.

Maria fastened her seat belt as Paulo drove out of the parking lot. He turned on the air conditioning full blast and directed the vents toward her. She was impressed with his honesty. He could have easily collected an additional fare from her as well.

Maria looked out the window as the airport faded from view. It was just a short ride to the dock so Maria checked her phone. She was anxious to call her mother and Jorge, but she didn't want Paulo to hear her conversation. She would just have to wait another few minutes and call from the yacht. She wonder

Chapter 38

Maria took a few swallows of the refreshing iced tea Captain Jack had served her before he went up to the flybridge to start the boat's engine. Looking out the salon window, she saw Manual releasing the heavy ropes that secured "Get Reel" to the dock. Captain Rick was busy putting the food and other supplies away in the galley. She leaned back on the couch and called her mother. She was anxious to hear about her father and hoped her mother had good news. Hearing her mother's voice mail, she simply hung up. She would wait another minute and try the call again. She took another drink of the iced tea and peered through the window again. She heard the shift in the fishing yacht's engine and realized they were now underway. It was almost six-thirty. She would have to ask Captain Jack when they would reach Aruba. She knew he didn't want to cruise at a fast speed at night, but she hoped he would make an exception once he learned the danger she was in.

Maria's cell phone rang and she saw from the caller ID that it was her mother.

"Mama, I'm so glad you called. I just tried your number, but got your voice mail."

"Your call went directly to voice mail. Why, I don't know. Enough about that. Are you all right?"

"Yes. I'm on the fishing yacht heading for Aruba. How is Papa?" Maria asked hoping for the best.

Your father is out of surgery and in the recovery room. The surgeons said everything was by the book. No complications. They let me see him for a minute. He wasn't awake yet, but seeing all those tubes frightened me." Anne Maria began to cry. "Oh, Maria. I'm so afraid for you. I'm so sorry I insisted on you coming to see us. I put your life in danger and I regret it. If anything happens to you, I don't know what I'll do."

"Mama, don't cry. I'll be fine. And I'm glad I came. I got to see you and Papa. It was important that we were able to talk in person. By tomorrow I'll be on a plane heading back to Miami," Maria said, wishing she was already there. "So please don't worry about me. Is Sal still with you?"

"Yes, he's here. He'll stay until they bring your father to the ICU. I told the nurse that I want to stay overnight, so she said she'd make up the sleeper couch. I didn't know the couch pulled out."

Maria heard the rustle of a tissue as her mother wiped her eyes and blew her nose. Then she said, "Mama. Are you going to wear one of the hospital gowns that open in the back?" Maria smiled at the visual that came into her mind.

Anne Maria laughed. "I don't think so. But if that's my only option, I'll put on two, one over the other to cover the gape in the back."

"That's my mother. You've got a creative solution for everything," Maria said, happy that she made her mother laugh.

"Except how to save you from the rebels. Maria, I'm frightened. I wish I could trade places with you."

"Mama, I'm going to be fine. They may not know where I am. I'm just hoping for an uneventful cruise back to Aruba. The sky is clear and the sun is starting to set."

Maria looked out the window and saw Santa Marta's shoreline fading from sight. She thought she'd better call Jorge while she still was in range of a tower signal.

"I better hang up and call Jorge. We're out in the ocean and it's possible I'll lose my cell phone service. I'll call you when I arrive in Aruba to let you know what flight I can take to Miami."

"Call Jorge. Give him my love and to my granddaughters. I'll talk to you tomorrow and you'll get a full report on your father. Stay safe. You know I love you."

"I love you, too," Maria said as she ended the call. She looked at Captain Rick who was in the galley busy preparing food for their dinner. After taking another drink of the iced tea, she called Jorge.

He answered on the third ring. "Maria, are you on the boat?"

"Yes, I am. I just got off the phone with my mother. I thought I better call you before I lose the signal."

"How's your father? Is he out of surgery?"

"Yes, he's now in ICU. My mother got to see him for a minute, but he isn't awake yet. She's spending the night. I really wish I could've stayed with her."

"We both know that wasn't possible. You nearly got yourself…" Jorge stopped before completing the sentence.

"Are the girls there?" Maria asked figuring that was why Jorge stopped talking in mid-sentence.

"Yes. Do you have time to say hello?"

"Of course. In case I lose the signal, I'll call you tomorrow from Aruba so you know my flight plans. Don't worry. I'll be all right. I already left Colombia."

"I just wish I could be there with you and …" Jorge stopped again, and then said, "The girls are waiting to talk to you."

"Hi, Mommy," Julie and Paula said in unison.

"Hi Julie. Hi Paula. Am I on a speaker phone?" Maria asked.

"Yes, Daddy got a new phone that shows the caller ID on the screen and it has a speaker on it," Paula said. "Pretty cool, don't you think?"

"It's a great idea. So you can both hear me at once. No more taking turns talking to me on the phone."

That's right, Mommy. Daddy said you're coming home now. We can't wait to see you," Paula said.

"I can't wait to see you both, too." Maria felt a catch in her throat as the thought of never seeing them again entered her mind. Her eyes began to fill with tears and Maria blinked them away. She had to be strong and not give the girls the impression that she was afraid. "I'll call you tomorrow."

"Are you all right, Mommy? You sound funny," Paula said.

Remembering how intuitive Paula was, Maria lied, "I just got something in my eye and it's tearing. I'm okay. Is your Daddy there?"

"Yes, I'm right here," Jorge said.

"Are the three of you taking care of everything while I'm gone?"

Jorge said, "Everything is fine. But it will be so much better when you're back home with us. We miss you and we love you."

"I love you, too. I'm going to hang up now. I don't know how much longer my phone will work."

"Okay, Mommy," the two girls said in unison.

Maria could tell the speaker phone was off when Jorge said, "Good luck, Maria. Stay safe. I love you. Be sure to call as soon as you can."

"I will. See you soon," Maria said before ending the call. She turned her phone off, put it into her suitcase, and took it to her stateroom. Now she had to steel herself to talk to Captain Jack. He was expecting an explanation why her trip was cut short. Should she tell him the truth: that the FARC rebels may still be pursuing her? He might just turn back and drop her off at Santa Marta not wanting to endanger himself and his mates. On the other hand, she could just make up a story. She could say one of her daughters got sick. Since he has two daughters of his own, he could relate to a mother wanting to return home quickly to care for her sick child. But lying went against Maria's values. She thought that was the worst sin of all. She had once said to her daughters that people who lie are cowards. They're afraid of the consequences that the truth may have. That was certainly true for her now that she was desperate to get back to Aruba. She was afraid that Captain Jack would not want to continue the trip with her aboard. She couldn't take the chance. She would have to lie. She would make it a point to go to confession when she got home. That is, if she actually made it home. She walked into the head and looked at herself in the mirror. Her brow was furrowed and she tried to relax. She washed her face and hands, then got her hair brush from her purse and fixed her hair. She put a little lip gloss on and felt better for it. Now she was ready to face Captain Jack. She couldn't show her fear or he would see right through her lie. But what if they encountered trouble with the rebels out on the water? What would she say then? Maria thought. Do I just act naïve? Maria prayed that there would be no trouble. She couldn't wait for this whole ordeal to be over. She took a deep breath, exhaled slowly, and walked back into the salon.

"Just in time, Maria," Captain Rick said. "I'm serving appetizers and drinks on the flybridge. What can I get you to drink?"

"A glass of wine would be nice."

"Do you prefer white or red?" Captain Rick asked. "I have both."

"White, please."

"Good. I have *Pouilly-Fuiseé*," he said, displaying the label. It was Louis Jadot, a white burgundy table wine imported from France. He opened the bottle and went up the stairs to the flybridge. "Come on up. Everything is set up there."

Maria followed him and would once again face the crew. She hoped no harm would come to any of them. As she emerged from the stairs, she saw Captain Jack and Manual. "Hi. It's so nice up here. With the sun setting and the warm breeze, it's delightful."

"Yes, it is," said Captain Jack. "Have a seat. I see Captain Rick brought up a very nice bottle of wine for you."

"That he did," Maria said as she sat down. She watched Captain Rick pour the wine in a sparkling crystal wine glass. She admired the straw color of the wine and she took the glass from her server's hand. She saw that everyone else had a cocktail or a beer in their hand raised in a toast. "Here's to your good health."

"*Salud*," the men said as they clinked each other's drinks and took a swallow.

"A good choice of wine that goes well with our dinner tonight – grilled chicken," Captain Rick said.

"I thought I smelled chicken. It smells wonderful." Maria sipped her wine and enjoyed the clean finish. She noticed a glass tray of appetizers on the table with small plates and napkins. She saw small French bread toasts topped with a chopped tomato mixture, tapenade or roasted asparagus and parmesan cheese. There was also a bowl of cashews and another dish holding grape tomatoes.

"Help yourself, Maria," Captain Jack said.

Maria could see they were waiting for her before helping themselves. She put her glass down and walked over to the table. Not having much of an appetite, she placed a couple of toasts and grape tomatoes on her small plate. She returned to her seat and took a bite of the toast with chopped tomatoes. "Aren't these called *bruschetta*?

"That's right. A great way to use day-old bread," Captain Rick said with a laugh.

He fixed a plate with a variety of the bruschetta and gave it to Captain Jack who was sitting at the helm.

"Thank you, Rick," Captain Jack said as he took the plate. He set the course on auto pilot and proceeded to enjoy the food and wine.

Maria noticed that now that Captain Jack had been served, Manual felt at ease to help himself to the appetizers.

"Captain Jack, thank you for getting your boat ready to leave so quickly," Maria said, figuring it was better to get her explanation out of the way so she wouldn't continue to fret about it. "My older daughter got sick over the weekend and I'm worried about her. I felt it was best to leave Bogotá early so I can be there to stay with her. Otherwise my husband would have to stay home from work to take care of her. I don't want him to miss work if it's not necessary."

"That's completely understandable. I hope you enjoyed your time with your family in Bogotá. How's your father? You mentioned he was suffering from kidney failure."

"I am happy to say that while I was with him this morning, he got the call for a kidney transplant. In fact, right now he's recovering in the ICU. I wanted to stay and I would have if it weren't for my sick child."

Captain Jack finished the last bite of his food and looked off to the horizon. Then he returned his attention to Maria and said, "I know. Sometimes you wish there could be two of you. I hope he has a speedy recovery. Maybe then he will be well enough so that he can visit you in South Florida."

Maria smiled at the suggestion. She hadn't given it any thought before because her father was ill and the relationship had been strained. But that was all behind them now. Once he recovered Maria would invite her parents to visit them. "I would welcome that," Maria said as she looked over the horizon for any go-fast boats coming their way.

"Excuse me a minute while I check on the chicken and the rest of the dinner," Captain Rick said as he got up from his seat. "It shouldn't be much longer until everything is ready. We can sit at the table in the cockpit."

Maria finished her wine and set the glass down on the table. Manual noticed the empty glass and refilled it. "Thank you. Captain Jack, what time will we arrive in Aruba?"

"It takes 16 hours, so since we left Santa Marta at 6:30, we'll arrive tomorrow morning about 10:30 as long as we don't come into any storms."

"Can we get there any sooner?" Maria asked wanting to put as much distance between them and the FARC rebels.

"Only by going faster and I'm not willing to do that traveling at night. You already know that. Another hour or two isn't going to make a difference. I'm sure you can get a flight out of Aruba tomorrow."

Maria frowned. Then she sensed Captain Jack looking at her so she turned to him and smiled. "I'm sorry for pouting. I'm just upset about my daughter."

Captain Jack simply nodded and turned his attention to his control panel.

I hate lying, Maria thought, but what choice did I have? I can only pray that the FARC rebels don't come after me out here. I know they can be heavily armed with guns and other weapons. The image of the grave the rebels dug for her flashed into her mind. Her eyes began to fill with tears and she tried to blink them away. She dabbed her eyes with her cocktail napkin and drank her wine. She took a deep breath and let it out slowly. She knew she had to stop projecting what could happen. The journey wasn't over yet and she was still alive and on the way to Aruba. She had to be grateful for that.

Chapter 39

"Manual, go out and pull up the anchors," Captain Jack said. "I'm going up to the flybridge so we can get underway. Maria, go ahead and finish your dessert and tea. Join me if you'd like or simply relax in the salon."

"Thank you," Maria said. She hadn't expected Captain Jack to drop anchor when dinner was served, but she thought if she objected, he might think there was something more to her wanting to get back to Aruba in a hurry than a sick daughter. They had only left Santa Marta about an hour ago so there was still time to turn back. She tried to act as normal as possible, but she was afraid that somewhere out there in the darkness there were rebels in hot pursuit.

Captain Rick got up and cleared the dishes from the table when he saw that Maria had put her napkin down on the table. Maria heard the yacht's engine roar to life once more and they were back up to speed in a matter of seconds.

Maria looked up at the twinkling stars in the clear night sky. Out on the ocean, there wasn't light pollution from city streetlights that reduced the visibility of stars. She looked back into the salon and saw Captain Rick stacking the dishes in the dishwasher. She wondered where Manual was, perhaps with Captain Jack. Maria climbed the steps to the flybridge and found the captain at the wheel. She noticed the control panel with all its gauges, GPS, and scanning sonar system illuminated.

Captain Jack turned to Maria as she stepped closer to him. "Have a seat, Maria. You seem tense. Rest assured we'll be back in Oranjestad in the morning."

"I'm all right. I'll be better once we're there and I can get on a plane." She looked out over the water and wondered who was out there. She couldn't hear any boats approaching since the flybridge was enclosed and climate controlled. "How do you know where you're going in the dark?"

"I've already charted my course so I follow that. I have the GPS — global positioning system, and I keep my eye on the sonar system at night. It's useful so I can see what lies ahead on the ocean floor. I had the sonar system installed to detect schools of fish when I take out fishing charters, but it's useful to detect reefs, wrecks, and other obstructions."

"What about other boats?"

"I told you about the radar," Captain Jack said pointing to the radar screen. "I see a few vessels out there. Now there's something I didn't notice before. It looks like we have a go-fast boat out there."

Maria's stomach tightened. She stared intensely at the radar screen. She saw the dot on the screen moving fast.

"Where is it heading?"

"It looks like it's coming our way."

"Then shouldn't you get out of the way?" Maria asked, worried that it was coming for her.

"I've got running lights on. The pilot of that boat can see me. He'll probably just pass us by to show off."

Maria saw the dot on the radar screen getting closer. She looked out the window and didn't see anything out there.

"Do you have any spotlights you can shine on the boat? To see who it is?"

Captain Jack had a puzzled look on his face. "Yes, I do. But why should I care who it is?"

Maria felt the fear grip her like a vise around her stomach. Her mouth went dry and when she tried to speak, she didn't know what to say. She looked at the radar screen and then back to Captain Jack. His eyes were searching her face for an answer.

"Maria, you're pale. Why do I care who's in the go-fast boat? Maria? Answer me!"

"Turn the spotlight on. Please!" Maria cried.

Captain Jack did as she demanded and they saw the go-fast was about 120 feet behind them. There were two men in the speed boat; one with his hands on the wheel, the other holding a rifle aimed at "*Get Reel*."

"Maria, what is this about? It looks as if those men are gunning for us!" Captain Jack shouted.

Suddenly, Captain Rick and Manual appeared in the flybridge. Captain Rick was the first to speak.

"What's with the go-fast? If I didn't know better, I'd say they're pursuing us."

"I agree. Maria, tell me," Captain Jack demanded. "You look like you know what this is about. If they're after us, I'll take evasive action. Now, Maria!"

Maria broke down in sobs. "I didn't want to tell you, but I had no choice. Those are FARC rebels. They kidnapped me years ago and I was rescued by the Special Forces. They threatened that if I ever returned to Colombia they'd kill me and make an example out of me. Somehow they found out I was in Bogotá. They kidnapped me again today when I was in the hospital while my father was in surgery. I managed to escape. I couldn't tell you about them, because I thought you wouldn't take me back to Aruba. I have to get home. If they get me they'll kill me."

Maria saw the three men look at each other. Captain Jack increased his speed from 18 knots to the max 36 knots. On the radar, it looked as if the go-fast was on a collision course with them. Finally a little more distance was put between them. Maria looked out at the go-fast boat and saw the tell-tale water fantail it left behind.

"Manual, get down to the cockpit and arm yourself. But no heroics. Only shoot if you have a chance to do damage to the boat."

Captain Jack then turned to Maria. "You don't think very much of me, do you, Maria?

"What do you mean?" Maria asked, wiping the tears from her eyes.

"Do you think I'd leave you in Santa Marta if I knew the rebels were out to kill you?"

Maria could see that she had insulted Captain Jack without realizing it. She failed to see his point of view. "I'm sorry. I didn't mean to offend you. I just thought..."Maria fell silent, not knowing what to say.

"You thought that if I knew you were putting us in jeopardy, I wouldn't take you back to Aruba."

Maria shook her head in agreement and looked down, feeling very ashamed.

The go-fast boat was now just 80 feet behind them. Captain Jack had his eyes on the control panel and Captain Rick faced the stern watching the progress of the go-fast boat as it gained on them.

They saw the rifleman shoot several rounds. Captain Rick said, "He's aiming low, going for the propellers."

More shots rang out, this time from Manual who aimed to disable the speed boat. Then the go-fast boat veered left and right so it was a meandering target.

"Oh shit." Captain Jack shouted.

"What is it?" Captain Rick asked.

"Hang on. The sonar shows we've got a submerged container up ahead." Captain Jack turned the wheel sharply starboard to avoid a disaster.

The go-fast boat stayed the course. It turned slowly following *"Get Reel"* but suddenly it stopped dead in the water.

"The submerged container! They hit it. They're dead in the water now!" yelled Captain Rick. "That's the end of their propellers. The hull may have also suffered some damage. They won't be going anywhere."

Manual appeared at the top of the step to the flybridge. "That was a close call, Captain Jack. They hit something in the water."

"Yes, one of those shipping containers. The sonar system saved us," he said as he reduced the yacht's speed back to 18 knots.

Captain Rick added, "Only because you were paying attention. Nice going, Captain. I hate to think of the damage that could have been done to your yacht."

Maria sat in shock. She realized that if the yacht had hit the container, they would be sitting ducks. Disabled and maybe even taking on water, the FARC rebels could have easily come aboard and killed them all. Maria felt a hand on her shoulder. It was Captain Rick, his intense blue eyes looking into hers.

"Maria, we're in the clear now. I think you should come down with me to the salon," Captain Rick said as he took her hand and led her to the stairs. "I'll get you something to drink to calm your nerves."

Maria followed him, holding onto the handrails to steady herself. She sat down on the couch feeling numb. She looked up to see Captain Rick offering her a cordial glass.

"Here Maria. Sip this Amaretto. I'll get you a glass of water as well."

Maria took the glass from him and took a sip. Captain Rick returned with the water and placed it on the coffee table in front of Maria. As he sat down in the swivel chair, she noticed he was holding a brandy snifter in his hand. She watched as he brought it to his nose, inhaled the aroma and took a sip, closing his eyes as he swallowed. She thought of her father who occasionally enjoyed a brandy after dinner, but that was before he got sick. She wondered how her father was. She pictured her mother holding his hand at bedside comforting him. Tears rolled down Maria's cheeks. She brushed them away, not wanting to cry in front of Captain Rick.

"It's all right, Maria. You've been through a lot in one day. I'd like to hear the whole story when you're up to it."

Maria shook her hand, thinking if he only knew half of it. She took another sip of the cordial. She wondered if the rebels would radio their comrades for back-up. She wouldn't feel safe until she was home with Jorge and her little girls.

Chapter 40

Maria woke up panic stricken until she realized that she was in her stateroom aboard the fishing yacht, *Get Reel*. She slept fitfully, due to nightmares when she was held captive by the FARC rebels. She saw the morning light from the small window and now could smell the aroma of freshly brewed coffee. She went to the head where she took a quick shower and got ready to face the day. She wore comfortable jeans, and a cotton knit top in pale blue embellished with some beadwork along the V-neck. She made her bed, packed her suitcase, and left it on top of the comforter.

When she entered the salon, Manual was pouring a cup of coffee and offered it to her. She thanked him, took the cup from him and helped herself to cream and sugar that was set out on the polished counter. She took a sip and then walked up the stairs to the flybridge.

"Good morning, Maria," Captain Jack said. "How did you sleep?"

"Not well, but I can take a nap on the plane later."

Maria sat down and took another sip of her coffee.

"I'm sorry about last night, that I purposely deceived you. I don't blame you if you're angry with me."

Captain Jack looked at her and after a moment he said, "Your apology is accepted. When Captain Rick and I were changing shifts up here, he told me your story. I must say I can understand your actions, and why you didn't want to tell me the truth. You were too distraught to think that I would want to help you."

"What are the chances of them coming to Aruba?" Maria asked.

"It depends on how much manpower they have. Once they leave international waters and enter Aruba's coastline, they might be sighted by Aruba's coast guard who might take an interest in a go-fast boat. But if they just sent those two goons, you're probably safe. Also they don't know your destination, do they?"

"I wouldn't think so. My parents are the only ones who know where I'm going, besides my husband, of course."

"There are quite a few islands out here in the Caribbean Sea," Captain Jack continued. "Plus my vessel is registered in St. Vincent which is another island east of Aruba. That might throw them into thinking that's where we're going. But how did they know to go to Santa Marta?"

"I was wondering the same thing. I think that my traveling alone makes me stand out. I think the mastermind figured I wouldn't have gone directly to Bogotá because of the US customs issue. They would have gotten that information from my sister-in-law. They know my father is wealthy so a private jet is affordable. I think they used the same thinking that I did. I bet they went to the private jet terminals and bribed people for information. You've heard the expression, *"plata o ploma"* meaning take the bribe or take the bullet. There are only a handful of private operators at the airport so they could have found out that a woman traveling alone was going to Santa Marta. With that information, the rebels would use their radios or cell phones to contact other rebels who are headquartered along the coast in cities such as Cartagena and Baranquilla. I remember they were always on those things when I was held captive in the farmhouse. Once they got news that I was in Bogotá, I believe they got their orders to track me down and kill me," Maria said.

She looked at the radar and caught Captain Jack's eye.

"Everything is copasetic," Captain Jack reassured her.

The two of them sat silent for a moment. Maria looked out across the Caribbean Sea turning around so she got a 360 degree view. There was an occasional fishing boat that she saw along with one sailing yacht. This was only her second time out on the open sea and she had mixed feelings about it. She decided under better circumstances, she might actually enjoy going out on a boat again but for now, she was too nervous.

"Captain Rick mentioned that you think your sister-in-law was behind all this. To me, it seems like her problem is more serious than just being jealous of you. She sounds very dangerous," Captain Jack said.

"That she is," Maria said. She finished her coffee and put the cup down. "That's why I am still worried. What if someone is waiting for me at the airport?"

"I know you're worried."

"Yes, I am. Money is no object with those damn rebels," Maria said, her voice breaking with emotion. "They want to kill me and show Colombians how powerful they are."

"Does your mother know how you feel about Silvana, about your suspicions?"

"Yes, she does."

"We'll be getting into Oranjestad earlier than I predicted. I decided to push the throttle because you're under such duress. We should be arriving in another hour. You should be able to use your cell phone soon. Maybe your mother will have an update about your father. And also Silvana. She may have talked to her or seen her."

"My mother probably talked to her. Silvana may have even come to the hospital to see my father last night. But Silvana will continue the role playing. And my mother would not confront her either. There is no proof."

"Not that you know of. But she has a connection to FARC. Find that and you have your proof."

"As much as I'd like to see Silvana go to prison, I'd much rather get home to my husband and daughters and put this whole nightmare behind me."

'What Silvana did is unconscionable, to betray her own family. I'd like to see her get her just desserts," Captain Jack said as he looked at his watch. "It won't be long before we'll be at the marina. You can see Aruba on the horizon. Why don't you have breakfast? Manual will prepare anything you want."

"Thank you, but I'm not hungry. Maybe I'll have a glass of juice," Maria said. She stood up and went down the stairs to the salon, her mind a ping-pong game of thoughts that ranged from Silvana, to her father's surgery, to her husband and daughters and to continuing her journey home. She would be ever thankful if she made it home alive.

Chapter 41

As soon as Maria's cell phone had a signal, she called American Airlines to change her reservation. She got a seat in business class departing Aruba at 9:05 am and arriving in Miami at 12:05 pm. If she didn't make that flight, the next one was at 2:45 pm. Since it was only seven-thirty and they would be docking in a matter of minutes, she decided the first flight was her best option. Both Captain Jack and Captain Rick said they would take her to the airport and see her off so that she would not appear to be traveling alone. Having them accompany her allayed some of her nervousness.

Next she called Jorge to tell him her flight information. She kept the conversation brief because he was getting ready to leave for work and she still had to call her mother. She also kept that conversation short as well because once the fishing yacht was secured to the dock, they would need to get to the airport quickly if she expected to make the flight on time. Her mother told her that her father was recovering well after surgery, and Silvana had come to the hospital. Her mother thought Silvana was very anxious and when she asked her what was wrong, she said she was worried about Don Pedro. Although she was elated to learn that her father was doing well, Maria had to bite her tongue to keep from saying what she really thought so she simply promised her mother she would call her once she was home in Pembroke Pines. Maria didn't mention the hair-raising encounter with the go-fast boat to Jorge nor to her mother. Thinking about it now made it seem like a nightmare. She knew she was lucky she had made it this far.

Maria sat in the yacht's cockpit with her suitcase and purse ready to go. Oranjestad was already bustling with Monday morning traffic. She looked around the marina wondering if a FARC assassin was waiting for her among the many boaters and fishermen. She heard the engine cut off and the yacht drifted toward the dock. Manual jumped out of the vessel and threw a line to Captain Jack to secure the bow and then another line for the stern.

"Manual, stay here until we get back. We're taking Maria to the airport. Call me on my cell phone if you need to," Captain Jack shouted.

Maria noticed that Captain Jack conveyed an unspoken meaning to Manual. She believed that "if you need to" meant if there was trouble. She hoped that there would be no more problems for these men who had saved her life.

"Let's go, Maria," Captain Jack said as he took her suitcase and stepped onto the dock. He extended his hand to help her out of the cockpit. Captain Rick followed and the three walked briskly past the many yachts and pleasure boats. She noticed supplies being loaded aboard the boats since many of the fishing charters left right after sunrise.

Maria looked at everyone around her to see if anyone took notice of her. She wouldn't relax until she was back in the states.

When they reached Captain Jack's car in the parking lot, the men took the front seats while Maria got in the back. Once they were on the road to the airport, Maria looked out the back window to see if they were being followed. There was a black car that was behind them.

"I think someone is following us," Maria said.

She noticed Captain Jack looked in his rearview mirror while Captain Rick lowered the vanity mirror in front of the windshield.

Captain Jack said, "We can test it out. I'll slow down and see if the driver passes me."

"But what if the driver cuts you off so you have to stop? Then we all could end up dead," Maria said.

"Good point. Then I'll try varying my speed. If the driver is tailing us, he'll keep up. If not, out of frustration, he'll just pass me."

Maria sighed and said, "Okay. I just hope you're right."

Captain Jack increased his speed another ten miles per hour. Maria watched as the vehicle behind them maintained its speed. The gap between the two cars widened. Then suddenly the car sped up and closed the gap. Captain Jack kept an eye on the car and slowed down to the posted speed limit. The car slowed down to keep a safe distance. Captain Jack accelerated once more and the other car trailed behind, keeping up the pace. Captain Jack slowed down again by braking and the other car had to do the same or run into the rear of their car. Maria looked ahead and saw no oncoming traffic. The car behind them took the opportunity to pass them. Maria looked to see who was driving as the car passed them by and it was a young woman who glared at them. Maria sighed with relief.

"Maybe she's late for work," Captain Jack speculated as he watched the car pass him. "Let's hope that's the end of the excitement this morning."

"I guess I'm acting paranoid, but I can't really help it. Not after all that has happened." Maria said as she sat back in the seat and tried to relax by taking deep breaths and exhaling slowly. The airport was just ahead and she would be happy to board the plane.

"Don't worry about it, Maria. You should always follow your gut instinct. I'd rather err on the safe side. I think that intuition is the Lord's way of keeping us safe."

"Yes, but sometimes there is no intuition. Things just happen. Like the night I was kidnapped," said Maria remembering that awful night.

"I bet there was something you found amiss, Maria. You told me your husband normally picked you up from class in the evening, but he was home sick. Instead your sister-in-law arranged for a classmate to take you home. Did you sense anything odd that night?" Captain Jack probed.

"Now that I think about that night again, I remember thinking that Silvana was very quiet. She's normally very talkative. She likes being the center of attention"

"That's it, right there. In fact, if she was behind the whole abduction, she was probably deep in thought anticipating when you would be ambushed," Captain Jack said.

Captain Rick interrupted, "But at that point you were already in the car so there wasn't anything you really could have done about it. To me, staying safe is to be aware of your environment and not distracted by other things."

"Maria can't fault herself for that night. She trusted her sister-in-law," Captain Jack said.

"I have no argument with that. She was betrayed, no doubt about it. Something like that changes a person forever," Captain Rick agreed.

"Too bad she got away with it," Maria said.

Captain Rick said, "I'm a firm believer in what goes around, comes around. There will be justice. You can find solace in that."

"I suppose," Maria conceded remembering how many weeks of counseling she went through to help her let go of the intense anger she had over the whole kidnapping. Now those feelings were surfacing again. She would have to work on controlling those intense emotions so that she could continue to live in the present and be there for her husband and daughters.

Captain Jack parked the car in the short-term lot so they only had a short walk to the terminal. When they got inside, Maria put on a navy fleece hoodie over her yellow knit shirt and jeans to ward off the deep freeze effect of the air conditioning. The three of them walked to the gate and Maria checked in with her boarding pass. Then they found seats facing the expansive picture window affording them a view of the plane. They could see baggage handlers loading the luggage into the hold of the plane. She wondered how careful they would be if they didn't have the public watching them. Finally Marie turned to her protectors.

"I appreciate all that you've done for me. You saved my life and I won't forget it. Captain Rick, give me your card so I can stay in touch. I have yours, Captain Jack," Maria said, thinking she would send them each a bonus when she returned home, God willing. "If you decide to visit Florida, be sure to let me know."

"I just might take you up on it, Maria. My daughters want to go to Orlando and South Beach," Captain Jack said.

"My wife has suggested it as well. It's just a matter of taking the time off. You know how that is when you're self-employed," Captain Rick said.

"I hear you," Captain Jack agreed. "Maria, please call me when you get home. You've made it this far. I'm sure everything will be fine."

"From your lips to God's ears," Maria said, meaning it earnestly. "I will call you."

The flight attendant at the gate announced that passengers could now begin boarding. Maria looked around as the crowd rose from their seats to queue up. There were some very obvious Americans who were sunburned, probably returning from vacation. There were some families and like the flight over, collegians wearing t-shirts and baseball caps with their college logo. Maria spotted two men who gave her pause. They were in their thirties, needed a shave and looked Hispanic with a dark complexion and black hair. They were both wearing olive green cargo pants, grey t-shirts and army camouflage jackets. She couldn't tell if they noticed her since both men sported dark aviator sunglasses. She found some solace in the fact that they had to go through the security screening for weapons before being allowed to come to the gate. But she knew she was naïve to think that there aren't other means to kill someone. After all, she had seen enough movies. She took a deep breath and exhaled slowly so that she would not be overcome with a panic attack.

She felt Captains Jack and Rick's eyes focused on her.

Captain Rick said, "Don't worry. If you're seated near them, you can ask to have your seat changed. But I don't think you have anything to worry about."

"All right, I better board now."

Captain Jack said, "They're getting up. Let them board first so you know where they're sitting. Then you can have your seat changed if you find they are too near you."

Flanked by Captains Jack and Rick, Maria waited until she saw the men go down the gangway. She rose from her seat and turned to her bodyguards. They got up from their seats as well. She saw genuine concern in their faces and tears welled up in her eyes. She looked to the ceiling and blinked them away.

The flight attendant made another announcement that all passengers should now board the plane.

"I better go. Thank you again for everything. I'll call you this afternoon, Captain Jack."

Maria hugged each man and managed a smile before turning and walking toward the gangway with her suitcase on wheels trailing behind her. After she presented her boarding pass to the attendant and was waved on, she looked back at the men. They both smiled at her and said, "Stay safe."

Maria smiled and swallowed hard. She then turned and continued walking down the gangway to board the plane that would take her to safety: the home she shared with Jorge and her beloved daughters. Before she crossed the threshold of the plane, she said a silent prayer that she be kept out of harm's way.

Chapter 42

Maria was greeted by the flight attendant who directed her to business class. The 737 jet only had twelve seats in this section and she was glad that she could have the extra room and privacy. She noticed a young couple sitting in the first row and a senior couple sat right in front of her. Before taking her aisle seat, she turned to look into economy class and noticed that there were many unoccupied seats. She couldn't see the two men dressed in camouflage. She figured that they must be sitting in one of the last seats.

Maria sighed and looked up at the overhead bin. She struggled to lift her suitcase and stow it in the compartment. Then she sat down and opened her purse. There was the framed photo of her daughters and Jorge. It seemed like weeks, instead of days that she had been gone from them, but she found comfort in knowing that in just a few hours they would be reunited. She closed her purse and fastened her seatbelt. She suddenly had a hot flash and opened the air vent over her head. Her palms were wet and she cooled them from the blast of cool air. She turned her head to look down the aisle once more, trying to see where the men were seated. She finally gave up. The only way to find them would be to walk down the aisle.

She heard a male flight attendant make the standard safety announcement and finally the jet taxied down the runway. In just moments the plane was airborne. Finally the seat belt sign was turned off so Maria was free to get up from her seat. She struggled with the idea of walking back there. She thought it would look odd for her, a business class passenger, to stroll through economy class and for what purpose. The flight attendant would find her behavior unusual since business class had its own lavatories and galley.

While she was deep in thought, the flight attendant distracted her by offering a choice of a Mimosa, Bloody Mary or champagne. Maria declined the cocktails and asked for coffee and orange juice. She wondered how people could drink alcoholic beverages so early in the morning. She remembered the American expression, "a little hair of the dog that bit you last night" as a cure for a hangover. Supposedly an alcoholic drink would cure it. Maria shook her head, realizing she was not focused. She knew she needed to relax because she was obsessing over the men who reminded her of the FARC rebels. It was all because of the way they were dressed. She found comfort knowing that in just a few hours, she would be safe. She thought about her father and yearned to be near him while he recovered from transplant surgery. She knew her mother would welcome her support. But that just was impossible. The FARC kept her from her family and she hated them for it. It was a miracle that she managed to escape from them yesterday. If they had given her more of the drug that rendered her unconscious, she would be dead at their hands. She felt grateful to be alive and tears welled up in her eyes blurring her vision.

When she opened her eyes, she turned to the year of the cabin and saw one of the men she feared looking into the business class entrance. Holding her breakfast tray, the flight attendant confronted him, "Sir, is there something you need? The other flight attendants are serving breakfast in your cabin right now."

The man mumbled, "No, *nada*." As he turned to return to his seat, Maria forced a smile. She pulled out the tray inside the armrest and allowed the woman to place her breakfast in front of her. She drank her juice and realized she was thirsty. When the aroma of sweet smokiness from the Canadian bacon hit her nose, she realized that in spite of being nervous, she was also hungry. She cut into the bacon and took a bite of it along with the mushroom omelet. She sipped the coffee and thought it must be Colombian, the best. She was beginning to feel somewhat normal sitting there eating breakfast along with the other passengers. Once breakfast was over, she could leaf through a magazine or watch an in-flight movie. She knew she couldn't sleep. She'd have to occupy her thoughts and let the time slip away. She glanced at her watch. In just two hours she would be reunited with her loved ones. It couldn't come soon enough.

Chapter 43

Maria sighed with relief when the plane finally landed. She was eager to see Jorge, Julie and Paula. How she missed them! And to think that she came so close to dying again at the hands of the rebels. Her eyes welled up with tears, so she remained there even after the seat belt sign was turned off and the other passengers rose from their seats. She blinked and dug a tissue out of her purse. She dabbed at the tears and released her seat belt. She waited for the passengers to disembark. With no place to move, there was no sense to standing up right now.

Finally when she was sole passenger on the plane, she stood up, retrieved her suitcase and left. She trailed behind the other passengers, following them along the long corridor. She saw the two men she had feared; only now they were embracing their families. As she passed them, they didn't even glance at her.

She continued to walk and saw the escalator down to the first floor of Miami International Airport where she would go through customs. She hoped the line for processing would move quickly. She wondered if Jorge would try to pick her up outside the airport terminal or come inside to meet her in the lobby.

It took an hour waiting her turn to go through customs. Now cleared, she stood in the lobby and called Jorge to find out where he was. She fished in her purse and found the phone, but just as she dialed his number, she heard, "Mommy!"

She turned and saw her sweet daughters running up to her followed by Jorge.

Maria burst into tears. It was like *déjà vu*. She felt as though she was in the Bogotá police station when they made the announcement of Maria's rescue by the special police force. It was the most wonderful memory when all of them embraced, hugging her and kissing her.

When they released her, Maria said to her daughters, "My, look at you. I am so happy to see my girls. I missed you so."

In unison, the girls said, "So did we, Mommy! Don't ever go away again."

"I won't," Maria said, meaning it with all her heart.

Jorge tilted her chin up so she could look into his eyes. "You look a little worn out, Maria. I think you need a vacation."

"Yes, I am worn out. I have a lot to tell you, but that can wait until tonight," she said as she leaned up and kissed him. She put her arms around his neck, hugged him tightly, and whispered in his ear. "That's the last time I will ever leave you and the girls."

He looked in her eyes and said, "I believe it."

Maria took each girl by the hand and Jorge led the way, trailing Maria's suitcase behind him out of the airport to their waiting car.

Epilogue

It was just a week before Christmas and the new house looked festive with all the holiday decorations. There was a Christmas tree in the formal living room as well as in the family room. The girls wanted to know if Santa would put presents under both trees and Maria laughed. It was something she hadn't even considered, but she just might do that since her parents were visiting for an extended stay.

Because of Don Pedro's generous gift, the family had moved into the five-bedroom, four-bath home in August after searching for the right house for more than a month. Maria wanted to make sure the girls could attend the same school. The home was located within the school's boundaries.

When they found this house, Maria and Jorge knew instantly this was their dream home. It had the square footage they wanted, almost four thousand, and the lot was oversized by Florida standards at a half acre. There was a built-in swimming pool with a whirlpool spa. The backyard was fenced so they had their privacy. Jorge loved the idea that there were plenty of fruit trees on the property: grapefruit, orange, key lime, avocado, and mango.

While Jorge focused on the backyard, Maria fell in love with the open and airy kitchen. It was a cook's paradise with French country cabinets painted cream and sea foam granite countertops. All the electric appliances were stainless steel. There was even an island in the middle of the kitchen that had four stools on one side, making it a convenient place for the girls to do their homework while Maria prepared their dinner.

With five bedrooms, each girl had her own room leaving two rooms available for guests. As soon as they were settled into the home and every box was unpacked, Maria invited her parents to come to her new home for an extended stay. Don Pedro had recovered from his kidney transplant with "flying colors," as his doctor said.

Maria's parents had arrived the day before Thanksgiving and were planning the visit for at least three months. Anne Marie fell in love with the kitchen and made herself right at home. She insisted on cooking every night and loved having her granddaughters take instruction from her. She also helped Maria decorate the house and they frequently went shopping to see what bargains they could find on Christmas decorations.

Maria walked into the kitchen and found her mother seasoning an eye of round roast for their dinner.

"Mama, you're always busy. Why don't you sit? I can take care of that," Maria said as she hugged her mother and kissed her gently on her cheek.

Anne Marie returned the hug and said, "I have it. Make yourself a cup of tea and we'll chat."

Maria put a kettle of water on the burner and took out a canister of tea bags. Then she sat down on a stool at the island counter.

"I was thinking about Silvana. How long has she been missing?" Maria asked.

"She disappeared just after you left Bogotá. We were expecting a demand for ransom, like what happened with you. But nothing. Strange, isn't it?"

"So what do you think happened to her? What does Roman think?"

Anne Marie hesitated, swallowed hard, and said, "He thinks she ran off with another man."

"Why does he think that?" Maria asked, clearly surprised.

"For one, there was no phone call demanding a ransom. Naturally Roman reported her missing. The detectives on the case questioned the saleswoman who worked in her boutique. She said that Silvana took extended lunches several times a week and had a guilty look on her face – like she was trying to hide something. She thought Silvana had a lover."

"What will happen with the boutique?"

"Silvana's parents hired a manager to run it temporarily. They asked if anybody in the family wanted to buy it, but so far, no offers."

There was a long pause as both women were thinking their own thoughts.

Anne Marie was first to speak.

"I wonder if Silvana really was pregnant that day she got sick in front of the building. Maybe Roman was not the father and it was her lover's baby."

"So you think she left town to have this baby with her lover?" Anne Marie speculated.

"It's a thought. I don't know. I think she got in over her head. I know in my heart she is the traitor who set me up. Maybe she did something stupid and she made someone really angry. You know, what goes around comes around."

Anne Marie was silent and looked at her daughter.

Maria caught her mother's expression and said, "Of course, I feel bad for Roman. He doesn't deserve to suffer and have this heartache, not knowing what happened to Silvana. What will he do? Just wait and hope she comes back?"

Anna Marie said, "I suppose he will for a time. If she doesn't turn up, my guess is that he will divorce her by publication."

"You mean file a notice in the newspaper?" Maria asked.

"Exactly."

"Enough about Silvana for now. I know I brought it up but she still haunts me. I just want you to know I'm so happy that we're living in this wonderful home and that we're all together once more. I'm so grateful Papa is healthy and we have more years ahead of us. I'm particularly happy that you two are back together, permanently."

"Yes, I love your father and I'm grateful things turned out the way they did," Anne Marie said as she put the roast in the oven. "Didn't you say you will be taking the TOEFL test after the holidays?"

"Yes, I pass that and I can enroll at Broward College and get my associate degree. Then I'll go on to either Florida Atlantic or Florida International University to get my bachelor's. I still plan on being a CPA you know."

"Yes, I know. You're determined. Once you set your mind to something, you chart your course."

"I guess you can say that." Maria hugged her mother and the both of them laughed.

THE END

Acknowledgments

I never know where an idea for a novel will come from, but I am grateful that my inner voice compelled me to apply for an adjunct teaching position at Broward College in South Florida teaching English for Speakers of Other Languages (ESL).

My adult students were from many parts of the world, but the majority were from South America where dictators ruled, civil wars and political situations made it intolerable to live under dire conditions. Each chose to petition the United States to grant them political asylum status so they could emigrate with their families. The majority of them were professional people such as physicians, attorneys, and entrepreneurs who fled, sometimes only taking two suitcases.

They were anxious to learn from me as they desperately wanted to belong to a community of free people who could speak their minds, find employment and live the American Dream.

But it was me who would learn from them. I listened to their amazing stories and admired their determination to leave everything behind in order to start a new life for themselves and their families. One day in class a young woman admitted to the class of her kidnapping by the notorious rebel group known by the acronym FARC. Not wanting to put her in an awkward position, I asked if I could interview her privately. She agreed and invited me to her home where I would meet her beautiful daughters and multi-lingual husband who would help her relay the ordeal.

In this novel, I relayed her experience in the flashback scenes. Then I said what if she wanted to go back for one reason or another. If you have a green card that has granted political asylum, you go back and forfeit the card because the US interprets that you no longer feel your life is in jeopardy in your homeland.

In the opening pages, Maria is challenged with that decision. And now you know the rest.

I did a lot of research once I figured out a way for Maria to circumvent Homeland Security. For that I owe Christine Kling my gratitude for her knowledge about passports, clearing immigration and the perils of sailing on the open seas. As a seasoned sailor, she is the author of the nautical thrillers, the Seychelle Sullivan Adventure Series and the Shipwreck Adventure series. Christine and her husband sail around the world on their custom-built aluminum expedition boat *Mobius*.

Thank you to my friend Rita Cohl for reading *Saving Maria* in the early stages of development and offering pertinent comments. I also recognize my favorite cousin Judy Johnson, a retired New Jersey supervisor of court reporters, for proofreading the manuscript.

Thank you to Hugh Williams of Just2Creative.com for his talent in designing the cover of *Saving Maria*.

Last but not least, I am grateful for the support of my family and friends from Florida, California and Connecticut.

Lynn Sheft

A native of New Jersey, Lynn Sheft earned her bachelor's degree from the University of Miami and established herself as a professional copywriter and creative director in South Florida. During her career, she won numerous awards for her campaigns for regional and national consumer accounts. In addition, she wrote articles for magazines, provided editing services and was an adjunct instructor teaching ESL classes.

When she relocated to Connecticut, she turned to writing fiction full time, including short stories and novels. "A Tryst with Fate" appeared in the anthology *Seascape: The Best New England Crime Stories*. THE DEADLY GAME was her debut novel and received five-star reviews on Amazon Books and Goodreads.

She is a member of Mystery Writers of America and Sisters in Crime. She lives in Madison, Connecticut with her husband Barry.